Also by Samantha Russell

Social Craze

Down to the Riptide

The Riptide Series

Book 1

To the ones who've ever been told their big deal is no big deal.

Content Warning

Dear Readers,

This book was written with a young adult audience in mind. It does not have a lot of spice or swearing, but there are other triggers I think some of you may want to be aware of before reading.

The contents of this book touch on sexual misconduct, loss of a parent, high school bullying, intimacy, and thoughts of death.

I know these issues are common in the real lives of people young and old. I put a lot of research and thought into how to tackle these issues as they arose in the storyline, and it is my most genuine hope that I have addressed each subject with the respect it deserves.

If you find that you need help with any of these issues, the following national organizations are available by phone 24/7 and have the best resources for you.

National Sexual Assault Hotline: 1-800-656-4673

Mental Health & Suicide Crisis Lifeline: 988

Take care of yourselves, readers.

With love,

Samantha Russell

Down to the Riptide

The Riptide Series

Book 1

Chapter One

Huntington Beach, CA

"You know, Kai, Rip Tide's golden child, Ace Madden, is about to jump in here for the Triple Crown title match, and I have to say, she needs to rip it if she's going to pull out on top. We have yet to see her really let loose and show us what she can do out there on the water. I hate to say it, because—like the rest of Surf City—I am an Ace Madden fan, but if it weren't for that interference call in the semi-finals, she might not have even made it into this final heat."

"You're completely right, Tripp, and I might add, I've been watching her with her coach, Graham Gentry, in warm-ups; they're not in sync today like they usually are. They've been a powerhouse team all season, so I really hope they can get in line and show us what they've been working on. Both are major athletes for the Rip Tide brand, so in a way, this event should feel like home turf to them. I'm hoping that puts a little heat under Ace's board, if you catch my drift."

"On that note, I don't know that I've ever seen a better coach-athlete duo. These two joined forces about a year and a half ago, and they've been unstoppable ever since. You don't ever hear of an athlete coaching another surfer, but it just works here. Graham really knows how to bring the froth out of that one, and people love watching these two take over the surf world. If they can pull this off, Rip Tide is going to be very happy with the Ace Madden team."

Masyn—Ace, as she's known in the surf world—scowls and puts her earbuds in to block out the commentary from the press box. Two large hands clasp her shoulders from behind, hands she knows well—too well. She flinches at the touch.

"Don't listen to them; we're fine, Ace." Graham's voice, so close to her ear, sends ice down her spine. "We'll come out of today just like we always do—on top of the podium."

"Don't touch me," she spits, unable to meet his eyes as she shrugs him off.

"Hey, A-babe—" Graham starts, but his concern turns into a smile as he meets eyes with someone over Masyn's shoulder. "Kennelly."

"Honey, you look like a nervous wreck. You're so tense; let Graham warm you up." Masyn turns to face her mother, who's once again butting into a conversation she has no part in. "Rip Tide has a trailer for you if you guys need to go in for a private pep talk, whatever you need to do."

"Mom, no. I'm fine," Masyn snaps.

"You barely made it out of that last heat. You're not fine."

Graham raises his hands, palms facing out, to calm the tension. "We're good. I'm going to go chat with Kai up there in the press box.

See if I can get him to keep our names out of his mouth 'til Ace hits the water again."

As he walks away, Masyn stretches her neck to one side and addresses her mother. "I want to be alone."

"Oh, Masyn, stop. It's just nerves. Shake it off. Your coach can help. He always does. Sometimes I think you forget he's a world-championship surfer."

"He's not helping, Mom. You have to believe me, he's . . . he . . ." Masyn struggles against the weight pressing in on her from all sides. She rests her head against the surfboard propped up in her arms, trying to draw out the strength to tell the truth. "The other night, when we were surfing late—he went too far."

Kennelly frowns, but quickly scoffs and rolls her eyes. "Masyn, you've been in athletics long enough to know the relationship between coach and athlete. When it comes to a big competition like this, of course he's going to push you harder and in different ways than you're used to. Stop pouting and learn to respect that. If it weren't for him, you wouldn't have gotten anywhere close to qualifying for an event like the Triple Crown this year. Nor would you have scored the top sponsorship in the industry. He's given you everything. Toughen up and show some gratitude. Better yet, forget the past and think about what you want your future to look like."

Masyn looks down at her bare feet, trying to decipher the larger truth. If she wins this competition, she'll have an automatic spot on the Junior Tour next year. It would be a dream come true to surf in the biggest competitions around the world, and yeah, it would be because of Graham, but the overwhelming knot in her stomach is a weight she can't ignore.

"Look honey, I don't mean to be hard. We're so proud of you, and I know we're all grateful for Graham. He's turned you into a name to remember, which has helped in ways we didn't even expect; it's even boosted our sales at the surf shop exponentially. Now, a win for you is a win for the business. So many people are rooting for you in this competition. Let's not let them down."

A buzzer breaks through the conversation, signaling it's almost time for the final heat to start. Masyn hears the announcers say her name, sees Graham hold her rash guard out to her, but she can't focus on any of it. The sound of the buzzer has evolved into a persistent ringing in her ears, one that continues to flood into her body and vibrate down her extremities.

She flicks her fingertips against the numbness and wills herself to keep it from taking over her senses.

I can't do this, she thinks. She turns to her mom.

Kennelly grabs her by the shoulders, narrowing her gaze as if to halt the frenzied searching of Masyn's eyes. "Go get 'em, Ace. We're all counting on you."

Chapter Two

Ellsworth, MA—Two Months Later

THERE'S A WEIRD THING about trauma: the essence of it can be enticing. Like returning to the scene of the crime. Masyn almost wonders if she's a bit of a masochist as she walks down the boardwalk scaling the bluff outside Aunt Nat's beach house on the East Coast. She stops at a large deck halfway down the cliff and rests her forearms on the railing, looking out onto the dark sea. This is a completely different ocean than the one she knows, but she hates it all the same.

Or at least she tries to.

The salty sea breeze feels heavier at night as it wisps the hairs framing Masyn's face. She rakes her fingers through her wavy locks and rubs at her temples with her thumbs, squeezing her eyes shut against a sudden wave of emotion. She doesn't want to think about what happened the last few times she was in the ocean, so why can't she resist coming out here?

When she opens her eyes, a new dim light tries its hardest to splay across the deck. She turns and tilts her chin up to the few houses on the bluff. The streak of light clicks off. Beneath the porch light of one house, she can see the shadow of a man standing with a beer bottle in his hand, looking down at her.

Apathetic to the man's investigation, Masyn simply turns and looks back out over the ocean. She'd dare anyone to come at her right now. Although, she doesn't actually know what she would do. She might fight back with more vengeance than any seventeen-year-old girl has ever had, or she might surrender without a shred of concern. Even so, her need for solitude carries her down the remaining steps to the sand. She stands with her bare feet just outside the waterline and loses herself in the sound of the ocean waves breaking on the shore. Each crashing throb clenches her heart tighter, clarifying the pictures of *that night* flashing in her mind. The night her surf career, her dignity, her whole self was stolen from her. The memories that forced her to run away from her future as a Rip Tide athlete on tour.

It makes her wonder if the Atlantic Ocean harbors the same demons as the Pacific, if it houses the same pull, the same power. Before she knows what she's doing, she runs into the whitewash, hurtling herself into the swell of an incoming wave before it crashes. She floats on her back, focusing on the faint yet formidable tug of the sea, listening to the underwater rumble of the next wave coming in, and letting the following surge sweep her up, knowing full well the perilous potential it holds. She braces for the crest to break, willing herself to let it take her, to feel what this ocean is made of—to feel *something*—but the release doesn't come. Two strong hands clench around her biceps and pull her upright, stabilizing her against the shore break. Salt bites at her eyes, blurring her vision against the dark figure hanging on to her, and the smell of alcohol burns her nose.

She fights against him, but he holds firm until the next wave crashes into them, sending them in a heap into the shallows.

"Kat," he calls out, his voice hoarse. "Kat, let me help you."

She shoves against the intruder, more out of anger than fear.

"Let me help you," he repeats.

Masyn knows he's a stranger, but the stench of alcohol and his firm grasp twist visions of Graham into her mind. "I'm not Kat. I don't know who you are. Now, get lost. Leave me alone."

The guy loses his balance against another impending whitecap and falls into the water, letting out a string of curse words. Masyn trudges up the beach and flops onto her butt on the dry sand. She watches as the man, who looks to be in his late twenties, brings himself to a stand, sweeps his wet hands down his face, then bends down to fetch his trucker hat and place it back on his head. He tilts his chin to the sky before looking in Masyn's direction.

She should feel scared. She should be worried about the intoxicated stranger, angered and walking toward her on a dark, abandoned beach. But she feels nothing—annoyed, maybe, but mostly nothing.

"What were you doing out there?" he rebukes as he approaches.

Masyn stands. "It's none of your business. Leave me alone."

From this angle, the moonlight illuminates the sharp features of his face as he stops at her feet and scowls down at her. The silver glow reflects in his eyes and highlights the intensity burning beneath them, an intensity which only seems to grow as he studies her. Worry flares in Masyn's belly. Does he recognize her? A beachside dweller wearing a trucker hat, he fits the mold. But luckily for her, Ace

Madden isn't a household name in East Coast beach towns like it is in California.

"What? Don't just stare at me. Say something," Masyn demands, hopefully interrupting his thought process before recognition can click in.

He yanks off his cap, runs a hand through his wispy hair, and looks away, his shoulders deflating on an exhale. "Nothing. Sorry. You just—you remind me of someone I used to know."

"Kat?" Masyn challenges.

The man swallows hard and his scowl returns, but this time his eyes are dull with the weight of a memory. Masyn holds his gaze. She recognizes that weight—the heavy temptation to give in. Close your eyes, and let the memory sweep you away so you can be done with it.

"You shouldn't be out here. You have no idea what could happen out there in dark water. Whatever that was," he says, pointing at the ocean, "don't ever do it again. You'll get yourself killed."

Masyn scoffs, leaning down to grab the bottle the man dropped on his way out here. "Speak for yourself, buddy. You and me, wherever it is we're at, we're on the same level."

"You don't know me," he hisses, fighting against the frown tugging at his lips.

"I don't need to. I'm looking at you right now. Watching you stumble around and try to save someone who's already gone. We're both prisoners, dude. Puppets to a past that does nothing but hold us up and push us down all at the same time. The only difference is you might have your key," she says, raising the glass bottle and shoving it against his chest. "Or at least you'd be able to get some control back if you tried," she adds before she turns to walk away.

He catches her by the wrist, pulling her back to face him. "Wait," he blurts. His eyes search hers in desperation, dipping down to her lips and back up. "I think I want to know you."

"Don't," Masyn spits.

"Tell me who you are," the man tries again, his voice cracking.

Masyn rolls her eyes and pulls away. "Nobody worth mention."

Chapter Three

The next morning, Masyn's in a daze. Her dry clothes signal that she must have returned to Aunt Nat's at some point in the night, but it can't have lasted long. Masyn sits on the beach at the end of the peninsula, just a ways away from where she entered the ocean last night, and watches as the morning light colors the ocean's hue while stretching out the kinks in her muscles that only a night sleeping on sand could have caused. There's a sole surfer out on the water—a decent rider for a middle-aged man—the only surfer she's seen in Ellsworth so far. It's not long until he walks up the beach and starts unzipping his wet suit. Though the swells here pale in comparison to the West Coast, the surf is still high—he's missing valuable waves.

As he walks past her to get to the parking lot, he stops. He takes one long look at Masyn and cocks his head. "Whatcha doin'?"

Masyn pulls at her sweatshirt sleeves. "Watching."

"And?"

"You're leaving at the wrong time. The best sets are starting to roll in."

"You surf?"

She winces, shakes her head, and gets up to leave.

"Hey," he calls out, throwing his arms up in confusion, smiling. "What was that for?"

Masyn shrugs one shoulder. "No, I don't surf," she finally answers, torment obliterating her brain fog as it slices through her.

She sits back down a distance away and looks out on the ocean as the man walks past her without another word and puts his board in the back of a pickup truck.

"Kid," he shouts from behind her.

She looks back to see the man propping a purple surfboard up against the wooden fence lining the parking lot on the small bluff. He silently studies her for a beat, something between pain and longing shadowing his smile, before slapping the *No Surfing* sign. Then he points at her and tosses some wax her way before retreating to his truck and speeding down the gravel road, headed toward the nearby houses where Aunt Nat lives.

After several minutes of solitude, Masyn looks around hesitantly. The series of stickers climbing up the side of the purple surfboard catch her attention. There's a skeleton hand holding up a hang-loose sign, a cat with sunglasses, and a retro Rip Tide logo. Masyn rolls her eyes, but the quote in block letters under the Rip Tide wave has Masyn on her feet and walking toward it. She's seen this sticker before, on one of her dad's old surfboards. Scanning her surroundings once more, she collects the board and retreats to her spot, where she falls to the sand with a thud and rests the board on her thighs. She runs her fingers over the peeling vinyl letters that read *Just Surf.*

Just surf, Masyn thinks, looking out over the ocean. *You* can *just surf.*

Minutes pass as she tries to clear her mind, but thoughts of *that night* encroach without warning.

Masyn and Graham had a pact to go night surfing at every full moon. That night, Graham had showed up tipsy after a dinner with friends, and Masyn toyed with him. She enjoyed the feeling of teasing him, daring him to make a move. She had even worn her cheekiest swimsuit, hoping it might entice him.

They were messing around on longboards when he freed his leash and hopped on her board, letting his own flee to shore. He grabbed her for balance, holding on longer than necessary. She ignored the tang of alcohol tingling her nose. It felt nice to be held by him. She thought about every time they made contact during practices. She'd cherished every playful nudge, every time Graham put a hand at the small of her back when pointing out a wave, every congratulatory hug that lingered just a beat longer than necessary. But that all changed in an instant when he pulled her back to him and splayed his hand across her stomach, his fingers dipping into the hem of her bottoms, and she realized she was flirting with something far beyond her scope of maturity. He felt too big, too strong. Everything about their proximity suddenly felt wrong—violating, even. She pushed him off the board and jumped into the salty water, kicking to put distance between them.

"Oh, come on, Ace. You can't leave me out here to swim back. The current's too strong. I was just catching my balance. I'm sorry," he'd called.

Masyn stopped, giving him the benefit of the doubt, and extended the board out to him.

Masyn squeezes her eyes shut and blinks away the memory. At some point, she had begun rubbing the wax over the board on her thighs. She's grateful for the jolt of pain that pulls her back into reality when her knuckles scrape against the rough surface. Remembering the events that followed would be too hard. She's not ready to relive the memory of Graham mounting the surfboard behind her to tandem paddle—her butt caged between his shoulders.

But now she can't stop it.

Masyn grabs the board and hauls it as quickly as she can toward the water in an effort to reshape the memory. She duck dives and crests the waves without turning back, but once she's in position to claim a wave, she can't bring herself to pop up onto her feet. Now, every time she's on a surfboard, she relives that night like an out-of-body experience—being overpowered in the water and just as debilitated by panic. If this wave were to do the same, she wouldn't have the strength to save herself.

Who am I kidding? she thinks. She can't allow herself to play the victim when she set Graham up to do what he did. Masyn stares at the water under her board, and in her mind's eye, it turns dark, like it was that night.

Though she suddenly felt naked in her cheeky bikini, his elbows slick against her hips, she convinced herself she was overthinking and relaxed her body beneath his. They'd done this plenty of times in training. It was part of surfing.

He slid up her body to whisper in her ear. "There you go, Ace. You're okay."

"Yeah, sorry I almost left you hanging."

"You always like paddling this way. I know you do. I think it's time we both admit we fit. I know you feel the same things I do."

She stilled. She had thought about it when she shouldn't have. But she never expected to feel as violated as she did in that moment with him against her, urging her to do more than she felt comfortable with.

"We're good together. Let me show you."

Masyn remained frozen. "Graham, this isn't right. You could get in trouble. We could get in trouble . . . with Rip Tide."

"Relax! Rip Tide has no business in our personal lives. Just hear me out. We've crushed it this season. We're a team—a great team. And the Triple Crown is coming up. What if taking us to the next level makes us unstoppable? Legendary, even?"

There was nothing she wanted more than to win the Triple Crown. It would secure her Rip Tide sponsorship for another year, maybe even more. It would put her in line to compete in the Junior Tour . . .

Maybe he was right.

Masyn snaps back to reality and cranes her neck to see a wave rolling in behind her. She has to get away from the memory, and she's in the perfect position to drop in on what looks to be a massive swell. Paddling as hard as she can and forcing herself to think about her technique, she pops up on the board, refusing to hold back.

Bottom turn, snap, carve, cutback.

But these mediocre maneuvers don't keep the memories at bay. Masyn ducks into the barrel of the wave and sees herself that night, face down on the surfboard, looking sidelong at the black water and nodding her head in response to Graham.

Graham didn't wait to close the distance between his mouth and her neck. His forehead pinned her cheek against the board. His hand lifted her hip and resumed its position on her stomach like it hadn't at all been an accident before. Once more, her subconscious was triggered by his brawny adamance. In an effort to throw him off her, she grounded her forehead and knees into the board and lifted her butt into him, but he was too heavy, and the motion only seemed to make him want more.

"That's it. You and me, A-babe."

Masyn slashes her hand into the wall of the wave, angered by the intrusive memory. She leans forward to propel out of the barrel, over the crest of the wave, and throws a 360 without thinking twice. The subsequent landing is jarring. The wave twists over her board.

And then she's down.

Now, just as she predicted, the memory aligns with her current circumstances. Water floods into her nose and mouth, the salt sting unbearable as it takes over her senses. She tries one more time to gain control. She fights until the sting is too much, numbing her senses.

Everything went black.

REALITY WASHES OVER MASYN when the sensation of floating crashes with what she can only describe as what it would feel like to be trapped in a washing machine. She doesn't know what's up and what's down, but she's felt this before—she's been swallowed by a wave. She doesn't fight it, just curls into a ball and waits. White-wash pummels her into the sand, and she drives her hands and feet down with all the force she has until she breaks the surface. She gets one insufficient gulp of air before she's pulled under again, but this time she knows it's almost over. When she hits the sand, she crawls as fast as she can and lets the current take her to the shoreline, where she coughs up more seawater than she thought possible before rolling onto her back.

She hears her dad's voice in her mind. *That's it, kid, you survived it. It only gets easier from here.*

You survived it, she repeats in her head. She keeps her eyes closed, hoping more memories of her dad will come to cover up the memories that just tore her down.

"Kid! Hey, kid! You okay?"

Masyn furrows her brow, trying to place the voice. When a warm hand rests on her shoulder, she flings herself into sitting upright and opens her eyes to find the surfer from before crouching in front of her. They stare at each other for a moment.

"I'm Redford. I live just up the bluff. You can call me Red."

Masyn scans her surroundings. "Your board! The leash snapped," she says, moving to stand. She has to find it.

"It's fine. It's fine. Don't get up. Here, take this." The man pulls a damp towel off his shoulders and blankets it around Masyn.

She wipes at her face only to find the saltwater running into her mouth isn't ocean water, but tears. A sob escapes as she pats her eyes with the corner of the towel. "I'm sorry. I'm so sorry."

Red looks briefly over his shoulder, then whips his head back to get a closer look. "What in the . . . ?"

A younger guy, muscular but lean, charges down to the beach, his head angled down at the ground. Masyn takes in the tips of his hair flaring out from under his cap and the Rip Tide logo on his t-shirt stretching against his pecs.

Surfer. Great. She rolls her eyes and averts her gaze, now seeing the blood dripping down her legs. She hadn't realized she was bleeding, but it only makes sense that her limbs have some road rash from scraping against the sand.

"What the hell were you thinking?" the younger guy implores once he's close enough. He crouches down to grab the surfboard from where it washed up on shore a short distance away, its tip bent forward and broken.

"Tate, lay off."

"I can't believe you gave this to her. How could you? You didn't think something like this could happen? Do you just hand this out to any reckless kook you see on the beach?"

Red stands, pulling the other guy—Tate—to the side. "Don't say things you don't mean. We both saw the same thing."

Masyn rips the broken leash from her ankle. "He's right," she says, standing. "I don't have any business using it. I don't belong out there."

She holds the leash out to Red. When Tate finally looks at her, he does a double take, his eyes boring into hers.

Masyn groans. Now that she can see his face—sharp nose, sunken cheeks hidden under a shadow of dark stubble, haunted eyes—he's easily recognizable as the guy from last night. Considering the state he was in, she's surprised he even remembers walking down to the beach.

"What were you doing out there? And throwing a 360?" he questions.

Masyn grips her torso and shakes her head, moving away. "I guess I was looking for somebody I used to know."

Tate whirls on Red before Masyn is out of earshot. "Who is that?"

"Don't know."

"So, you just decided to give Kat's board to some strange girl on the beach?"

Redford narrows his eyes. "The heck you care? You haven't so much as looked at this thing in years."

Tate holds the board at arm's length to assess the damage, then tosses it at Red's feet.

"I saw Kat when I looked at her," Red admits. "I felt her even before I saw the similarities. That girl and Kat, they have the same spirit. I don't know what that was out there today, but I'd be damned if she doesn't know her way around the waves. You saw it yourself, all of it. Don't try to deny it."

Chapter Four

Masyn catches sight of herself in the full-length mirror of the women's restroom at Wingate Forbes Academy, the most prestigious boarding school on the East Coast, and the school she's attending starting today. She looks too tan, too sun-bleached against the amber glow of the building, her very cells a reminder she doesn't belong here. The only reason she's been accepted is because her grandfather—rather, step-grandfather—is the headmaster. She combs her fingers through her still-salty hair and pulls at the hem of her plaid uniform skirt. Looking down at her scuffed high-top Vans, she lets out an exasperated sigh and walks straight out of the bathroom, not stopping until she reaches the headmaster's office.

A woman is waiting at the door, and even her easy smile falters when Masyn faces her. "Masyn, welcome to Wingate Forbes Academy. My name is Karina Kensington, and I'll be your guidance counselor this year. The headmaster is ready to see you now."

Masyn's returning smile is minimal at best.

Mrs. Kensington opens the heavy wooden door to reveal a large office with stone walls, bookshelves, and mahogany furniture. The headmaster, an older man with salt-and-pepper hair and piercing grey eyes, snaps his gaze up from where he's looking down at his desk, then slowly tips his chin and leans back in his chair.

"Ace Madden, on the East Coast. I never thought I'd see the day," he booms.

Masyn looks nervously at the woman who brought her in. When she tilts her head down and steps out of the room, Masyn forces her gaze to meet the headmaster's once more and clears her throat.

"Headmaster Wingate," she responds, because that's the only name that feels right in this moment. In their few encounters, "Granddad" never fit, and she can't call him James here. She doesn't want to draw attention to their family ties, nor would he allow it.

He pulls his lips tight and nods. "Please, have a seat."

When Masyn sits, her eyes catch on the file with her name sitting open on his desk.

"Oh, yes. I was just reviewing some details your parents and previous school sent over. Don't worry, I won't spill any of your secrets to your classmates," he says with an incriminating wink. "However, I did give a file to each of your teachers."

"Why is my personal life any of their business?"

Headmaster Wingate narrows his eyes in challenge. "Because when they see your work—or rather, your lack of it—every one of them is going to wonder how you got into the most elite college-prep academy in the nation."

Masyn looks down at her sneakers. She knew she wouldn't fit in here, but she didn't expect to feel so unwanted. "I'd prefer if they didn't know who I am or why I'm here."

"There's no compromising information in this folder. It's more of an FYI file. I'm not one to spread the family's dirty laundry around. Here, this will be your schedule," he says, handing over a white slip of paper.

"Isn't this a little long?" she asks, scanning the class list. "I'm a junior. There's like ten credits on here, and I've already taken some of these classes."

"WGA only produces top-tier college candidates. You might have sat through some of these courses, but your grades don't suggest you've *taken* them. Besides, every class here is an even more superior version of the honors courses at your last school. You'll thank me for allowing you the extra experience." Headmaster Wingate pulls out another slip of paper and slides it to Masyn. "This is a list of extracurriculars and volunteer opportunities. You'll need to select one from each column. Your counselor will be checking in to make sure you're fulfilling whatever it is you choose."

Masyn bites the insides of her cheeks and raises her eyebrows in response.

"Well, class is about to start. You better go. But please, tomorrow, try to be a little tidier. Besides, I thought they weren't allowing you to wear those surfer brands anymore."

She looks at the slouchy pullover hoodie she threw over her uniform. "It's a free country. I can wear what I choose, even if they don't like it."

"Not at this school." The headmaster clears his throat. "Now, you best be getting off to your first class."

As Masyn nears the door, she turns around. "With all due respect, Headmaster, don't call me Ace. You know, dirty laundry and all."

Masyn stops in the doorway before entering her second period AP Chemistry classroom. Her stomach churns at the idea of walking into a classroom full of students already in their seats.

"Okay, class, rumor has it we have a new student," the teacher hollers from his desk. "Is there a, uh . . ." His back is to her while he shuffles through paperwork to find a manila folder. He cocks his head to read the name on the outer tab as he stands and rounds the desk. "A Masyn Madden here today?"

She looks at the room of students lounging every which way in their seats, as if daring her to try to enter the cliques they've already solidified in the first few months of the school year . . . or rather the first two years. Spots at Wingate Forbes Academy don't just open up. These students have likely been here since they were freshmen. Masyn steps into the room and clears her throat, too nervous to offer even a slight smile. The teacher turns to face her, and they both freeze.

He's wearing chinos and a button-down shirt, and his hair is styled in place, but there's no mistaking it. There's the shadow of a permanent hat dent in his hair, and when he looks at her, the flare of silver in his eyes shoots straight to her heart.

It's the guy from the beach. The one who pulled her out of the water the other night and yelled at her for being reckless the day after. Tate?

Isn't he too young to be a teacher? He can't even be thirty. Teachers at this school are like forty-plus, Masyn thinks.

He clears his throat. "I'm, um, Mr. Houghton," he stammers, his discomfort causing Masyn to break eye contact. She looks at the file in his hands, taking in just how thick it is as he flips it open.

"Please don't read that," she blurts, but she can't bring herself to look him in the eye.

Tate raises an eyebrow and studies her features for a long beat before snapping the folder closed and tossing it back on the desk. "Okay. Tell us, then, what's your deal?"

Masyn pales and looks down at her feet as she searches for an answer. He can't seriously be asking her to talk about her emotions in front of the class, can he? "My deal?" she finally asks, looking up and silently pleading with him not to make her answer the question.

"You know, your thing," he responds slowly, uncertainty shadowing his voice. "What do you do in your spare time? What's the one thing that takes up all your extra brain space? Everyone has one, so what's yours?"

Surfing. Graham Gentry. The thoughts come instantaneously, like a neurologic reaction. Panic rises in her chest, not just because she can't share the only things that come to mind, but also because he already knows. He saw her surf. If she doesn't say something, he'll blurt it out to the whole class. She tilts her chin to her shoulder, pivoting ever so slightly away from the class. She feels his eyes on her—everyone's eyes on her—as she mentally pushes past her issues. Before she comes to her senses, someone grabs Masyn by the elbow and forces her out of the room.

She looks up to see Adison Wingate, her cousin-in-law, flashing a fake smile. "We'll just be one minute, Mr. Houghton," Adison calls over her shoulder.

"What are you doing here?" Masyn demands after being pinned to the wall outside the classroom.

"What am *I* doing here? I own this school. *Wingate* Forbes Academy. What are *you* doing here? This is the last place you belong, *Ace*," she taunts, singsonging Masyn's surfing nickname.

Masyn rolls her eyes and shrugs out of Adison's grasp. "It's not like I *want* to be here. Don't ever call me that again."

"My dad said your family had beef. Didn't say they were trying to get rid of you."

Masyn clenches her jaw. Adison doesn't need to know the details. There's no doubt she'd flaunt any morsel of information all over the school.

"Oh, I see. After your little party-girl rampage, they excommunicated you from Surf City *and* your own household? I guess that checks out, you know, now that you're a nobody."

"Ladies," Tate—err, Mr. Houghton—interrupts, leaning around the doorjamb, "class has started."

"One second, Mr. Houghton. We're almost finished," Adison instructs, as if she really does own the school.

Mr. Houghton pulls away from the door but pauses, studying Masyn. She gives a small nod and moves to walk around Adison and into the classroom.

Adison grabs Masyn's forearm and leans in close. "Listen to me. You are a nobody here, too. Understand? Nobody," she hisses. "If you tell a single soul who you are, I will make you royally regret it."

Masyn yanks her arm away but doesn't say a word.

As the girls walk in, Mr. Houghton puts a hand out to stop them. "Your family may own this school, Miss Wingate, but you do not own this classroom. That little escapade has gotten you a tardy for today."

Adison rolls her eyes and addresses the class, putting one arm around Masyn. "This is my cousin, Masyn Mad—just Masyn. She moved here from California. And no, she doesn't lay out on the beach all day, and she doesn't know anyone famous. Don't bug her," she deadpans, then turns to Masyn with the world's fakest smile plastered across her face. "You can sit with us at the back."

"Masyn will sit there," Mr. Houghton interrupts, pointing to a lab table at the front, "with McCall. Seats have already been assigned."

When she looks at him, Masyn finds his expression is firm—anchoring—and she can't help but feel like maybe he's pulling her out of the water here, too.

"West Coast, best coast," a broad-shouldered boy shouts. Adison swats his shoulder as she storms down the aisle to her seat.

"Okay, anything else you want to add, Masyn Madden?" The tone of Tate's voice, and the way he says her full name, makes Masyn feel like the contents of her file are written all over her face.

She tries to smile at the class, which turns out to be more of a wince. "Happy to be here."

Tate coughs out a laugh. "Right. You don't have to lie to us," he says, earning a collective chuckle from the class. "Okay, well, welcome to class. Let's move on."

Masyn takes her seat next to a smiling brunette, grateful to be far away from Adison's rowdy group in the back and a safe distance from the teacher's desk.

The *teacher's* desk. She still can't believe it. He looks so young, and he was so angry at her the other day. Teachers don't get angry at innocent people.

When the class ends, Mr. Houghton walks over to Masyn's desk, reminds everyone of the homework assignment, then looks directly at her. "Stay put for a minute, if you don't mind."

She sinks back into her chair and picks at her nails, refusing to look at him. Throughout the class, she thought about their run-ins on the beach, which made her think about surfing, which made her angry. But once she catches sight of the manila file folder in his hands, her eyes snap up to his, ready to defend herself.

Before she can say anything, he drops the file on the lab table with a slap. "Why don't you want me to read this?"

Masyn bites her lip, then lets out a sigh and shakes her head. "Go ahead, I don't care anymore."

"Oh, come on. That's the second time you've lied to me. You weren't scared to speak the truth before." His words are laced with a hint of the anger she saw the other day.

Masyn flicks her gaze to his, wondering once more how this guy is a teacher.

"I won't read it," he continues, this time softer. "Just tell me what you're thinking."

"Why were you so mad about the surfboard? Who's Kat?"

Tate grabs his neck and pivots on his heels. "No. Not that question. Not here."

"Why are you doing this?" Masyn tries again, gesturing to the file. "Because now that I'm your student, you feel bad about your outbursts? You regret wanting to *get to know* me?" She stands and pulls her backpack over one shoulder. "Seriously, go ahead. Read it. But don't treat me differently, and don't talk to me about any of it—don't talk to anyone about any of it. I have to go. I'm late."

"I'll write you a slip."

"I'll be fine." Masyn storms past him.

"Madden!" Tate shouts, causing the hairs on the back of her neck to stand. He holds the file out to her. "Take it."

Masyn slowly walks back to him, pausing with her hand clasped around the file. "Thank you," she whispers, swallowing the lump in her throat.

Tate bites his lips together and offers her a slight nod.

It's not until the final class of the day that the tension in Masyn's shoulders eases at the thought of going home to an empty house. However, ten minutes before the final bell, the school-wide intercom beeps, signaling an impending announcement.

The headmaster's voice penetrates the classroom, eerily clear for an intercom. "Masyn Madden to the headmaster's office. Urgent." He says her name with such emphasis, he might as well just call her Ace.

Masyn bites her cheeks, willing herself not to make eye contact with the two dozen classmates craning their necks to look at her. Her British Literature teacher frowns, then gives Masyn a dismissive wave.

Masyn can sense the reason for the summons is not good. Even still, the headmaster might be her stepfather's father, but he has no power over her. He wouldn't kick her out of his own school. Mostly because that would reflect poorly on him, but it would also stress out her parents and jeopardize the cherished family surf shop they're so busy rebranding. The very same family surf shop James Wingate recently purchased shares of.

Masyn doubts he's ever so much as touched a surfboard.

Karina Kensington is standing at the door again when Masyn approaches. She wonders if this is her sole job as her guidance counselor—to keep an eye on the family's dirty laundry and clean up any messes she causes.

Karina smiles and holds the door for her. Before the door closes, the headmaster starts. "Did you like it?"

Masyn stops, looking to Mrs. Kensington for context. Apparently, she's joining the meeting this time.

"That's what you wanted, isn't it? For the whole school to hear your name?" the headmaster says with derision.

A hint of defensive anger flares to life inside Masyn. Instead of acting on it, she fidgets with the sleeve of her sweatshirt, letting the emotion flicker out as she wonders how long she will have to wait for this meeting to be over.

"Headmaster," Karina scolds as she guides Masyn into a seat and takes the one beside her.

"I just got out of a meeting with one of your peers, distraught that you were unkind to her in chemistry class because she didn't parade you around as Ace Madden."

Masyn's eyebrows fly skyward. "Adison?"

"It doesn't matter who, but now that we're placing blame, I might add that I thought you'd respect the family ties in this school since she and I are only doing you favors."

"Favors? You think Adison wants to do me favors?" Masyn rears back in astonishment. "She hated me before I even met her."

"She invited you to meet her friends, did she not?"

Masyn opens her mouth to retort, but snaps it closed again. She's not an idiot—after the lecture Adison gave her about who rules this school, she knows Adison was only inviting her to sit with her friends so she could manipulate what information Masyn shared with them. But there's no point in trying to compete with the clear favorite in this situation. "I already told you. I'd prefer if no one knew about . . ." She pauses, glancing toward Mrs. Kensington, who just winks and quirks her mouth knowingly. ". . . Ace Madden."

"Yes, you said that, but it is certainly not in line with what I heard is happening out in the halls. On top of disrespecting your family and fellow classmates, how is it you already have one tardy and one request for a class transfer? Have you no dignity to at least put in a morsel of effort on your first day? It's a lucky thing you don't share my last name or else . . ." He trails off and shakes his head. "Nonsense."

"Who requested I transfer classes?" Masyn asks, ignoring his outburst.

"Houghton. Your second class of the day. Your *second* class." His face grows redder with every word. "You know what? No. I'm not going to save you from this. You'll participate in his class, or you'll pay the consequences."

Masyn picks at one of the many bracelets on her wrist. "That stupid file."

"What is that supposed to mean?"

"Every one of those teachers today looked at me like I was already a disappointment. All of them, except the one that didn't have the chance to read the file. Now he's probably looked me up, and he doesn't want to have to deal with me."

"Consequences, Ace. You should be familiar enough with them by now. All that file says are the choices you made. People not wanting to put up with more of your delinquency? That's just another consequence of your actions."

"Headmaster, may I?" Mrs. Kensington speaks up.

He motions with his hand for Mrs. Kensington to speak, but Masyn keeps her glare pinned on him.

"I—You know what, I think this might go over better in private. Would you mind?"

Masyn moves to get up, assuming Mrs. Kensington is speaking to her, until the headmaster huffs and rises from his desk, aggressively fastening the second button of his suit coat before storming out. Masyn has to roll her lips inward to keep from smiling at the counselor's dismissal of the man.

Once he's shut the door, Mrs. Kensington turns in her chair. "I don't think he should have given out those files. I think it was his way of trying to help out his granddaughter, but it didn't have quite the effect he'd anticipated."

Masyn scrunches her nose. She can't help the reaction. Hearing that title—granddaughter—feels like swallowing a foreign object. A rancid one. "Is that in the file? He told everyone I'm . . . related to him?"

"Not that part, no. I know, because I'm well acquainted with the Wingate family. If you'd like me to, I will have a conversation with all your teachers asking for a fresh start."

Masyn shakes her head. "I'm fine. I can handle *the consequences*," she says in a mocking tone.

Mrs. Kensington stifles a smile and nods in response. "Do you like horses?"

"Umm, I don't know. I've never been around them."

"My family owns an equestrian center not far from here. Lots of students take lessons there. Why don't you come and check it out after school?"

Masyn looks her in the eye, really looks at her. This woman might be the most genuine person she's ever met. "What time?"

Mrs. Kensington shrugs and leans over to write the address on a sticky note. "I'll be there 'til sundown. Just ask for me—Karina," she says with a wink, handing Masyn the paper.

Chapter Five

Wingate Forbes Academy is primarily a boarding school. While some local students choose to live at home, the vast majority dorm on campus. After her meeting with the headmaster, that fact leads Masyn to suspect her mom didn't have her stay with Aunt Nat for constant surveillance, but rather the headmaster didn't want Masyn's reputation tainting his high-class students. Either way, she got the better end of the deal.

Nat is her stepfather's sister—the only one of his relatives Masyn halfway likes. She's a few years younger than him and even younger at heart. She always shares wild stories of her trips abroad and used to bring Masyn foreign candies when she visited California. Masyn hadn't fully believed Aunt Nat traveled so frequently until now. She's only seen her aunt for about three hours in the week since she's been here, but Masyn doesn't mind. She's been begging for some solid alone time for months now, and this house is about the best place for it.

It's a midsized, wooden-shingle house positioned between two enormous estates on the bluffs. The inside looks like a Pottery Barn showroom, but the outside is what Masyn loves most. Large hedges and hydrangeas line three sides of the property, and the backyard opens to a sweeping view of the ocean below. Each house on the street has a wooden stairway cascading down the ocean-side hill until the individual paths join into a single boardwalk that weaves through grassy dunes before leading to the open sand. The cove is relatively small, but it brings in some of the best waves Masyn has seen on the East Coast. Even keeping her distance from all things surfing, the salty air and the murmur of ocean waves are comforting to her soul.

As Masyn pops the top off one of Aunt Nat's fancy sparkling waters and sits on the back porch swing, her mom calls. She ignores it, but the screen immediately lights up with a follow-up call.

"Hi," she says, already wishing she'd ignored this one, too.

"Honey, Granddad called. He said the first day didn't go as hoped."

"It was fine."

"It was not fine, Masyn. One of your teachers has already tried to kick you out of class, for Pete's sake. It's embarrassing. I knew it was a bad idea to send you to WFA. Maybe I should come and get you. Or I could send Graham to pick you up."

Masyn chokes on her sparkling water. "Why would you send Graham?" she coughs out.

"Because he's Graham. You guys are . . . he's practically family."

"No, Mom. He's not. Graham and I are no longer a team, so just forget about him. Don't talk about him, and don't you dare talk *to* him, either."

"Masyn Madden! You don't mean that. I know you're stressed, but don't worry. We'll find a way to get you back into Rip Tide's good graces."

"Mom, no! You can't."

"Well, if you don't shape up, I will have to, Masyn. We won't stand for this."

"Why not? Because it's embarrassing?" Masyn's mom doesn't reply, giving each new beat of silence a piercing effect. "I'm so sorry I've embarrassed you in front of the preppy East Coast family you've cared so much about recently."

"Masyn. Cut it out. I'm having Graham call you—" Unable to muster the energy to care, Masyn zones out for the rest of her mom's lecture. Graham can call all he wants. She blocked his number. "Is that clear?" Kennelly adds at the end.

"Sure. I'll try harder."

"I just don't understand. You're a very likable girl. You used to be a straight-A student. What changed?"

"I don't know. I guess, just, surfing maybe. It just got too stressful. Too competitive. I can't go back." Masyn parrots other people's speculations about her with no meaning behind her words. There's no such thing as too competitive to her. She thrives off competition. And she knows exactly why she can't go back.

Graham Gentry.

"You need to make friends, do normal teen things, start posting on social media again. I want to see that you're liking it there, that you're okay."

"Okay. I will, Mom," Masyn says, hating that phrase. *I want to see that you're okay.* That's all that's important to her mom—that Masyn is, at all times, and even in her current state, "okay."

She's not okay. Why isn't it important to anyone that she's *not* okay?

"Thank you. Have you met any friends? Do you like your teachers? Have you picked your extracurriculars yet?"

Masyn takes a deep breath and looks out at the setting sun as she considers the events of her first day. She grasps at the one thing that could get her out of this conversation. "Actually, yeah. Which reminds me, I have to go. I'm supposed to meet someone at the equestrian center down the road."

Chapter Six

When Masyn drives through the gates of Kensington Equestrian Center, she slows to take in the view. The last sliver of the setting sun illuminates bright-green pastures backed by woods and divided by white split rail fences. A grouping of large white barns with black tin roofs and ebony doors sits in the middle of the green space. When Mrs. Kensington said she owned an equestrian center, she severely downplayed the situation. This looks more like the Ritz-Carlton for horses.

Masyn parks and walks toward the hazy light peeking out of the open barn doors. As she nears the entrance, the boy who was sitting at Adison's table in chemistry comes out of the barn wearing tight riding pants and tall boots and scowling down at his phone.

It's not until he nearly bumps into Masyn that he looks up. "Hey. It's Masyn, right?"

Masyn has to force herself out of the trance his sea-glass-green eyes have put her in. "Umm, yeah. Hi."

"I'm Clayton," he says, wiping his hand on his pants and offering it to Masyn.

The combination of his friendly grasp and the way his eyes crinkle at the corners under wavy blonde hair catches her off guard. It's almost as if she wants to smile, something she's not sure she's done genuinely for weeks.

"I was hoping I would catch you at school sometime today, but I didn't see you after classes. I looked for you at lunch."

"Oh, that's nice of you. I had . . . meetings. You know, admin stuff to get settled in and everything," Masyn lies. She was sitting in her car during lunch.

A black BMW rounds the corner and stops just inches from her. The rear window rolls down to reveal a beaming Adison. "Clayton VanDamme. Shouldn't you be getting to that homework, so we can hang out this weekend?"

"Um, yeah. You know, I better go get on that," he says, patting the windowsill. "Masyn, it was nice to officially meet you. Sit with us at lunch tomorrow?"

Masyn doesn't have to look at Adison to know she's balking at the invitation. "I'm not sure if I can. Meetings and all," Masyn says with a shrug.

"Here, let me see your phone." He sticks out his hand, and Masyn hesitantly places her phone in it. "I'll find you," he says, handing the phone back with a crooked smile.

Once Clayton's a safe distance away, Masyn turns her attention to the heat of Adison's glare. "Are you trying to take over my life? Why are you even here?"

"I was invited. Not that it's any of your business. Your life has no interest to me. And by the way, thanks for feeding your granddad lies about me," Masyn responds, already walking around the BMW.

"Ace!"

Masyn whirls around. "Stop calling me that!"

"If you want me to keep your little secret, you better stay away. Got it?"

Masyn checks over her shoulder to make sure Clayton can't hear their conversation, then returns her attention to Adison. "Don't worry. Boys in tight pants aren't really my type."

"I don't know, wet suits are pretty tight," Adison quips back with a sinister smirk. "Especially those Rip Tide ones."

Masyn flinches, her face falling flat, and she has to focus to wash away the memories brought up by Adison's implications. *She doesn't know about Graham, does she? No. Nobody knows why she left surfing.*

"Equestrian is mine," Adison barks.

"I'm not here to ride ponies, Adison. I'm following through on an invitation. That's all."

"I guess I believe you. After all, riding things hasn't worked out for you in the past. Boards or people," she adds before she rolls the window up, and the BMW takes off.

Masyn groans and closes her eyes against the dust. The night she ran away from the Triple Crown title, she ended up at a string of parties that were the epitome of sex, drugs, and alcohol. It was out of character for her, but she didn't care. She was with Graham's friends, who were all over drinking age, so when the cops came, she was the only one that got taken in. But did she get in trouble? No. Because when you're famous—even a little bit—you're seen as an adult, and everyone likes to do famous people favors by sweeping things under the rug. She'd even told the officers about Graham coming on to her, but it was all chalked up to young love and mistakes and brushed to the side. Everything except her reputation. In just one night, the press transformed her from surfing's golden child to wild child.

Thinking back on it now, she wishes she could say she regretted going to the parties, spoiling her reputation, and getting taken in by the police. But she doesn't, because that was the final straw that convinced her mom to send her to boarding school on the other side of the country—as far away from Graham as she could get.

When she opens her eyes, she sees a dark chestnut horse peeking out from its stable. She walks up to it, wondering what one does when interacting with horses. For a minute or two, she just stands there, staring at the horse as it stares right back at her. Finally, the horse bows its head, so Masyn places her hand on its nose. Then, she leans in and rests her forehead against the horse's, its warm breath calming her frustration as a vague memory of her dad's stories about the horses he had growing up pops into her head.

"I see you've met Phoenix." The voice startles Masyn, and she looks up to find Karina walking hand in hand with the man from the beach, Red. "You must be one of the chosen ones. He doesn't take to most people. Isn't that right, Phee?" Karina says as they approach.

Masyn looks at the horse and smiles, scratching him under the cheek. Phoenix looks to the side and sputters before retreating into his stable and turning his back to them.

"He has a certain distaste for me, that's for sure," Red says and offers his hand to Masyn. "Redford Kensington. Although, I believe we've already met."

Masyn takes his hand and shakes it, but he doesn't let go. Instead, he stares at her like he's seen a ghost. Masyn looks at their clasped hands, unsure of what to do.

"Oh, I'm sorry," Karina jumps in. "Red, this is Masyn Mad—"

"Madden."

Masyn's eyes snap to his. He might recognize her from the beach, but she never told him her name. Karina was in the headmaster's office when he called her Ace. Did she tell her husband?

"Dingo," Red says, his voice barely above a whisper.

Now Masyn's the one staring in disbelief at the reference to her dad's surf nickname.

"Dingo Madden and I were best friends growing up. We were practically brothers before he ran off to California and got married," he says with a shaky laugh. "I used to travel to see him surf."

Masyn's heart clenches, the sting that always comes at the mention of her dad poking at her eyes. He'd died in a surfing accident in Hawaii nine years ago. If Red followed her dad's career, he likely knows of the tragedy. Nobody in the surf world missed it.

Before she knows it, he embraces her in a hug.

"I'm beyond honored to meet you," he whispers.

Masyn can't bring herself to speak, but she nods and hopes he knows she feels the same.

MASYN HAS TO BLINK back tears more than once as Red and Karina show her around the barn, sharing stories along the way. She has no doubt Red and her dad were as close as he says. He even has the same mannerisms as her dad.

When they finally lock the barn doors and head for the parking lot, Karina pauses. "Masyn, forgive me if I'm overstepping, but would you like to join us at our home for dinner tonight? I know you're staying with your Aunt Nat, but I also know your Aunt Nat, and—well, we'd just love to have you, if you'd like."

Red turns and nods his agreement, offering a pleading smile.

Masyn considers for a beat, twisting her keys in her hand. "I'd love that, thank you. I mean, as long as I'm not imposing."

"Not in the slightest. You can follow us home. We live really close to Nat," Karina responds with a wink.

Masyn is slightly confused when they pull onto the gravel road that leads to Aunt Nat's before she remembers Red had been surfing on these beaches. Then, Red turns their truck down the brick-paved driveway leading to the large estate directly beside Aunt Nat's.

Masyn parks in Aunt Nat's driveway and jogs around to the Kensingtons' driveway. "Wait, are we neighbors?" she asks as the Kensingtons hop out of their truck.

Karina smiles. "Surprise!" she says, leading Masyn inside. She doesn't hesitate to put Masyn to work in the kitchen, and together the three make chili, which they take out in bowls and eat on the back patio. As they sit in their Adirondack chairs, the crisp autumn air at combat with the warmth of the built-in firepit, Masyn realizes she has that feeling again—like she could smile without even trying.

Things are different here. This evening wouldn't have existed in her previous California life, and something about that feels refreshing. She even goes so far as to wonder if this is what her life would look like if her dad had survived. *Would her family have somehow ended back up in his home town?*

The blissful feeling pushing up the corners of her mouth drops when Mr. Houghton walks out onto the patio. He's changed back into his normal attire, boardshorts and a hoodie with a trucker hat atop his head. Masyn eyes him with panic. He had been kind for a few brief minutes after class, but then he tried to get her transferred. *Does he even know the headmaster rejected his request yet?*

And then there's the fact that she knows he's suffering inside—she saw it firsthand the night they met. But most of all, she can't shake the sight of him holding her by the wrist and looking down at her lips with an expression of torment and lust from her memory. It doesn't make him a predator; it just makes him a guy who didn't know how old she was or that she would soon be his student, who wanted to forget his pain. And maybe would have forgotten it by kissing her.

When he sees her, he freezes, a beer halfway to his lips.

"Tate! Join us for dinner?" Karina asks, surprised but pleased.

Tate hesitates, lowering his beer. "Red said you were making chili. I didn't know you had company."

"Oh, Masyn, you've met Tate . . . Houghton? I think you're in his chemistry class," Karina says, her expression twisting. She must be remembering how Tate tried to remove Masyn from his class.

"Umm, yeah. Hey . . . Mr. Houghton," Masyn says.

"What is this?" Tate spits, anger flashing across his features as he looks at each of them.

Karina screws her face up at Tate. "Don't be rude," she hisses. "What is going on with you?"

Red moves to Tate and puts a hand on his chest. "We had a run-in down on the beach. The three of us," he clarifies to Karina, urging Tate back inside.

"The beach? A run-in of what kind?" Karina asks, worry etched on her face. "Tate, you were on the beach?"

"The complicated kind," Red hollers.

Karina's eyes go wide as she turns her attention to Masyn. "Complicated how?"

Masyn shifts in her seat. "It was nothing. Just a difference in opinions. How do you know Mr. Houghton?"

"Tate is my younger brother. He lives out in the guest house for the time being. He and Red are thick as thieves—he just hasn't been coming around as much, so it surprised me to see him for dinner. I didn't realize you'd met outside of school."

Masyn winces. "I upset him . . . kind of. That's probably why he tried to transfer me when he realized who I was."

"What happened?"

Masyn sets down her half-empty bowl and folds her arms around herself. "Red saw me on the beach the other day and loaned me a surfboard. I wasn't planning on using it, but I did. I biffed a wave and broke the tip. Tate was really mad about it."

"Why would Tate be mad about that? Red has plenty of surfboards. And why was he on the beach? He refuses to even look at the ocean," Karina wonders more to herself than to Masyn.

Masyn picks at the sleeve of her sweatshirt. "Who's Kat?"

A mixture of realization and disbelief washes over Karina's features. "He talked about Kat?"

"I think it was her board." Masyn shrugs. "I'm sorry?"

"Purple?"

Masyn nods.

"Don't be sorry," Karina says, voice barely above a whisper, but that's all she says as she stares into the fire.

After a few minutes, Tate's voice grows louder inside the house. "She's not Kat! You can't just replace her."

Karina and Masyn turn their attention toward the large sliding glass door. Tate is walking out of the kitchen toward the front door, and Red is bracing himself against the island, head hanging between his shoulders.

"I think I should go," Masyn says, standing and grabbing her bowl. "Thank you for having me. I'm sorry I . . . I'm sorry."

"Kat is our daughter. She passed away five years ago." Masyn pauses, shocked by Karina's words. "Those three would surf every morning together. Red still keeps up the tradition, but Tate . . ." Karina shakes her head.

Masyn sits back down, chewing on the insides of her cheeks. "Mrs. Kensington, I'm so sorry. I didn't know," she says. "I shouldn't have used the board. Had I known, I never would have."

"Listen to me, Masyn." Karina leans forward and places a hand on Masyn's knee. "I don't know what Red saw or felt when he found you on the beach, but I know without a doubt that he wouldn't have given you that board if he didn't want you to use it." She pauses for a minute. "You know, we all heal from trauma on our own timeframes. I think that was part of Red's healing. *You* helped him."

After a moment of stretched silence, Masyn asks, "He's still healing even after five years?"

"Aren't you? From the loss of your dad?"

Masyn swallows. "Yeah, I guess I am." When Karina doesn't respond, Masyn works up the courage to ask another question. "Does Red know? Did you tell him who I am?"

Karina shakes her head. "I'm your guidance counselor. It's not my place to tell anybody anything that you might want kept private, not even Red."

"Thank you," Masyn says, flicking a nonexistent piece of lint off her knee. "How do you know when you're ready to heal?"

Karina takes a deep breath and tilts her chin to the stars. "It's hard to say, but I think it starts when you recognize that you're experiencing life through the filter of your trauma, and then you decide to get rid of that filter so you can see and feel the world for yourself. So you can live, and not just exist."

Masyn sinks deeper into her chair. She doesn't feel filtered by her trauma; she feels buried under it, the weight of it even audible in the heavy sigh she lets out.

Karina leans forward, collecting the bowls on the table and gently stacking them. "I'm sorry about Tate. He's just . . . He's still struggling with it all. I don't know what he said to you, but he tends to call it as he sees it, so—he can be blunt, is what I'm trying to say. I hope he didn't offend you."

"It's fine," Masyn cuts in before Karina can question her about the other night. "Blunt is a nice change," she adds with a shrug, then stands and heads for the descending porch steps. "I better go get ready for bed. Thank you for dinner."

When Masyn is out of sight, Tate steps onto the porch with Red on his heels, lovingly squeezing Tate's shoulders.

"That girl is hurting," Karina says, empathy clear on her face.

Red walks across the patio to sit next to his wife. "You should have seen her in the ocean. She wasn't just surfing. She was running from demons."

Tate gulps his beer and shakes his head. "No." Karina and Red look up at him, confused. "She was chasing them down." He swipes a hand down his face and hangs on his chin. "She's not a runner," he says, tossing his half-full beer in the trash and jogging to catch up with Masyn.

"Just like Kat," Karina and Red say in unison.

Chapter Seven

MASYN IS STANDING ON Nat's back porch, looking out at the darkening ocean, when the movement of Tate ducking through the gap in the hedges catches her attention. He straightens and stares at her, taking her in with an ever-deepening scowl before walking up to the porch.

She hurriedly wipes her tears away before turning to face him. "What do you want? It's getting cold," she says blankly, arms wrapped around herself for warmth.

"Grab a blanket. I need to talk to you." He motions to two chairs among the patio furniture.

Masyn ignores his order and sits, shooting him a death glare all the while. "I'm fine."

Tate rolls his eyes. "You *are* just like Kat," he mumbles, ripping his sweatshirt over his head and tossing it at her before taking the other seat. It lands with a thud on Masyn's face, the smell of beer mixed with cologne making her stomach swirl. She sets it beside her, refusing to put it on.

"You're a surfer," Masyn says, pointing to the Rip Tide shirt he's wearing, less of a question and more of a statement.

"No," he says with distaste.

"Right. That's the second time you've lied to me." She gets up to walk inside.

"When was the first?"

"When you pulled me back on the beach. You didn't want to get to know me. You just wanted to lose yourself in something stronger than alcohol."

"I used to be," he divulges. "And you said the same thing, that you don't surf, but clearly, you do."

"Not anymore." Masyn stares at him before looking out onto the black water that blends in with the dark shadows of the yard and the dull night sky. "At least, I don't want to."

"Well, there's one thing we have in common." Tate rests his elbows on his knees, unperturbed by Masyn's attempt to exit the conversation. "Look, I'm sorry. Truly. I'm sorry for how I acted on the beach . . . both times. And for trying to transfer you," he adds. "Kat and I were close, and Red is right. You and Kat are freakishly similar. I thought it might be too painful to have a reminder of her every day."

Masyn nods and sits back down. She pulls her knees to her chest and blankets the sweater over herself, subconsciously hiding from the idea that, without even trying, she's already become a burden to the people in her new life.

"Why don't you surf anymore? Or why don't you want to?" Tate asks.

Masyn looks at him, trying and failing to hide the pain that grips her. Before she has to answer, Tate saves her from his own question.

"Kat . . . Red and I used to surf with her every day. I didn't even like surfing until I surfed with her. It was all fun, all the time. The ocean was a blessing." Tate swallows hard.

"Just surf. Right?" Masyn says, thinking about the sticker on Kat's purple board and how it got even Masyn back in the water.

Tate closes his eyes and nods. "Now that she's gone, it doesn't feel right."

Masyn closes her eyes and rests her chin on her knees. "Is that why you were out on the beach the other night? You really thought I was Kat?"

Tate sighs. He opens his mouth to speak, then closes it again, shaking his head.

"You don't have to explain. I get it," Masyn says, running her finger along the Rip Tide logo at her knee. "Some memories are too hard to hide from, so you become desperate to manipulate your ability to feel them. I don't blame anyone for wanting to forget something with that kind of power."

Tate scrunches his brow and looks at Masyn, *really* looks at her, like he did the first time they met. Like he's looking at her soul and not her sins.

For the first time, someone is listening to Masyn, and it doesn't feel like Tate will judge her. So she continues. "Kat was right. It is a blessing. And I do want to. Surf. But I don't *want* to want to."

Tate cocks his head, trying to understand.

Staring into the darkness, she says, "I thought I knew what I wanted once before, thought I could handle it, but all too fast a power bigger than me took over, and I'm too afraid that it'll happen again to get back in the water. It'll never be just surfing for me . . . not anymore."

They sit in silence before Tate speaks up. "I haven't known you long, Masyn Madden, but I already know you're stronger than you think you are." He pats his thighs and stands. "And don't forget, waves reward bravery." He sighs. "Or so I've been told. We'll get there someday. See you in class?"

Masyn looks at him but keeps quiet. The waves she's thinking about carry more than just saltwater. She's not sure she'll be in class—all of a sudden it feels as if too many people know too much about her past.

Tate stops in line with her shoulders, searching her soul once more. "Madden, promise me you'll be in class tomorrow." When Masyn doesn't say anything, he reaches his pinkie out to her. She looks at it for a long beat before hooking her pinkie in his. Warmth shoots through her.

Warmth. Since when did that feeling become foreign? she thinks.

Their interconnected pinkies feel like a lifeline that Masyn wants more than anything to cling to and not let go of, but she quickly drops her hand back into her lap and watches as Tate turns and walks back to his house.

Masyn stays on the porch, unable to move, and puts on Tate's sweater to fight the numbness beginning to set in, whether from the cold or her body's natural reaction to the memory of Graham that's taken over her. Or maybe from Tate's absence. When that doesn't work, she gets in the shower fully clothed and turns the water up until it's scalding hot.

Chapter Eight

THE HIGH SUN BEATS down on Masyn as she sits on the sand in her bikini and an oversized tee, knees curled to her chest, considering the neon-yellow board in front of her. Maybe if there weren't a giant black spade—the official Ace Madden logo—marking her boards, she would be able to surf without thinking about Graham. Rip Tide created a whole line of gear with that thing splattered all over it. She was their pride and joy. And now what does it symbolize? A castaway, a liability. A mistake.

She flips the surfboard over to hide the monstrosity and stares out at the waves, trying to clear her mind. She didn't think she'd actually put her board to water, but coming out here felt like a good start. A step toward bravery.

Shouts echo down from the bluff, but she doesn't bother to investigate. That's the thing with her lately—she can't bring herself to care about things outside of survival. The thought hurts, because she wasn't always like this. She used to feel more than just the weight on her heart.

She kicks her board and buries her head in her hands.

It didn't used to be like this.

If only she could tell somebody everything. Get it all out. But she doesn't think she can, because some part of her wanted some part of what happened. And besides, she already told the police. They didn't care about anything other than saving the reputations of the two biggest stars in their beloved Surf City.

Before she knows it, Masyn is shaking with sobs. Trying to get a grip of herself, she rakes her fingers through her hair and yanks. Then she hears the shouting again, this time closer, and it sounds familiar. She wipes at her wet eyes and turns to find Tate Houghton stalking up to her in his khaki slacks and gingham button-down shirt.

Masyn grabs her board and hurries to get up, prepared to walk right past him and up to her house without answering a single question. It's been two days since she told him she'd be in class.

He clutches the board, stopping her in her tracks. "What the hell, Madden? You're supposed to be at school. You promised me."

"Let me go," she retorts, trying and failing to yank the board back.

He glances at the bright-yellow surface, his eyes catching on the spade. "What are you even doing with this? We both know you're not going to use it." His eyes don't leave the Ace logo, and Masyn watches him. She has to remind herself that even if he's figured out who she is, he wouldn't know the worst of it.

"Thanks for the support," she says, meeting his eyes for the first time. "Why are you even here? You're supposed to be at work, *Mr. Houghton.*"

He grabs the back of his neck with his free hand and looks out at the ocean. His mouth opens and closes like he wants to say something.

"What?" Masyn blurts.

"I'm not letting you go. Not after I just—" He takes a deep breath, interrupting himself. "You're not a runner."

"You don't know anything about me."

"Bull! How can you say that after the other night? Or the first night we met?" he says without missing a beat. "We're the same, remember? I want to know more of you. We all do. Red, Karina, me, and so many other people want to know *you.*" His eyes flash to the Ace logo once more.

A tear drops down Masyn's cheek and she wipes at it with the corner of her t-shirt. She looks at Tate, holding his gaze.

"What is it, Masyn? What is holding you hostage out here? What are you looking for?"

She lifts her arms halfway before dropping them in a deflated shrug and turns her attention to the ocean, watching the crest of a wave rise higher and higher before curling in on itself and crashing with a roar. Masyn feels that release of power like a shock of terror coursing through her. "Me. I'm looking for me. But there's no point. I don't think there's anything left to find."

Tate drops the board to the sand and wraps both arms over Masyn's shoulders in a hug so tight she couldn't get away if she wanted to. "People need you, whatever you have left . . . You have no idea how much we've needed you." Masyn shakes her head against the cage of his arms, but he doesn't let up. "Don't go. Don't run."

After what feels like a lifetime of silently crying against his chest, she pulls away.

Tate dips his head down to catch her eye. "Trust me," he whispers. "And if you don't want to trust *me*, then trust Karina and Red. Please."

Masyn nods. "I'll see you at school."

"I'm taking you," Tate replies, giving her a look that doesn't leave room for debate. "Go get changed. I'll meet you in your driveway in ten minutes."

TATE PULLS UP TO the school to let Masyn out on the curb. She hops out of his Jeep and faces him. She should say thank you, but she just lifts one corner of her mouth in as much of a smile as she can muster and turns to walk away.

"Karina's waiting for you in her office," he calls.

Masyn doesn't respond. She doesn't want to let him down if she doesn't show up in Karina's office. But as she walks, Tate's words echo in her mind. *"You have no idea how much we've needed you."*

She knocks twice on the thick wooden doorjamb of the office.

Karina waves her in and stands to close the door behind her. "Hi! It's good to see you," she says, giving Masyn's shoulder a gentle squeeze. The warmth in Karina's eyes says she means it. She's not passive-aggressively harping on Masyn for skipping school.

"Thanks. You too." Masyn smiles as she takes a seat and Karina moves back to her desk.

"Pardon me while I send out this last referral. One email, and I'll be all yours."

Masyn nods, taking in her surroundings. The large grid windows glow with natural light that highlights the wooden accents throughout the room. The bookcase behind Karina shows off collector's edition books and small trinkets. Her eyes catch on a driftwood picture frame with a photo of Red and Karina smiling down at who she can only assume is Kat. The girl in the photo has the kind of natural blonde, beachy waves that people spend a lot of money trying to recreate. Her expression is shocked, happily so, with the kind of open smile that makes you feel her joy. But it's her eyes that Masyn can't look away from; completely unguarded, brimming with the surety that the people surrounding her will support her, take care of her, trust her.

Masyn might share a handful of physical features with Kat, but that earnest look has been long past extinguished from her. If Red, Karina, or Tate are looking to fill the cracks that Kat left, they won't find it in Masyn.

Karina looks up, sees Masyn studying the photo, and reaches back to grab it. "That's our Kat. Tate took this picture."

"She's radiant."

Karina smiles down at the picture. "She is," she agrees, running her thumb over the driftwood and setting the frame back in its place. "So, Tate said he found you on the beach this morning."

Masyn exhales. "Yeah. I'm sorry."

"You don't owe me an apology. I was just inviting you to talk about it if you want to."

Masyn stares at the photo for a few more minutes before finding her words. "Surfing used to be my everything. My life didn't just revolve around it, my life *was* surfing. And I liked it that way because . . ."

"Because?"

"It felt like the bad stuff couldn't get to me out on the waves. Now it just seems like it's all waiting for me out there. Waiting for me to pop up on the board so it can trap me and drag me down."

"Can you tell me about the bad stuff? Memories? Feelings? Sharks?" Karina winks.

Masyn looks up at Karina and smiles until her lips start to tremble as if playing tug-of-war with a frown, and she shakes her head.

"I had to read your file. As your guidance counselor, it's my job to read your files. I know you are an amazing surfer with even greater potential. But it seems not too long ago you suddenly didn't want to surf anymore. Is that right? Your sponsors pulled out?"

Masyn nods.

"How do you feel about that? I want you to know that this is a safe space. Anything you share, unless it's causing physical harm to you or others, will be kept completely confidential. You have my word."

Masyn takes a deep breath and picks at the hem of her skirt, clinging to the safety of the knowledge that her hardest truth is not in that file, but also fearing that it could never remain confidential if told to an ethical person like Karina.

"Is that what happened out there during the Triple Crown Finals? The bad stuff trapped you out on the waves?"

"You could say that. It was the first time I had surfed since—" Masyn bites her cheeks and rubs her temples.

"Masyn, hey. Masyn." Karina's voice penetrates the numbness darkening Masyn's mind. "You're okay, you're safe," she repeats as she stands and sets a hand on Masyn's back.

Masyn flinches and shakes her head. "I'm sorry."

Karina raises her hands in front of her and backs up until she's in her chair again. "Don't apologize. If you feel like you can, I think letting out some of those thoughts, feelings, or memories that are fighting against you will help. Release some of the pressure in there. Whatever you think you can give."

Masyn chews on her lip and thinks for a moment before shaking her head once more. The action frees a tear, and Masyn swipes at her face.

"Is there a reason that you feel like you can't talk about it?" Karina asks.

"I don't want to admit to something that's only going to cause me to hurt more."

"How do you mean?"

"I'm old enough to know the protocols. Believe me, I've done my research on what I *should* do, who I *should* tell, and I know what will happen. I won't be able to survive the guilt, or the shame, much less the publicity. It would make things far worse for me than if I had just dealt with the situation privately. And since the situation happened to *me*, I think I'm the one who should get to decide how I heal from it."

"So, the bad stuff is bad enough to involve law enforcement?"

Masyn shrugs. "Depends on who you ask. I told the police, because that's what everyone teaches you to do, but they didn't see the need to step in."

Karina nods against her frown and opens her mouth to speak.

"Before you say anything, I'm not in danger. Nobody else is in danger. Nobody else will be in danger. I'm not hurt, nor did I get hurt . . . well . . . it doesn't matter. I'm fine now." She closes her eyes against the recall of her face pressed into the surfboard, salt stinging her nose. "I straddled a line for a long time, and when I realized I'd fallen to the wrong side, I sprinted back. The ethics protocols are made for people with far worse circumstances, not for me."

Karina tilts her head. "As a guidance counselor, I'm obligated to tell authorities if I believe someone is in danger or has been hurt. And I know you said you haven't been, but I also know that sometimes, we can't see everything when we're the ones in the depths of pain."

Masyn takes a deep breath in an effort to stifle her defensiveness. "Did the file talk about my hospitalization? The week before the Triple Crown."

"Yes, but Masyn, we need to talk about this."

"I'm not changing the subject. I'm trying to prove to you that I'm seeing clearly."

Karina nods and hands Masyn her file, pointing to the page. Masyn looks it over.

Hospitalized after injuries sustained in a rip current. Masyn huffs out half a laugh.

"I was with Grah—" Masyn stops, swallowing hard. She can't bring herself to say his name aloud. "I was with my coach that night—Graham—" Her voice is shaky, but she continues. "We were out on the waves, and that's when . . . that's when we . . ." She blows out another breath and closes her eyes. "We crossed a line."

"We?"

Masyn shrugs. "I led him on."

"So he made the first move, and then what? How far past the line are we talking?"

Masyn takes a deep breath. "Far enough to ruin me, but not so far that anyone else would care. I couldn't get him to stop..." Masyn looks up to see Karina nod, and moves forward, motivated by the woman's willingness to listen. "When a teenage girl is brought into the emergency department by a man after she's gone unconscious, they automatically screen for physical and sexual abuse. At least, that's what they told me. The exams came up clear, so there's your proof. I know what I'm talking about, and I didn't get hurt like that."

"You told the police about this?"

"Yes."

"Okay." Karina taps a finger against her lips for a minute before speaking again. "I'm here for *you*. I can tell you've done a lot of thinking and studying about the right way to go about this, and I want to support you in healing the best way you can. Seeing as you've already spoken to authorities, and the screenings have come up clear,

I don't think there's any need for me to report anything. But if you ever change your mind, you tell me, and I will advocate for you. Hurt doesn't have to be physical, Masyn."

They sit in silence for a moment before Masyn feels like talking. "The Triple Crown was my first time surfing since . . . the hospitalization. I sucked in the opening heats, but I hung in. I just couldn't shake what happened between Graham and me. I tried to tell my mom, and she shut me down. It was like she didn't want to hear the truth because then she would have to do something about it. She didn't want to have to deal with my problems, so I went out with the heat.

"I sat there and let the sets come in, watching my competitor rip into one wave after the next. Then, right before the heat ended, I decided that the repercussions of not trying would be worse than facing the truth, so I paddled out for a wave, and I surfed my best wave ever. I caught air twice, and I felt so good. I was sitting at the back waiting for priority to turn to me when I caught sight of Graham on the sand. He had this sign he would do when he was proud; he would hold his arms up high and make an upside-down heart, a spade, with his thumb and forefingers. That's when I knew that he didn't care. He didn't think he had done anything wrong. He thought he was bringing us closer, strengthening our team bond so we would win. I didn't want to make him right. If I got the title . . ."

What he did would have been worth it.

Masyn shifts in her seat. "That's when the bad stuff closed in. I caught another wave and surfed my hardest to get away from the memory, but it kept encroaching. That wave scored a perfect ten. I could hear the excitement from the beach before I even finished, but the only thing worse than succumbing to the blackness that was starting to fog my mind again would have been running into the arms of the people who knew I was drowning and didn't care. So I ran. I surfed as fast as I could to hit the sand before the buzzer rang to close the heat. I ran. Under the pier and as far away as I could."

Masyn crumples, holding her head in her hands and shaking it back and forth.

"It sounds like you feel guilty about that, but I'm not sure it's warranted. Can you help me understand? What part of all of this are you regretting?" Karina asks.

Masyn looks up at the ceiling and bites her bottom lip to quell the anguish in her chest. "All of it. I shouldn't have even surfed the title match. I should never have trusted my coach. I shouldn't have run away when it happened. I should have pushed harder, fought harder." She stops, covering her face with her hands, slowly dragging them down as the darkest, most naked truth escapes her. "Or maybe I should've just given up. Then I wouldn't be haunted by the feeling of being trapped in the water. I wouldn't have to feel that first dose of numbness take over my senses time and again." Masyn quiets, flexing her fingers against the sudden tingling and letting the sobs roll through her. Terrified by what she just shared, she stands and eyes the door.

Karina makes no move to stop her. "I'm really glad you told me this. Do you think this way often?"

"I don't want to die, truly—when I woke up in the hospital, I was so grateful to be alive. But with every day that passes and I still can't get back to myself, I can't help but think maybe I was *supposed* to let the ocean take me. It's like by reviving me, Graham interfered with that, too, and now I'm stuck in this tormentingly empty shell of myself."

"Why do you think you feel this way?"

"Because I can't surf. It's not just that I'm too afraid of the memories it brings. I don't really know how to explain it, but I used to meditate before surfing, kind of like soul-searching. And every time I would feel the ocean lifting me up; I would see myself on the waves. Now, all I see is the view from the ocean floor—dark, and heavy, pressing directly onto my heart. I can get over some silly little kiss; what I can't get over is all the other unexpected, unexplainable things that night did to me. All the parts of me it took away."

Karina nods in understanding. "It's not about the kiss. At least not anymore."

"As much as I try to, the truth is that I don't know what happened in the water. Maybe there was a riptide. Maybe there was," Masyn repeats in a daze, trying to convince herself.

"You feel like all control has been taken from you. Graham betrayed you, but maybe the ocean did, too. It was your only safety net, and it took advantage of you just the same."

Masyn furrows her brow against the gut-wrenching zap of confirmation that shoots through her core. That is exactly how she feels. She moves to wipe away the tears streaming down her face only to find her whole body is trembling.

"Masyn, look at me," Karina says, her voice soft but firm. Masyn struggles to lift her gaze but holds it there until she can see through the blur of her tears.

"You are more than a surfer. You *are* Ace Madden, and you are *still* more than a surfer. Nothing outside of yourself, not a person, not even the omneity of the ocean, can alter your identity. But you can." Karina watches with empathy as a sob rolls through Masyn, but she continues. "If you want to surf, surf. If you don't want to surf, that's fine, too."

Suddenly the weight on Masyn's heart bursts like the salty spray of a crashing wave. She itches to run out to the ocean or anywhere else that might free the terrifying, vindictive release now bouncing around inside her. It's all she can do to stay seated in that office.

When Karina dismisses her from the meeting, she bolts out of the office and down the corridor, but she stops in her tracks when she comes face-to-face with Headmaster Wingate.

The bell rings and students swarm the hallways. The headmaster is scolding Masyn, she can see his mouth moving and his brows furrowing closer together with each second, but all she hears is buzzing in her ears. Behind him, Adison struts out of his office with a manilla file folder in her hands, grins, and walks in the opposite direction.

She can't hear what the headmaster is saying over the roar of the halls, but she can read his lips. "Ace, listen to me, Ace!" In her peripheral vision a classroom door swings open. Mr. Houghton stalks to Masyn's side. Masyn snaps her head in his direction, and suddenly her senses catch up.

She sees the way Tate analyzes every inch of her in a matter of seconds. "Don't run, Madden. You don't have to run," he says under his breath. But all the individual particles of the weight that crashed down inside her are still bouncing around, trying to find a way out. If she stays here, she will burst.

She takes off and runs back the way she came, out the front administration doors and into the woods surrounding the school.

Chapter Nine

MASYN TRUDGES THROUGH THE wooded area until it opens into sweeping pastures lined with white fences. The enormous white barns of Kensington Equestrian Center stand like a beacon in the distance. The few horses out grazing don't pay her any attention as she walks across the pasture, except Phoenix, who walks right up to her. She stops to pet him before continuing toward the barn. The horse follows, nipping at her blonde waves flying in the wind. When she reaches the far end of the fence, she sits atop it, and pets Phoenix as he sniffs her. It's not until a pair of tan and weathered forearms rest next to her on the fence that the horse chuffs and trots away.

"I tell ya, he really doesn't like me," Red jokes, making Masyn smile. "Shouldn't you be at school, Little Madden?"

She sighs and quirks her mouth to the side. "I kind of ran away," she says, noting how easy it is to be honest with him.

Red lifts his brows in question.

"I'm not good at counseling, or being counseled, or whatever. I blew up."

"You know, I always thought I learned more about myself when I was with horses than anywhere else, anyway. Don't tell my wife." He winks. "Your dad did, too."

"Really? I vaguely remember him talking about horses," Masyn says, her features lightening as she scans the pasture, picturing her father trotting around on a Thoroughbred. "I was only eight when he died."

"He and I were out here all the time. I'll admit I practically had to drag him out here to ride a horse instead of a surfboard, but he always liked it in the end."

Phoenix whinnies and pads his feet in the distance.

"What was he like? When he was my age?"

"Trouble."

They both laugh until Red's phone rings. Masyn can hear Karina's frantic voice on the other end.

"Hold on just a sec. I've got her right here," Red says into the phone.

Masyn snaps her attention to him, wide-eyed, and Red holds up one hand to reassure her. "No, I don't think that's necessary. Put him on the phone." Red makes a face before speaking again. "Headmaster, James, I've got this. Trust me. Call off your dogs. Well, that's her decision. Okay. Yep. Goodbye, Jim."

"How bad is it?" Masyn winces.

"It's fine. Something you have to understand about Wingate Forbes—it's full of wealthy tightwads." Masyn's mouth drops into a surprised smile. Red continues, "Sometimes you have to swallow your pride and give them what they want. But this—today—this is fine."

"Thank you."

"So, you want to ride?" Red asks, offering her a hand.

"A horse?" Masyn asks with a taste of disgust.

"Or a surfboard." Red winks. "I'll let you pick."

Masyn looks toward the ocean. She can't see it beyond the trees, but she can visualize the swells crashing just like they did inside her not even an hour ago. "A horse might be a good start," she says, taking his hand and hopping off the fence.

ONCE RED HAS TWO horses saddled, he helps Masyn on one and leads her out to the largest pasture before mounting his own horse.

"What do I do?" Masyn asks.

"It's not hard. Just hold the reins and let the horse teach you. Your legs determine your speed, but squeeze too tight and you'll get thrown off. Kind of like surfing."

After rounding the pasture a few times, Masyn trots, then finally gallops. The wind flies through her hair and against her skin, breathing life into her. She brings the horse to a stop and leans down, draping herself over its neck and praising it. With her cheek pressed to the horse's soft mane, she notes the feeling spreading through her. The warmth of the horse seems to seep into her, clearing out the debris and bringing new energy. She closes her eyes and breathes in the horse's musky scent, allowing her soul to relish in the warmth it's been lacking for so long.

"Okay kid, are you hustling me? There's no way that was your first ride. You're a natural," Red says as he guides his horse to circle around Masyn.

Masyn smiles. "I guess I've been missing out. I feel like I could take over the world right now."

"Feel like you can go back to school tomorrow?"

Masyn sits upright and shivers against the chill that runs through her as she stares down at her horse. "Did Karina talk to you? About me?"

"How do you mean?" Red comes to a halt beside her.

"About what was in my file."

"And breach student-counselor confidentiality?" He raises his eyebrows. "Karina would never. I, on the other hand, cannot keep a secret."

Masyn nods, already zoning out thanks to the sapping fog that sweeps over her mind whenever she thinks about her baggage. Any warmth gained from the horse ride has been extinguished. She's torn between wanting her secret locked up tight and thrown into the ocean, and wishing Karina had told Red who she was, so the weight on her heart wouldn't feel so heavy.

"She did talk about you, though. Hasn't stopped. She says you beam brighter than you even realize. That she can already tell you're stronger than most adults she knows."

Masyn rolls her eyes and tries to smile.

"Look, Masyn, I'm gonna tell you a secret. See, I can't help myself. You ready?"

"Shoot."

"I already know who you are, if that's what you're getting at."

Masyn flinches, spooking her horse. She pulls on the reins and brings the horse around to face Red.

"You can't tell me you're my long-lost best buddy's daughter and not expect me to Google you, Ace."

The color drains from her face. She sits up a little straighter, squeezing her thighs just to the threshold of a command as she decides whether to bolt or face Red's judgments.

"Woah," Red bellows, whether to her or the horse she's unsure. "You're really talented, you know? And you work hard. I know this doesn't make sense coming from me, but I'm so proud of you."

Masyn looks down. "You don't know the half of it. I screwed up."

"I know everything the internet has to offer."

Masyn was wrong to think she wanted Red in on the secret. He might not know everything, but he knows the tainted stories the internet tells of why she ran from the biggest surf sponsorship there is. Shame pricks at her, but she forces herself to meet Red's eyes.

"And that half of it I don't believe for crap," he finishes. "If you want to talk about it—the reason you stopped surfing—I'll listen."

And just like that, the fog clears. Out here with Red, the lies can't bring her down—they're nothing but a salty sea spray dissolving into the wind.

Would the same happen with the truth?

Masyn shrugs. "I'm not . . . I can't be Ace Madden anymore."

Red tilts his chin, squinting against her comment.

"I can't surf like I used to," Masyn continues, shaking her head. "I just need a break, I guess."

Red nods. "There's nothing wrong with a break. Breaks are good. But surfing for you isn't just a talent. It's a gift. Don't give it up, Ace."

Masyn sighs and looks into his eyes. They sparkle just the way her dad's did—so full of emotion. And the way he says her nickname is different from how the headmaster and Adison say it. He's not trying to weed out the power of her secret identity—he's trying to put the power back into it.

"Hear me out. Your dad wouldn't forgive me if I didn't try to help you see things differently." Red hooks the reins on his saddle horn and crosses his arms.

Masyn nods, permitting him to go on.

"Innate gifts aren't just sprinkled around to land on anyone they please. They're given to us, *for* us. They help us learn more about the purest form of ourselves when we need it the most. I'm not saying that surfing is the only thing that defines you, because that's just not true, but you're a Madden, and I know there's not a thing that anyone in this world can do to take the saltwater out of your DNA."

Car horns honk in the distance, signaling the rowdy WFA students are pulling up for polo and equestrian training. Red clicks his heels and his horse walks away from where Masyn sits atop hers.

"Wait," she shouts.

Red guides the horse back around and stops in front of her.

"What if my gift feels more like a curse right now?"

"That can only mean someone else tainted it." He adjusts the reins in his hands. "Whatever turned you off from surfing, you survived it. Now it's time to conquer it." He turns back and trots away.

Goosebumps coat Masyn's skin as the terminology her dad once used cuts straight to her heart. *You survived it.* Had he also used to tell her to conquer it and she'd just forgotten? Maybe he was saving the second half for future life lessons he never got to be a part of. If he were here, he would be the person Masyn told everything to. What hurts even worse is she knows he would also be the one to listen. He'd be the one to fix it.

Unable to let this piece of her dad go, Masyn trots up behind Red. "Where are you going?" she calls.

He points to her horse, then the one he's sitting on. "That's my horse. This guy is one of theirs, and if they find out I'm riding it, they'll be ticked. Stay out here, take your time. I'll send Phoenix out to flirt with you."

Masyn reluctantly lets him go, trotting the horse around the pasture until her phone chimes incessantly, signaling incoming text messages.

Mom: No time to call today, but this can't wait. No more absences, no more tardies, no more missing assignments. Granddad will be following up with teachers daily. Also, I want you in a team sport, I don't care what it is as long as there's a team relying on you and vice versa.

The second message includes a screenshot of a flight from Boston to LA.

Mom: Any slip-ups, and I'll hit purchase without a second thought.

Love ya too, Mom, Masyn thinks.

Clayton: You didn't tell me you rode.

Masyn looks up to find the polo team warming up in the next pasture over. Clayton's sitting on the fence with his phone in his hand. When he catches her looking at him, he points cockily and waves.

Masyn: It's new.

Clayton: Doesn't look like it. Can I give you a ride home?

Masyn: I have a car.

Masyn hits send, then realizes her car is at her house. She didn't drive here—she didn't even drive to school—but how would Clayton know that?

Clayton: I'm giving you a ride. Just accept it.

Masyn: I didn't know we were friends . . .

Clayton: It's new.

Masyn watches Clayton watching her as she rides toward the stables where Red meets her at the hitching post. As she dismounts, she catches sight of Adison, who levels a glare at her while strutting over to Clayton. Masyn ignores her and helps Red put the saddle away. She even stays to watch some of the polo practice and wash the horses before packing up her things and heading home. She doesn't so much as look around to find Clayton. If Adison thinks he's hers, Masyn wants nothing to do with him. Who knows what Adison would tell the headmaster if Masyn made a move on her man.

She only makes it about halfway to Aunt Nat's before a shiny black truck pulls up in front of her.

The passenger's side window rolls down to reveal Clayton in the driver's seat. "You didn't wait for me."

Masyn scrunches her nose. "I'm fine to walk."

"Get in, Masyn," Clayton growls, leaning over the passenger seat to flick the door open.

Masyn hops in and turns toward Clayton. He looks like he's having trouble concealing his smile. "What?"

"I thought you'd put up more of a fight."

Masyn flashes him a sidelong glance and makes to get right back out of the truck, but Clayton reaches to keep the door closed, both of them laughing. However, when a black BMW pulls up next to them, Masyn's eyes go wide. "Is that—"

Clayton groans. "Yeah, she does this every time she sees me driving."

Masyn doesn't wait a beat before crouching down to the floorboard.

"What the—what are you doing?"

"She can't know I'm in here." Masyn tugs on Clayton's pant leg to make him look at her. "Got it?"

"Okay, okay. Who's the creeper now?"

She smiles to herself before she hears Adison's voice ringing out through the window.

Clayton keeps his window up halfway. "Sorry, no time to chat," he shouts as he salutes with two fingers and peels out.

"I might have overreacted," Masyn admits from the floorboard.

"Yeah, ya think?"

"Well, I didn't know what was going to happen. Better safe than sorry." Masyn emerges from her hiding place, leaning an elbow on the center console and directing Clayton where to go.

"What's with you two, anyways? Don't think I didn't notice the tension between you guys in class the other day."

"We've never really gotten along. More of a her-thing than a me-thing. I don't know, I'm just trying to stay out of her way, since I'm coming onto her turf and all. The change is still new for both of us."

"So basically, she's jealous that she has to fight for attention every minute of every day when you come in unannounced, and everything you touch turns to gold."

Masyn freezes. "That's not true."

"Seriously? Did you not notice that half the girls at school have started wearing beachy waves and a fraction of the amount of make-up they normally put on? I've been at this school since freshman year. Preppy has been the only style until you got here."

Masyn scrunches her face. He must be exaggerating.

"Oh wait, you probably didn't notice because you were only at school long enough to diss the headmaster. Nicely done, by the way. Care to explain what that was about?"

"Ugh, not really." With everything that has transpired today, the run-in with the headmaster feels like days ago.

"Also—I'm not done—you said riding a horse was new, but you looked like you were born on that thing out in the pasture today. Like I said earlier, just accept it." Then Clayton leans toward her, pinning his sparkling green eyes on hers and sings along with the Harry Styles song playing on the radio. "You're so golden."

Masyn can't suppress the surprised laughter that bubbles up. "You're too much of a cool kid to sing to the radio."

Clayton's face falls flat. "You're right. Where's my phone? We need handpicked songs."

She laughs and hands him his phone from the cupholder. "I don't sing."

"Yet another thing you can do for the first time and be perfect at," Clayton teases, swiping the screen until the opening notes of "Build Me Up Buttercup" ring through the speakers. Within the first few lines, they're both belting the lyrics out the windows as they drive down the gravel road to her house.

Clayton grabs her hand and pretends to sing into a microphone between their interlocked fingers. As they sing the lyrics to each other, Masyn notices her smile is there without force. But all too soon, her inner voice turns on her. *You're not golden anymore. You don't deserve this.*

Masyn closes her eyes.

Conquer it, she recites.

One look at Clayton, head tipped back and neck veins bulging as he sings up to the sky, brings her back. Masyn allows herself to stay in the moment for as long as it lasts, taking in the wind in her hair and the sunshine on her face.

What she doesn't see is Tate Houghton walking down his driveway and stopping dead in his tracks at the pure joy plastered across her face.

Chapter Ten

MASYN SITS ON THE floor of Aunt Nat's garage, staring at the quiver of surfboards propped against the far wall. Just this morning she sat tormented on the beach, but after her meeting with Karina, her afternoon with Red, and her ride home with Clayton, she feels lighter. It makes her think maybe she could loosen her hold on the Ace secret a little bit. Karina and Red know, and she hasn't combusted. Maybe she could tell more people. Tate? Maybe Clayton?

She smiles at the thought as the lyrics to "Build Me Up Buttercup" play on repeat from her phone's speaker. She lays back to gaze up at the ceiling, tossing a wax block over her head, the cold epoxy floor creating goosebumps on the flesh of her midriff where her cropped t-shirt has risen.

"Madden!" Tate's voice rings out through the open side door.

Masyn springs to her feet, wedging her body between the door and the jamb to block Tate's view.

He stops short, looking her up and down. "What are you doing in there?"

She glances over her shoulder at the boards on the wall, the rack of wet suits, and boxes of Rip Tide apparel all marked with the trademarked spade of the Ace Madden logo. The very one he seemed to notice on her board the other day.

This is her chance. She could tell Tate.

"None of your business," she deadpans, stifling her panic by pulling the door shut just a little more and inching forward as much as she can without coming chest to chest with him.

Thinking about telling him is a whole lot easier than actually doing it. Thinking about it doesn't have consequences, which is good, because consequences never seem to go in Masyn's favor.

Tate doesn't budge. "You're acting suspicious."

"It's *my* garage."

He folds his arms across his chest, causing their arms to brush, and narrows his eyes at her. Masyn nonchalantly rubs at the goosebumps spreading up her forearm and steps back.

"What's with the song?" Tate pushes.

"Also none of your business."

Tate raises his eyebrows and points at the wax disc in her hand.

Masyn raises her eyebrows right back, daring him to say something.

That silver gleam sparks to life in Tate's eyes. "Planning on shredding?"

"Why are you here, Tate?" Masyn demands, shoving the wax into his palm.

"Karina wants to know if you'll be joining us for dinner. She's making fried chicken." He leans his head down ever so slightly, coming further into her bubble, and adds, "So you've got some time.

Fried chicken takes forever." He's taunting her, challenging her to surf.

Masyn bites her lip, remembering everything she revealed in her last conversation with Karina. "I might be."

Tate lifts his chin, trying once more to see what Masyn's hiding behind the door.

"That's it," she says, nudging him back with her forearm and slamming the door shut. "This is private property. I'll see you at dinner . . . Maybe."

Tate straightens, and a smile overtakes his face.

"What?" Masyn snaps. "What are you doing?"

"Nothing," he replies, the grin illuminating his features. "This is called a smile. You should try it sometime."

Masyn pinches her lips together and tries to glare at him, but she can feel the corners of her lips tugging up and softening her stare until she's almost smiling at him as he looks at her like she commands the tides.

"I can't believe it," Tate says, shaking his head.

Panic flares to life in Masyn's chest. "No," she snaps.

He can't know. If Tate knows about Ace . . . somehow she knows she won't be able to keep the rest of her secrets from him. It feels like admitting this to him could break down all her protective barriers at once. With one look, he'll know everything.

Masyn steps forward, grabs a now highly suspicious Tate by the biceps, and turns him around, pushing him back toward his house. "There's nothing for you here."

"Hold up, hold up." Tate wheels back around. "I also came over to check on you."

"Why?"

"We haven't talked since I found you on the beach. You okay?"

Masyn looks down, picking at her nails. "I think so." She shrugs.

"I saw you with the VanDamme kid," Tate admits, his voice more gravelly than before.

Masyn looks up at Tate from under her lashes. "And?"

He blows out a breath, shaking his head. "If you ever need someone on your side, you can come to me."

"I'm not sure what you mean."

Tate steps toward her, forcing her to look up to meet his eyes. "If Clayton VanDamme, or any one of those other WFA fools hurts you, you tell me. I don't care who it is. I'll take care of them."

Masyn briefly wonders if Tate would take care of Graham, too, if he knew. "Clayton's a nice guy," she answers, rubbing at the flush of heat on her neck. Tate's jaw pulses. "But I'm not really in the state of mind to date around, or to date anybody in general. I'm not that kind of girl."

"Trust me, Masyn, the boys at this school aren't going to accept that answer. Not from you." Tate turns to walk away.

"Hough," Masyn says, pulling him back. "Why do you care?"

"You don't have anyone out here. Now you have me."

"But why? Why do you care about *me*?"

Tate clenches his jaw and looks down at where her hand still clutches his arm. "You and me, we're the same. Isn't that what you said on the beach?"

Masyn nods, searching his features.

Tate swallows hard. "I felt it, too."

Once Tate leaves, Masyn walks right through the hedges and knocks on the Kensingtons' back door.

Karina waves her in with floured hands. "Did Tate find you? I just sent him over."

"Just talked to him. I think he went back to his place." Karina smiles, and Masyn walks to the sink to wash her hands. "Does he know? About me—the Ace version of me?"

Karina passes Masyn the dishcloth from her shoulder to dry her hands and shakes her head. "I haven't told him anything."

"He probably talked to the headmaster or read the file before he gave it to me."

Karina laughs. "Tate doesn't talk to the headmaster. But I did hear that he collected all the files from your teachers."

Masyn smiles to herself and opens the fridge to look for salad ingredients in the crisper. By now she doesn't even have to ask what she can do to help.

Karina hands her a knife. "Something you should know about Tate—he's a protector. If or when he does find out, he'll be on your side."

They work on their respective tasks side by side for a moment. If Masyn didn't know that about Tate before, she certainly felt it a few minutes ago.

Finally, she speaks up. "I'm sorry for causing a scene today."

"Masyn, honey, please don't apologize. I'm really proud of you for making the progress that you did. I know it's not easy to open up hard memories."

Masyn sighs. "You're the only person who knows those details. I didn't exactly expect to share them."

Karina sets the latest batch of fried chicken aside and turns to face her. "How did it feel?"

"It sucked. I know what it feels like when something rips you apart from the inside out, but replaying that out loud was . . . It was tormenting."

Karina wraps her in a hug, careful not to touch her with messy fingers. "I know. I've been there. I know."

"I thought talking about my feelings was supposed to make me feel . . . I don't know, lighter? More like me, or the me I used to be? Isn't that what everyone always says?"

Karina pulls away with a sad smile. "You'll never be the you you used to be. None of us will. We're all changing every day with each new experience we face. For better or for worse, we get to decide."

Masyn bites her cheeks, and Karina goes back to the frying pan, thinking for a minute before speaking again. "You're right, though. Nobody tells you how much it hurts to start the healing process—the courage it takes to consistently confront your trauma until it doesn't scare you anymore isn't the kind of bravery that feels good. It's the hardest thing I've ever had to do." Her face is turned away from Masyn, focused on the frying pan, but Masyn sees her dab at the corner of her eyes as she sniffles. "Do you think you're ready to take on that kind of healing?"

"It's like standing up on a surfboard, letting go of the flimsy thing you call security, and giving yourself to gravity—forcing yourself to fall until you learn how the powers coming at you from all sides will try to take you down." When Masyn realizes she's talking out loud, she looks up to see Karina leaning against the counter, her full focus on Masyn.

"The waves reward bravery." Karina tilts her head. "That's what Red always says."

That's what Tate said, too.

"I think I'm ready to go on offense. To put energy toward something other than shutting out my memories every hour of every day. Because it's not working. The memories don't go away the more I shut them out, they just show up in more situations," Masyn admits, bracing the counter for stability.

"Let's do it. Together," Karina offers. "Or as together as you want to do it."

AFTER A HEARTY MEAL and countless stories about the mischief Red used to get into with Masyn's dad, Red grabs the plates and clears the table. Masyn thanks them for dinner, and starts to excuse herself, but Karina stops her.

"Masyn, Headmaster Wingate is expecting you to have chosen a sports team to try out for tomorrow after school. Have you thought about which one you want to join?"

"Umm, I used to play volleyball."

"The girls' volleyball coach is excellent. He's a fan favorite among the students, and he might be the best in the state. The team always competes in the upper-level tournament. I think you'd fit in great with the girls, too, but you'll have to prepare for a grueling tryout. It seems like every girl in the school wants to be on the team."

"Because the coach is a playboy," Tate scoffs.

Masyn's gut clenches, and she looks down at her feet. "Oh, umm. I haven't quite decided for sure yet. I also thought . . ." She tries to think of another fall sport, face flushing, and she catches Tate's eye. He cocks his head and scowls like he's on to her. She quickly looks down at the table. "Sorry, lost my train of thought. I thought . . ." Tate kicks her under the table. "Soccer? I've always wanted to try soccer."

Karina hesitates. "The soccer team's decent. Meg Nance is also a great coach, but I'll warn you the team's a little petty, it seems."

"Wonder why," Tate says with an eye roll.

"What the peanut gallery means is that Adison is on the team," Karina clarifies.

Masyn's eyes widen. "I thought Adison did equestrian."

"Equestrian and polo are clubs, so the students can technically do a sport at the same time."

Masyn quirks her mouth. "Well, it might be good for Adison and me to learn to get along."

Tate's confusion multiplies and Masyn doesn't miss the slight shake of his head as he gets up from the table. "Thanks for dinner, sis. I gotta go." He turns toward the front door, but not before pinning a hard glare on Masyn.

Masyn gives him a look. What's he so put off about? He's the one that kicked her into deciding on soccer.

Karina waves him off. "Soccer is great, if that's what you really want. I'll email Coach Nance to let her know you'll be joining them tomorrow for a tryout practice."

"Thank you." Masyn smiles and heads out the back door toward Aunt Nat's.

Chapter Eleven

It's lab day in chemistry, which means the class is set free to work with their respective lab partners at their own pace. Naturally, everyone is talking about anything but the lab project. Masyn notices Clayton making excuses on multiple occasions to chat with her and McCall. He's leaning both forearms atop their desk, poking at their test tubes, when Adison calls out from her seat at the back of the room.

"Mr. H, aren't we supposed to be working with our assigned partners?" she singsongs.

The class quiets, and Tate looks from Adison to Masyn and back again. "Yep," he says with a disinterested pop of his lips before turning back to his computer screen.

"So, are you going to monitor that?" Adison counters.

Tate sighs, leaning back in his chair. "It's not my job to babysit you. You work with your partner on the lab, you get a good grade. You don't, you don't." He flares his hands out before looking at Clayton and pointing his thumb toward the back of the room. Clayton salutes the teacher and walks to his chair.

"I know, I just would hate for anyone to miss out on the science of hydrogen. It's so interesting how one element can function as different states of matter. It's like it has a secret life."

Masyn sucks in a breath, willing herself not to give Adison the satisfaction of looking back.

"Miss Wingate, a word?" Tate drawls.

Adison stands and follows Mr. Houghton out of the room, only to re-enter moments later with a scowl.

The class has quieted now, so everyone hears Adison when she speaks next, this time her comment pointed toward Clayton. "I wouldn't waste your time. You're not her type."

Masyn just shakes her head and pulls her lab goggles over her face, turning back to the experiment. She refuses to let Adison get a rise out of her.

"She's into much older guys. Toned and tan, if you know what I mean. You should see her boyfriend back in California."

Masyn freezes, unsure what to do. Adison wouldn't bring awareness to the Ace situation. She wouldn't want that kind of attention on Masyn. Right?

She feels the eyes of the entire class on her as she lifts her lab goggles back onto the top of her head and looks back at Adison. Out of the corner of her eye, she catches Clayton looking between the two of them, clearly wondering who to believe.

"I don't have a boyfriend," she clarifies, futilely hoping the rest of the class will mind their own business.

Adison scoffs. "Oh please, your pictures suggest otherwise."

"Pics? Pull one up, I want to see the competition," Clayton's buddy Jake pipes in. "My boy C ain't afraid of the big boys."

Adison realizes her mistake the same time Masyn does, and Masyn was right. Adison doesn't want people to know she's Ace, she's just trying to make her sound like a slut so Clayton will back off. Graham Gentry is well-known as the best surfer in the nation, even among non-surfers. If they see Masyn with Graham, they could easily figure out the rest.

"There are no pictures. Well, there were, but they're gone. I deleted them from my social media when people who had nothing better to do started spreading rumors," she says, looking pointedly at Adison.

"So there was boyfriend *potential*! Who's the guy? Come on, you both know. What's with the mystery?" Jake taunts.

"Gentlemen!" Tate hollers. "Clearly, some of us don't care about our grades. Fs don't get you on the football field." His tone is just sharp enough to get everyone to drop the gossip and return to their experiments.

Thankful for the escape, Masyn pretends to read over the lab instructions again, though the flush on her cheeks only grows. She hadn't considered that Tate could overhear the conversation, too. He knows she surfs, but she can't ignore the way his eyes held onto the Ace logo on her board yesterday, and there's a good chance he saw all the gear in her garage. At 5'5", she doesn't exactly make a good privacy screen. If he's figured out who she is, he knows who her coach was—older, toned, and tan. Naturally, he'll make further assumptions from there.

Masyn looks up from beneath her lashes to find him glaring down at his desk, something between fury and concern twisting his face. His knuckles are white from clutching his pen so tightly. His eyes flick to Masyn's. When their gazes lock, he tilts his chin up and swallows hard, immediately releasing the tension in his fist as if he knows he's been caught, before standing and walking toward Masyn's lab table.

"You sure you want to try out for soccer with that?" he asks, pointing his pen toward Adison. "She's the captain," he whispers as he walks past her.

Masyn follows Tate with her gaze. She really doesn't want to get into this here. Part of her *is* wondering if volleyball would be better. Now that she knows what to look for, she could fend off a handsy coach, right?

But that's the thing. Throughout her relationship with Graham, she thought she was in full control. She was doing what she thought she wanted, only that very thing turned out to be too much for her to handle.

She can't trust herself, at least not with the coach/athlete dynamic. Not right now.

Soccer it is.

"Wait, you're trying out for soccer? I'm on the team, too." McCall beams at Masyn.

The bell rings and Masyn moves to pack up her things. "Yeah, umm, I don't know if I'm any good. I was hoping I could try something new," she says, standing up and scooting in her chair.

"Wait for me after school. I'll walk out to the field house with you."

"Thanks," Masyn says, a true smile brightening her features.

A long arm wraps around her shoulders, and she flinches before she's swept into stride with Clayton. "Jumpy much?" he asks, leaning down and pulling her closer to him as they walk toward the door. "I forgive you for maybe-dating someone older and tanner than me before we met. Although, I don't know, I'm pretty toned."

Masyn stops walking and glares at him, silently pleading this won't become an ongoing joke.

He clasps her shoulders and ducks his head to look her in the eyes. "Okay, okay. Too soon. I'm sorry. I'm on your side, Buttercup. Promise."

She tries to give him a thankful smile, and he pulls her back in as they walk past Mr. Houghton's desk and out of the classroom. Masyn doesn't dare make eye contact with Tate, but she doesn't miss the way his hand tightens into a fist as she and Clayton go by.

CLAYTON WALKS MASYN TO nearly every class for the rest of the day, so it's no surprise when she walks out of seventh period to find him waiting outside, slouched against the exterior wall.

"You don't have to do this, you know?" she says, stopping in front of him.

"Actually, I do."

Masyn cocks an eyebrow.

"I'm usually normal—with girls—very independent," he says with a cool-kid smirk, "but I can't stop myself. I'm always wondering what Masyn Madden is up to. Speaking of, you need to start texting me back!"

Masyn huffs out a laugh. "All you ever text me are lyrics to the buttercup song. What am I supposed to say to that?"

"I don't know, red heart emoji? That seems sufficient. When in doubt, red heart emoji," he jokes, pointing at her before pushing off the wall. "Headed home?"

Masyn takes a deep breath. "Soccer practice," she says and points to where McCall is walking toward them.

"Perfect. I'm headed to the field house, too."

"For?"

Clayton laughs. "I'm the best dang quarterback this school has ever seen."

"Cool and humble. Things are making sense now."

Clayton jokingly pushes Masyn to the side. When they bump back into each other, he wraps his arm around her again.

"Are you guys officially a thing?" McCall asks as she joins up with them.

"No," Masyn replies.

"Yes," Clayton says at the same time.

McCall suppresses a laugh and looks at Masyn.

"No," she reiterates.

"Yes," Clayton jokes.

"Whatever." McCall laughs, then points past them. "More importantly, why are all the sprinklers on out on the practice fields?"

OUTSIDE THE FIELD HOUSE, they run into Adison and a group of girls flirting with the football team. "Oh, there you are," she says, her saccharine tone contradicting the pointed glare she gives them as she notices Clayton's arm around Masyn. "Coach Nance told me you'd be joining us today. I went to grab you all the practice gear, but Trainer Joe was out of shin guards and cleats," she says, handing Masyn a practice uniform and socks. "I guess you'll have to wear your Vans. So sorry about that! He also must have forgotten to change the sprinkler schedule. I swear that guy does not know how to do his job."

Masyn notices the way the other girls snicker but won't look her in the eye. "Thanks," is all she says as she takes the clothes, refusing to play into Adison's scheme.

Soccer is not what she expected it to be. There's a lot more body contact than what she's seen on TV. Within the first thirty minutes of practice, Masyn is covered in mud, grass stains, and even blood—thanks to the wet grass and lack of cleats. They're running a three-on-three drill when an opposing player runs up to Masyn. She turns her body to block her opponent, just as Coach Nance instructed, and dribbles to the outside corner of the goal. As she's winding up to shoot, a sharp pain drags down her shin. Before she can react, she's simultaneously sliding across the grass and colliding with another body. Masyn rolls onto her stomach and lifts her head to see Adison prancing away, high-fiving one of her teammates.

After practice, McCall pulls Masyn's shirt up and angles her phone camera toward her.

"What are you doing?" Masyn shrieks.

"Umm, documenting this. I've never seen a raspberry this big! Just wait, the comments will roll in."

"You're not putting this on social! It's embarrassing!"

"It is not! You're BA. Besides, it will totally make Adison's plan backfire on her when everyone sees your six-pack."

"I don't have a—"

"Flex!"

Masyn rolls her eyes and does as she's told, just as Nance's voice cuts in. "Madden!" The coach throws a pair of old, worn-out cleats at Masyn's feet. "Put these on and come with me," she says, hoisting a bag of balls over her shoulder and walking out of the locker room.

"Where are we going?" Masyn asks, jogging to catch up with her.

"Dry ground. There are no sprinklers in the stadium."

"Isn't football practicing in the stadium?"

"They'll move."

Masyn fights the urge to shrivel in on herself as Coach Nance cuts right through football practice. She convinces the coach to allow them to use the far end of the field, but even then, Masyn feels the players' eyes on her.

Coach Nance drops the balls at Masyn's feet and starts walking backward. "Give me a fast dribble and then shoot. I want the ball to soar right over my hand," she says.

"What if I hit you?"

"Don't."

Masyn gives an unconvincing thumbs-up and turns to further the distance between them. Once again, she catches half the football team watching her.

This should be good, she thinks.

She drops the ball and starts to dribble toward Coach, keeping her eyes on her the whole time. Coach Nance raises her right arm. Masyn plants her left foot, squares her hips, and aims with her right foot as best she can. The ball arcs up and over Nance's fingertips.

"Nice! Again," Nance instructs.

Masyn runs the drill again, this time using her left foot to send the ball over Coach's left hand. After a few more times, she figures out how to angle her kicking foot just right to get the ball to curve, and even fakes Coach out once or twice. Once the bag of balls is empty, Coach Nance walks up to her, stopping to put her hands on her hips.

"So, tell me, Masyn, are you worth the trouble?"

"What trouble?"

"My field has never been drenched before practice. We both know that was no accident."

Masyn kicks at the turf and hangs her head, exhausted in more ways than one.

I don't turn things into gold, I turn things into trouble, she thinks.

Despite the good day she'd been having—overcoming Adison's schemes without shriveling in on herself—grief tugs at her like the current of a receding wave before the next swell barrels onto the shore. "That seems to be the question of the week," she says, tilting her chin to peek up at Coach Nance, wondering if she received a file, too. Masyn's eyelids feel heavy, and all she can do is lift one shoulder in a half-shrug. "I'm not sure I'd take a chance on me."

Coach Nance looks Masyn up and down. "Want to know what I think? Bringing you on is not taking a chance. It's making a change. Welcome to the team—you're our new center-mid."

Back in the locker room, Masyn unlocks her phone to find a text from Adison. She's included a screenshot of McCall's social media story.

Adison: What don't you understand? Back the hell up, you slut. Or I will let everyone know just how desperate you are. Keeping your secret seems to cost me more than it's worth.

The intense need to be out on the waves, to clear all the hardships from her mind bubbles under Masyn's skin. She hurries to her car, weighing her options. Does she really want to get back in the ocean? Is it worth chancing the haunting reminders? The weight?

Masyn lets out a self-deprecating chuckle. What's the point in healing from her trauma if no matter how far she comes, there's always someone there to take control away from her? Someone's always ready to retrieve the burdens she casts off and manipulate her with them.

In a snap decision, she throws her bags into the car, slams the door shut, and takes off toward home, hoping that a run will do for her what the ocean used to. As she turns onto the gravel road stringing together the few properties on the bluff, she blames the tears that fly off her cheeks on the cold wind and not the rogue wave of emotion that looms over her, threatening to break at any moment.

At the sound of tires crunching over the gravel road behind her, Masyn picks up her pace until she's in a full-out sprint. It doesn't matter who is pulling up—she's not in the mood to chat. Tate's white Jeep passes her as he peels into the Kensingtons' drive, stopping in just the right position to block Masyn's path, causing her to come to an abrupt halt. She braces against the sill of the open passenger's side window as she nearly collides with the vehicle, all the while holding eye contact with Tate. At first, Masyn thinks he might yell at her for running all the way home alone, but his features transform into solicitude. Suddenly, it feels as if their joined gaze is the only thing holding her up. She knows he sees the tears, but she doesn't move. The slight, pitying furrow of his brow is all it takes for Masyn to break. The strong line of her mouth bends into an uncontrollable frown. Tate literally jumps at the display of vulnerability, opening his door and rounding the back of the Jeep.

Masyn tries to go around him, but he reaches for her. "Masyn, wait."

She turns to run around the front of the car. He beats her there, so she reroutes, running down the Kensingtons' driveway and through the hedges that separate their property from Aunt Nat's.

RED POKES HIS HEAD out of the garage, looking from Masyn to Tate and raising his arms in question.

Leaving the Jeep where it is, Tate jogs after her. "Madden!"

"Let it be, Tate," Red grunts, intercepting him at the hedges.

Tate wheels on Red. "She's not okay. She needs us."

"Since when? Two weeks ago on the beach, all she was to you was reckless. What changed?"

"Have you talked to her? Have you had a real, one-on-one conversation with her?" Tate demands.

Red nods.

"Then you know. That's all it takes. I've had to watch her being fed to the wolves day in and day out. If she doesn't have us, she has nobody."

Red dips his head, but juts a hand out to stop Tate from going after Masyn. "Listen, she never was okay. Okay? From the moment she got here, she's never been okay!" he spits, grabbing Tate by the shoulders. Red hangs his head again, catching his breath. "But at least now she's trying. Let her try. She'll never be okay if we interfere with that."

Tate steps out of Red's hold, pulls at his collared shirt, and tilts his head to the sky. "You don't understand—"

"I do." Red's voice is firm. "She's a whole heck of a lot like Kat. I get that more than you know. But she's not. You hear me? She's not Kat. We have to trust her. Come on, pull your car in and meet me in the backyard, but only come if you're really ready to trust her."

"Why?"

"When a Madden flees, there's only one place they go—the ocean."

Chapter Twelve

THE TWO MEN STAND at the edge of the bluff in silence watching Masyn run down the beach and straight into the water, tossing her neon-yellow board over the foam. Red was right—nothing could stop her from breaking through those waves.

Even from their vantage point, they can see the purpose that propels every stroke of her arms as she paddles through the water, duck diving under and cresting over the swells until she's in the clear. For several minutes, she lies back on her board, arms spread on either side of her, letting the incoming sets bob her around as they please.

Finally, she sits up, checks her surroundings, and moves into position to drop in all at once.

Red braces his hands behind his head, elbows to the sky, and Tate bites down on his fist.

"Whatcha doin'?" Karina asks, startling them both from behind.

"Shh," they hiss in unison, pointing to the beach.

Karina squints. "She's surfing," she says with an awed smile.

Red clears his throat. "Not yet."

"She's trying," Tate whispers.

Craning her neck to look at Red, Karina laughs. "Are you tearing up?"

He and Tate snap their heads toward her, blinking in denial.

"Both of you!"

"Would you be quiet? She's going to hear you," Tate scolds.

"She can't hear us up here. You're the ones posted up on the cliff like scarecrows," she says, pushing them down into a crouch. "Are y'all planning on watching the whole thing, or are you going to give the girl some privacy to find herself again?"

"It's just a beautiful thing to witness," Red says. "Someone who understands the ocean so deeply she can't turn her back on it."

Tate rests his head on his fist. "She has the power to pull the tranquility out of the greatest force on the planet. She's just like . . . she's Ace Madden."

Karina and Red snap their attention to Tate, who's still focused on Masyn.

"How do you know that?" Red asks.

Then the three look at one another. "How do *you* know that?" Tate and Karina ask in unison. Instead of answering, they share a smile and turn their attention back to the beach.

Eventually, Karina heads back inside, but Red and Tate watch Masyn surf one wave after the next. There's no denying the swells aren't nearly as big as the West Coast waves she's used to, but one thing's for sure: Masyn Madden can make any wave look good.

By the time the sun has dipped below the horizon, Tate is the only one left watching from the bluff. It's not until darkness settles and Masyn trudges up the sand that he breaks out of his trance and heads toward the guest house. On his way, he catches sight of Clayton's black truck turning into Nat's driveway.

Masyn's still heading up from the beach. If she emerges from the backyard wearing a wet suit with a board in hand, Clayton will know she surfs. Worse, if Clayton looks in the garage—where Tate saw Masyn's quiver of surfboards—he'll know she's Ace Madden. Tate doesn't know why Masyn's keeping her surfing identity a secret, but he's not about to let it slip. Not after he just promised Masyn he'd have her back.

He ignores the internal voice that tells him to stay out of it and breaks through the hedges. To his right, the tip of Masyn's board peeks over the bluff. She's almost reached the top of the stairs. To his left, Clayton's making his way toward the open side door of the garage.

"Hey," Tate calls to Clayton, running out from behind the garage.

Clayton freezes and looks around. "Uhh, hi. Mr. Houghton?"

"VanDamme," Tate practically shouts while casually blocking the doorway, trying to look like he belongs here.

"I'm looking for Masyn." He points at the house and then back to Tate. "What are you doing here?"

Tate grips his koozie-covered can and gestures to the garage. "I'm moving some things around for Nat, Masyn's aunt. We're . . . friends."

"Oh, okay. Are they home?"

"Uh, yeah, no. They headed out a bit ago. Shopping, I think; could be a while."

After an awkward pause, Clayton nods. "Well, if you see them, tell Masyn I stopped by, I guess."

"I'll walk you to your truck." Tate flashes a tight smile and grasps Clayton by the shoulder, tighter than necessary, urging him back toward his vehicle as a light flicks on in the house.

WHEN MASYN CATCHES SIGHT of Clayton and Tate in her yard, she runs inside to create an alibi for herself. A million thoughts run through her mind as she throws on an oversized hoodie, wraps her wet hair in a towel, and adheres under-eye masks for added effect. *What could Tate possibly be saying to Clayton? Had she left the garage door open? Had Clayton seen her out on the beach?*

She flings the front door open and jogs up to Tate and Clayton, suspicious and out of breath. "What's going on out here?" Her eyes lock on the drink in Tate's hand. She can't help but wonder what is hiding behind the koozie. She hadn't noticed Tate drinking alcohol since that night they talked on the porch—but then again, she hadn't seen him much.

"You didn't answer my text, so I was coming to check on you. Whose sweatshirt is that?" Clayton asks.

Masyn eyes Clayton, irritated by the interrogation. What does it matter to him? Then her eyes go wide with realization. She grabs the Rip Tide logo of the sweatshirt and looks down at it. She's somewhat relieved to find that it doesn't say Ace Madden, but more embarrassed to realize the first hoodie she could find and rip over her head was Tate's sweatshirt she had yet to return. Had she not been secretly wearing it every night, this may not have been an issue.

Masyn's eyes flick to Tate's, trying and failing to assess his reaction. "It's my dad's?" she responds, more of a question than anything else.

Tate palms his forehead and turns, taking a few steps toward the garage before sweeping his hand down his face and walking back to them.

"Whatcha drinking?" Masyn blurts.

Tate scowls at her. "I'm your teacher. Buzz off."

Clayton chuckles, but Masyn presses on. "You're also . . ."

Tate gives her a look. "*Nat's friend,*" he says, finishing her sentence for her.

"Come on, tell us." Masyn smirks. "What's your Friday night drink of choice?"

"You have some nerve, you know that?"

Masyn shrugs.

Tate takes a long swig. "It's Pepsi. Clayton, why are you here, dude?"

He puts both hands up in surrender. "Can't a guy check in on his girl?" He points to the rash on Masyn's bare leg. It looks even worse now that it's been irritated by saltwater. "I'm here to heal the wounded."

"What is that?" Tate balks, seeing the rash for the first time.

"Apparently, it's what happens to soccer players. Why are *you* here?" Masyn replies.

"I'm finishing up my project in the *garage* for *Nat*. See how I left the door wide open?" he says pointedly, giving her a look that says she should be more grateful he was covering for her. "Ran into Clayton when he was headed in to look for you. Care to explain what *you* were doing?"

Masyn returns his glare. She saw him and Red standing watch up on the bluff. He's dangling her secret in front of Clayton on purpose. "Obviously, I was self-caring," she quips, pointing to her face.

"Obviously." Tate rolls his eyes, turning toward the garage.

"Where are you going?" Masyn demands, panicked.

"I'm not quite finished with my *project*. Tell Nat I expect to see her tomorrow."

Masyn takes a shaky breath to settle the war raging inside her. In her mind, there's still a small chance he doesn't know about the Ace stuff, but if he goes into that garage, it will be game over.

Can she casually intercept Tate before he reaches the threshold? Or should she stick with Clayton and get him out of the way?

"Don't count on it. She'll be gone for the weekend," Masyn calls out, grabbing Clayton's arm. "Come on," she says, pulling him toward the house. After only a few steps, terrified curiosity gets the better of her, and she peeks over her shoulder.

Tate's gaze bores into hers for a beat before it softens. He holds up a pinkie before ducking into the garage. The door clicks shut and Masyn freezes.

Tate is in the garage, no doubt looking at the spade on every one of her surfboards, reading the name Ace Madden on her wet suits.

When he goes home, he'll search the internet and see the slew of pictures of her with Graham. He'll read all the opinion articles on why she left.

He might believe them.

Masyn releases a stress-laden breath she didn't realize she'd been holding. The release feels like a wall crumbling inside her, only she's not sure who kicked it over—her or Tate. She waits for the numbness to crawl up her fingers, the ringing to echo in her ears, but it doesn't come. Maybe it's the way every time Tate looks at her, he seems to read a piece of her soul. Maybe it's how he's protected her secret since that first night, without needing to know the details. Maybe it's the drink in his hand—if Masyn lets him have this next piece of her secret, he might let her have the next piece of his.

Whatever the cause, one thing is for sure: it feels good to trust Tate.

"Everything okay?" Clayton asks.

"Yeah, sorry. Let's go inside."

Once inside, she removes the towel from her head and secures her hair in a messy bun.

"That was weird," Clayton says.

Masyn rolls her eyes. "He probably just wants to be able to tell Nat he was watching over me while she was gone. You know, chivalry and all."

"He said you guys went shopping . . ."

"We did," Masyn says, turning to avoid looking at Clayton while she lies. "We went earlier, and now she's off on a trip."

Clayton shucks off his shoes. "Do you really think he was drinking Pepsi?"

"Don't know, don't care. Hungry?" Masyn asks, changing the subject as she leads them into the kitchen.

"Sure, I could eat," he says, leaning against the marble island.

"Let's see." Masyn opens the fridge and shuffles through the meal prep bags Nat gets delivered weekly. "We have chicken alfredo or steak tacos."

"Tacos. I'll help."

As they combine the small packets of ingredients, Masyn figures she should try to start up a conversation, but with all that happened today, she can't bring herself to put forth the effort. Too many questions cloud her thoughts. Did Tate know about Ace before tonight? Is that why he watched her surf? Will he forgive her when he finds out what she did?

Clayton seems very aware of her, watching her read the recipe and following after her, already prepared to complete the next step. They shuffle around each other in the kitchen, bumping elbows and sharing small smiles. It's a comfortable silence, Masyn realizes once she stops obsessing over the unknown, making it easier for her to start a conversation when they sit at the island to eat.

Masyn turns to Clayton. "So, the best dang quarterback this school has ever seen, huh?"

Clayton laughs and wipes the corner of his mouth. "I was mostly kidding."

"Mostly," Masyn teases.

"Are you going to come to my games?"

Masyn takes a bite of her taco and thinks as she chews. "I might," she says with a shrug of one shoulder. "If I can walk by that time. This road rash is starting to feel stiff."

"Oh, I actually brought you something for that. It always works on turf burns, at least." He pulls a small tube of ointment out of the pocket of his sweatpants and gestures to her leg. "Here, let me."

Masyn turns her barstool to face him and gives him a nervous look.

"I'll be gentle, I promise," he says as he begins dabbing the ointment on.

Masyn winces and clenches the stool.

When Clayton finishes her leg, he moves to her stomach, scrunching the excess fabric of the large sweatshirt in his hand. "This okay?"

Masyn just nods, biting her lip. She looks at the faded Rip Tide logo of the hoodie and realization hits her. Clayton wanted to know whose sweatshirt it was because he wondered if it was her *older boyfriend's*. She bites her cheeks, trying to stifle both the sting of the ointment and the sense of betrayal.

Clayton looks up from where he kneels beside her. "If you come to the game, you can wear my jersey."

"Mmm, I don't know if that's a good idea." Her voice cracks, but there's no uncertainty in her mind. Especially not if Clayton is jealous of the *older boyfriend.*

"Because of Adison?"

"I literally couldn't care less about what Adison thinks anymore."

"Well then?"

"Because I don't want to give you the wrong idea." Clayton scrunches his face in confusion, and Masyn continues, "I'm not girlfriend material."

"Masyn, seriously?" he deadpans and stands up straight. "You're gorgeous and tough and independent and not worried about what people think about you. I don't know what girlfriend material is, but that all sounds pretty great to me."

Masyn shakes her head and looks at the ground. "I'm serious. I won't be able to give you what you need. Be there for you in all the ways you'll want me to be."

Clayton moves his hand up to dab the ointment on the redness at Masyn's temple. "How did this get so inflamed so fast?"

Masyn thinks about the burn of the saltwater and frowns. "Hot shower?"

Clayton studies her for a minute before accepting her answer. "Fine, don't be my girlfriend. Just be . . . you, and I'll be here in whatever ways you need or want me to," he whispers, bringing his lips to her cheekbone and leaving a soft kiss.

Masyn leans in and closes her eyes against his touch. "I'm just—"

"It's okay. We don't have to have a label. We can just be us."

Thoughts of Graham creep in even as goosebumps cover her neck where Clayton's steady breaths warm her skin. She swallows hard, trying to suppress memories of Graham's touch, and grabs the back of Clayton's neck, pulling his mouth to hers.

He deepens the kiss, sliding his hand to the small of her back and arching her against him. When he dips down to kiss her neck, Masyn squeezes her eyes shut. She *is* enjoying this—part of her is, at least.

She wants to be in the moment with Clayton, so why can't she get Graham out of her head?

What is wrong with me?

Clayton rubs her hip, hooking a thumb on her hip bone. Masyn flinches. She'd anticipated the memory of Graham holding her, arm wrapped around her waist on the surfboard. She knew it would come in intimate situations like this.

What she didn't realize until now was that Graham had touched that same spot on her hip bone on more than one occasion. Memories flood her senses—him hugging her after a win, helping her stretch, adjusting her surfing stance.

The spot singes under Clayton's touch. Masyn pushes him off and stands abruptly.

"I'm sorry," he says. "I wasn't trying to—"

"No, it's fine," Masyn says, shaking out her hands and pacing the kitchen. "It wasn't you. It's just . . . my burn. I think I caught it on something. My fault."

"You sure?"

"One hundred percent."

Clayton starts to lean in again, but Masyn stops him. "I'm sorry. It's been a long day. I have to get up early tomorrow, so I should really get ready for bed."

"Right . . . I better go."

Once he leaves, Masyn immediately jumps into a steaming hot shower, then lays in bed, listening to the sound of the waves. Her phone chimes, breaking her out of her stupor and yielding a photo of Clayton's navy-blue football jersey.

Clayton: All yours, Buttercup.

Masyn: [red heart emoji]

Masyn: Goodnight, Clayton. Thanks for coming over . . . I mean it.

Clayton: Night

Clayton: Also, your soccer practice . . . golden.

Masyn smiles, setting her phone on the nightstand and flopping back onto her pillow. She tries her hardest to focus on this feeling, the warmth that Clayton gives her, but she knows it won't last—she'll kill the sparks, just like she did earlier tonight.

Instead, she rolls over and turns on the bedside lamp to combat the nightmares she knows will come.

Chapter Thirteen

"Did you see that one?" Red exclaims, sloshing water over Masyn as he paddles by.

Masyn chuckles. "When was the last time you actually landed a 360?"

Red sits up and shakes out his hair. "Cut me some slack. We haven't had waves like this in years. You must have brought them from California. Now just give me some time to dust off my gnar."

"When you find it, let me know, old man," Masyn jokes, laying back on her board as Red paddles away to get in line for another wave.

Masyn watches the first rays of the sun paint the sky. Surfers are early risers, and when she saw Red walking down to the water this morning, she followed her impulse to join him, though she has yet to claim a wave. Surfing today feels like teetering on the threshold of triumph or tribulation; simply being out here is a leap of faith. She closes her eyes and focuses on the current beneath her fingertips. That liquefied muscle under the surface does its best to intimidate her, but she finds that out here with Red, someone she trusts, it has less power over her.

A few minutes later, she feels another splash across her belly. "Shouldn't you be finding your steeze?" she jokes before opening her eyes.

It's not Red on a board beside her. It's Tate.

Masyn sits bolt upright and looks to where Red paddles over until he's in front of them, forming a triangle. He says nothing, just sets his eyes on Tate and folds his arms against his chest, a small smile lighting up his features.

Masyn remembers last night. How Tate covered for her and likely found out about Ace. She looks out at the shore, but the feeling she's grown used to in these situations—the need to flee—doesn't come. "Did a jet ski pull you out here or something?" she deadpans. "I was beginning to think you were afraid of sharks."

Tate kicks a leg out and flips her board, dumping Masyn in the green seawater.

Red chuckles. "Welcome back, buddy. Wait 'til you see this." He paddles out, preparing to drop in on the next swell.

Masyn stretches her arms over her board and looks up at Tate, swaying her legs back and forth in the water. "You're really doing this?"

"Floating on a board and calling it surfing?" he teases. "Sure."

Masyn kicks at his board, throwing him off balance. But unlike her, he recovers.

"What can I say? I felt inspired after a certain turn of events last night. By the way, I don't think Nat would want you alone in her house with a boy."

Masyn's eyes widen. "You really don't know how to mind your own business, do you?"

"You mean, *thank you*? For concealing the secret identity you were going to tell me about . . . when, exactly?"

"It was in the file. I told you you could read it."

"I guess I was too busy minding my own business to get to it."

"But not busy enough to stay out of the garage."

"I'd already figured it out, that was just confirmation."

"And?"

Tate's teasing expression turns serious. "You could have told me."

"I know."

"So why didn't you?"

Masyn sets her jaw and stares past him, gripping the surfboard with white knuckles and shaking her head. "It's a thing of the past. There's no point in talking about it."

"If it's a thing of the past that's dictating your future, there's every reason to talk about it."

"Being Ace Madden is not as easy or enjoyable as it used to be."

"Why is that?"

The answer is on the tip of Masyn's tongue. She sees it in front of her as she looks down at the darkening ombre of seawater beneath her, but she tosses it back with the shake of her head.

"What are you afraid of?"

"You won't want to know, Hough. It'll change how you think of me."

"You're wrong, Masyn. I want to know everything about you." Tate dips his hands into the water, paddling closer. "I want to fix everything for you. I don't know what happened in your past, but I've seen you surf, so I know whatever it was that took that passion out of you, you didn't deserve it—and worse, you probably didn't expect it."

Masyn sighs, resting her forehead on her surfboard. She should be cold, sitting still in the ocean this long, but the conversation warms her from the inside out. When she looks back at Tate, he's studying the waves. "Is this the first time you've surfed since . . ." Masyn says.

Tate's jaw clenches, and he nods as a heaviness sets over his eyelids.

"I'm glad you're here."

At that moment, Red paddles up again. "Okay, gals, enough dilly-dallying. I have time for one more wave, and I want the three of us to drop in together."

Masyn smirks before sliding onto her board and pointing at the two of them. "Don't let your rusty steeze cramp my style."

Red heads out to line up, but Masyn stays put, looking down at the jade water as the ripples move her so close to Tate their boards practically touch.

"Hey," she whispers. When he looks up, she leans over, sliding her hand toward his until their pinkies interlock. She squeezes until Tate squeezes back, and then she turns and paddles to catch up with Red.

It doesn't take long for a swell to build up behind them, and the three of them paddle hard, popping up one after the other. Red whistles loudly and points to the cliff. A tiny figure, Karina, is jumping up and down, waving her hands. Masyn carves against the base of the wave and can't stop the huge smile creeping onto her face. She turns to look at Tate, who's completing a maneuver right behind her. When their eyes meet, Masyn's smile reaches full capacity—like the moment a comet gains enough heat to burst with light and streak through the sky.

Tate stands up straight on his board and stills, letting the white-wash suck him in, never taking his eyes off her.

Masyn abandons the wave, letting it take off in front of her as she crouches down to a seat on her board. She lets the next wave carry her in and kneels next to Tate, who's huddled on all fours in the surf. Masyn throws her board onto the dry sand and looks around. Red is already halfway up the bluff, running to Karina.

"Tate," she says, putting a hand on his back. He doesn't move. "Tate," she tries again, turning his face in her palm.

His eyes are red, from emotion if not saltwater, as he searches Masyn's gaze. Passion flows between them like everything Tate is enduring is being transferred to Masyn through an invisible current. Her heart hammers in her chest, trying to work overtime so Tate's doesn't have to. Masyn closes her eyes and dips her chin. It's too intimate to feel these things with him.

Tate shrugs her hand away from his jaw and stands, yanking at the zipper on his wet suit. "This was a stupid idea," he says, fighting his way out of the long neoprene sleeves. He shoves the material down to his waist and looks at Masyn before picking up his board and starting up the beach.

"Why?" Masyn's voice cracks.

He stops and turns toward her. She forces herself not to look at how his abs ripple, or the way his muscles striate across his shoulders. "Because . . ." He cuts himself off and shakes his head.

"Because I'm not Kat?"

Tate's eyes flash with pain.

"I'm not, Tate. I never will be." Masyn looks at the sand speckling her thighs. "If you're looking for a replacement, I . . ." Masyn sighs. "I'll never shine for you guys the way she did."

He stalks back over and squats down in front of her, their faces only inches apart. "Kat shined." He nods, his expression serious. "You, Ace? You burn," he says, pain crackling in his voice, before he turns and walks up the beach without looking back.

Chapter Fourteen

OVER THE NEXT FEW weeks, it's more than apparent something changed between Masyn and Tate that day they surfed. Masyn should have seen it coming; the beach seems to reinforce their affinity for one another every time they find themselves on it together.

But Tate had surfed for her. She'd held his face in her hands. He'd told her she burned, a phrase she's been searching for meaning within ever since.

Now, Masyn can't so much as look at him without feeling his stubbled jaw under her palm. She'd watched that jaw tense plenty of times before, but the way the masculine muscle pulsed under her touch shot its way straight through her and into her core memories.

Masyn and Red surf every morning. If Tate joins them, he keeps his distance—never makes conversation—and Masyn can't bring herself to poke the bear. At school, he doesn't even look in Masyn's direction. And the nights she joins the Kensingtons for dinner, Tate stays out in the guest house. Kensington Equestrian Center is the one place Masyn knows she won't see Tate—at least, she's never seen him here before.

It's a relief, not having to wonder if she'll run into Tate, not having to worry how she should react, why he's not talking, if she should leave. In its own way, this place is safer than the ocean.

As Masyn walks into the barn, kicks off her slides, and steps into the rubber boots Red gave her, she can't help but smile. She's still sweaty from a private soccer practice, dressed in an oversized t-shirt, athletic shorts, and long soccer socks under her muck boots with a shovel in hand. *Tate would get a kick out of me right now,* she thinks.

Phoenix whinnies and juts his head out of his stall as if reprimanding Masyn for thinking about Tate.

"I'm sorry, Phee. I know, this is our place," she says as she reaches a hand up to scratch behind his ear.

"Talking to horses now, are you?" Adison's voice calls from down the aisle. Masyn turns to find her strutting toward her in riding attire, slapping her crop against her palm. Masyn ignores her and resumes her duties, bridling Phoenix.

"What do you think you're doing?"

"Redford is short-staffed this week. I'm helping out."

"That explains why no one came to get my horse. I had to tie him to the hitching post myself." Masyn gives her a sidelong glance and continues her work while Adison gives her a once-over. "I'm surprised you're not mucking in your high tops."

"What do you need, Adison?" Masyn asks, moving toward her to open the stall.

"I wouldn't do that."

"Why not? I have to clean the stall, and I'm not going to do it with him in there."

"That horse is a jerk."

Masyn looks at Phoenix. "Don't listen to her. You know you're my favorite."

Adison scoffs. "Of course he is. What, do you just look for things that are mine to take over?"

"What are you talking about?" Masyn asks.

"That horse. He's mine. Or he was, before he proved himself useless and Daddy sold him to the staff." Phoenix widens his eyes and stomps his front hoof.

"I think he just doesn't like you," Masyn retorts, opening the stall to bring the horse out.

Adison looks like she has more to say, but Masyn ignores her until she hears Mrs. Wingate call down the aisle.

"Adison Elizabeth!"

Adison stiffens. "I said I'd be right out, Mom."

"You were supposed to be at your father's house prepping for the club an hour ago."

"Mom!" Adison shrieks, looking at Masyn with wide eyes. Masyn freezes, half tempted to hide behind the horse. *Her father's house?* Adison's parents prided themselves on their flawless marriage. Masyn would have heard if they were separated. Before Masyn can act, Shaylynn Wingate floats into view on the other side of the stall door.

She does a double take. "Masyn Madden, I heard you were in town," she says, tossing her hair back and squaring her shoulders. "You heard nothing. Are we clear, Ace?" The name sticks on her tongue like its articulation was intentionally weaponized.

Masyn shifts her glare from Shaylynn to Adison, who looks mortified. "I'm just trying to muck my stalls." She clears her throat. "Excuse me."

Shaylynn clicks her tongue. "Adison, in the car, now. We have a lot of work to do if we want to make you look presentable for dinner."

No matter how much she tries not to care, Masyn can't help but stare at Adison's submissive posture as she follows her mom out of the barn. When she reaches the door, she turns her head just slightly to meet Masyn's eyes. With a sigh, her shoulders slump and her eyelids flutter with defeat.

Masyn gets back to work mucking the stalls, but she can't shake what she heard about Adison's parents. It's clear they're living in separate houses, but apparently that's not public knowledge.

Maybe Adison has a few secrets of her own.

Once she's finished with the stalls, Masyn slips her slides back on and pokes her head into Red's office.

"There she is. How'd it go, kid?"

Masyn smiles and looks down at herself. "I smell like a barn."

"Glorious." Red smiles. "Karina's out at a charity event, but she said there's dinner for you in the fridge if you want to stop by. Dawn patrol in the morning?"

Masyn laughs at his surf lingo. "Wouldn't miss it. Hey, you know the Wingates, right?"

"Sure," Red says with a nod. "Which ones?"

"Adison's parents. They're not like . . . divorced. Are they?"

"Ahh, I don't know, kid. Wingates have a lot of drama, but they keep it behind closed doors. All I can say is, I know what a happy marriage looks like, and it's not that." Masyn nods, thinking to herself, and Red points at her. "Dawn patrol—can't wait! Now, go eat. It's already getting dark."

When Masyn gets home, she walks straight over to Karina's, but stops short with her hand on the doorknob when she catches sight of Tate through the back door. He takes a long swig from a beer bottle, then leans on the kitchen island, hanging his head. He looks more than tired—he looks weighed down. It's giving Masyn flashbacks of the night they met.

Masyn slips to the side, leaning her back against the house, contemplating whether to go in. She hasn't seen Tate drink since her first week here, but she can't just waltz in there and talk to him after he's been avoiding her. And she'd be lying if she said alcohol doesn't make her a little nervous. Graham had been drinking the last night they surfed together. If he hadn't been, she might not be standing here right now.

Besides, Tate wants nothing to do with her. That much has been painfully apparent to Masyn over recent weeks. Even so, she still feels the familiar tug to humor her curiosities. It's as if any shadow of darkness regarding Tate entices her soul.

She wants to go in there and find out what's wrong—why he's drinking—but she knows if she puts herself on his level, she'll stay there long enough to invite her own shadows to the party. She's supposed to be healing.

Masyn pushes off the wall and walks back to Nat's, pulling out her phone as she goes.

Masyn: Come over?

Clayton: Are you seriously texting me first?

Masyn: Is that a yes?

Clayton: Be there in 10.

Masyn: Make it 20 . . . I need to shower.

Clayton: Be there immediately.

Masyn rolls her eyes and twists the shower knob as hot as it will go before jumping in. When she gets out, she puts on a pair of shorts and an extra-large Rip Tide sweatshirt, double-checking it's not Tate's and it doesn't have the Ace logo on it.

Clayton knocks on the front door, and Masyn walks out of her room to get him but stops abruptly in the hallway when she finds Tate on the back patio. They stare at one another through the panes of the French doors. Tate puts a hand to the glass, barely touching it. He dips his head, shaking it before looking up and mouthing, "I need you."

Masyn takes one step toward him, but her focus is broken by the doorbell ringing. She searches Tate's face for some hint of what he's feeling, a glimpse inside his head. Her gaze drops to the beer bottle in his hands and back up to his glassy, sunken eyes and disheveled hair.

"Please," he mouths.

She can't be running to Tate right now. She has to overcome her own trauma, or she'll be forced to move back to California and look it straight in the eyes. Masyn shakes her head ever so slightly and drags herself past him to let Clayton in.

As soon as she opens the door, Clayton barrels in, looking at her wet hair and feigning defeat. "No! I missed it. I'm too late."

"Shut up," Masyn teases, smacking him on the chest and letting one small chuckle escape.

Clayton pulls her into a bear hug against his chest, and Masyn takes a deep breath, taking in the scent of his hot-guy cologne and trying her hardest to let the past thirty minutes melt from her memory.

"Hey, you okay, Buttercup?" Clayton asks, looking down at her.

Masyn nods. "Just tired," she says, grabbing his hand and leading him further into the house. "Come on, let's hang out in my room."

Clayton makes himself comfortable on the small chaise lounge in the corner of Masyn's room, and points at her sweatshirt. "You're always wearing Rip Tide. Do you surf?"

"I lived in a beach town. They practically hand these out for free down there," Masyn says, side-stepping the question. "It's like the Vineyard Vines of the West Coast."

Clayton looks down at the whale on his own t-shirt. "Makes sense."

"So, how was football?" Masyn asks, scooting in next to him.

"I have polo practice on Thursdays, which is why I couldn't watch you practice. I should probably check for new raspberries," he says, pulling at her thigh and lifting her sweater to inspect her stomach.

Masyn laughs. "Stop it! I had a private practice today. No collisions."

"Private?"

"Yeah, well, most of the team had equestrian, and I need all the help I can get."

Clayton dusts his fingers over her midriff. "That's not true. You're already the best one on the team, and you just started playing."

"You're biased . . . or delusional."

He makes a face and pulls her to him. The movement makes her sweatshirt ride up, exposing her stomach. "I'll show you biased," he says, splaying his large hand across her abs and leaning in to kiss her.

Masyn smiles against his lips and pulls away to look at him. He's exactly what she needs. Confident yet innocent in all the ways he should be.

Masyn closes the gap between them, kissing him because she wants to, not because she's trying to escape something. But when Clayton moves down to kiss her neck, thoughts of Graham massaging that very spot before a competition flash in Masyn's mind.

How long is she going to let Graham stay in the forefront of her subconscious? She forces herself to quell the memories.

She braces Clayton's face with one hand and his back with the other, pulling him into a kiss and taking in the curves of his back muscles. She slides her hand to his stomach, running her fingertips down the ripples of his abs. Clayton follows her lead, exploring up her rib cage. He runs his hand down until he reaches her hip bone and readjusts so his body covers more of hers, then rubs her hip again. Masyn shifts, trying to shake away another memory, but Clayton is pressed heavily on top of her. She focuses on their embrace, trying to calm herself and kiss him the way he deserves to be kissed. He continues his path down her hip bone toward her outer thigh.

"We fit together. It's you and me, Mase."

Clayton's voice blends into Graham's, the memory she's been working so hard to keep out flooding her mind as her ears start to ring. She clenches her jaw on instinct, her mouth suddenly tasting like saltwater.

"We're good together . . . you and me, Ace."

She has to get away, she has to escape. Before she knows what she's doing, she's standing beside the chaise lounge, chest heaving, looking down at Clayton as he holds a hand to his bloody lip. "What did you just call me?" she asks through heavy breaths.

"What the heck was that? You bit me," he says, dabbing his lip and sucking away the blood.

"I'm sorry, I'm so sorry." She pulls his hand away, looking at the red welts lining his bottom lip. "Clayton, I didn't mean to . . . I tried to tell you. I can't do this. I can't be who you need me to be." Tears streak her cheeks faster than she can stop them.

"Hey, hey, it's okay," Clayton offers, wrapping his arms around her. "I don't need you to be anything. Just talk to me."

Masyn buries her head in her hands. "I'm so sorry. You can leave."

"Do you want me to leave?"

Masyn separates her fingers to look at him. He looks concerned, not mad in the slightest. She shakes her head.

Clayton pulls her to him, readjusting so she's leaning back against his stomach, his legs on either side of hers. "I called you Mase. Is that bad? I won't do it again if you don't like it."

"No, it's fine. I misunderstood. Just please—let's forget it happened."

He rests his chin on her head. "I'm sorry if I went too far. We can go slower. However slow you need."

"It's not your fault, Clayton. Please, don't think any of this is your fault."

"Can you tell me what's going on? So I don't freak you out again."

Masyn pauses for a beat, holding Clayton's hand against her thigh and circling her fingertips around his open palm before she lets out a long sigh. "Back in California, I—"

The doorbell cuts her off.

"Who's here?" Clayton asks.

"I don't know, maybe it's Tate?" Who else could it be?

Clayton adjusts to look Masyn in the eyes and scrunches up his face, making her realize she called him Tate out loud.

"I mean, Mr. Houghton. You know, looking for Nat."

Clayton frowns.

"Just wait here, I'll go see," she says.

The doorbell rings two more times before Masyn reaches the door and whips it open, ready to reel on Tate.

But it's not Tate.

Adison stands on the porch, wiping her eyes. "Can I come in?" she asks as she walks right in without waiting for an answer.

"Adison, I don't think you—"

"They're not divorced."

"Adison—" Masyn starts, trying to quiet her before she spills her secrets to not just Masyn, but also Clayton, who is likely eavesdropping from the bedroom.

"They're living apart for the time being, but they're—"

"Would you shut up?" Masyn grumbles. This stops Adison with her mouth open wide. "I'm not alone, okay?" She pulls Adison toward the door by the elbow.

Adison sets her glare on Masyn. "Who's here?"

"I didn't tell you that so you could pry."

Adison moves around her, looking left to right from the kitchen toward the bedrooms. "Do you have a boy—oh, you've got to be kidding me." Her indignation mounts with each word as she storms down the hallway toward Masyn's room.

Clayton walks out with his hands halfway up in surrender. "Hey," he says as he meets Adison.

She turns on her heels and storms back toward Masyn until she's only inches from her face. "I told you to stay away—from him, from the equestrian center, from everything. And this is what you do. You two-faced whore! It's no wonder your family didn't want you. You're a disgrace."

Masyn bites the inside of her cheeks and closes her eyes against Adison's insults. They don't sting as much as they were meant to.

She already knows she's not wanted by the people she loves. She's accepted that, along with the fact that the only person who wants her is the person who hurt her most. What stings is the new realization that she's unworthy of anyone else. She'll never be able to give anyone the intimacy they need.

"How could you say that?" Clayton speaks up, wrapping an arm around Masyn.

Adison scoffs and moves to the door. "Oh please, she's..." She looks from Clayton to Masyn, vengeance igniting in her eyes.

Don't do it. Please, don't tell him.

"She's not who you think she is, Clayton," she spits, slamming the door behind her.

Masyn leans into Clayton's embrace, all too aware of the suspicion creeping through him like rigor mortis. "This night is a disaster."

Chapter Fifteen

TWO DAYS LATER, MASYN finds herself on the beach for a bonfire after the football game. She'd spent every spare minute of the last couple of days with Clayton, but all she can think about as she looks at the bright orange flames flickering back and forth is the last thing Tate said to her.

"You burn."

What does that even mean?

"Earth to Masyn." Jake waves a red cup in front of her face. "Drink this. You look like you could use a second wind. Party's about to start." He points toward the group of girls approaching the firepit, with Adison at the head.

Great, Masyn thinks. She takes the cup, looks at the bright red liquid, and downs it.

Clayton looks up from where he's lounging between her legs. "That's definitely spiked."

She scrunches her nose in disgust.

"Yaaaasss!" Jake cheers, handing out more drinks around the fire. When he comes back around to Clayton, he stops and pinches his lip. "Dude, you get bit by a vampire or something?"

Masyn dips her head, but across the firepit Adison chimes in, "That's what happens when you play around with a slut," making Masyn snap her head right back up.

"Are you kidding me?" she blurts.

"Sorry, *Mase*, secret's out." Adison shrugs unapologetically before adding under her breath, "This one, at least."

"Good for you, man!" Jake hollers, going in for a high five with Clayton.

"Bro, no. It's not like that," Clayton says, squeezing Masyn's calf.

"Oh, so you guys haven't . . ."

"Jake, dude. Drop it."

Jake throws his hands up defensively. "Sorry man, I just thought you would have by now."

Masyn stands, taking control of the conversation, and pats Jake playfully on the chest. "I'm going to kill you if you keep talking. Let's go get refills."

"Yaaaasss!" Jake repeats. "Slut, vampire, whatever . . . I like you, Masyn Madden."

Music blares through the Bluetooth speakers, and hours pass filled with games and dancing. Masyn, bored and weighed down but sufficiently tipsy from whatever was in that punch, pulls the cooler open to find a water. She grabs the first thing her hand meets in the icy chest and pulls out a bright-blue can.

"Pepsi." She giggles to herself, feeling a renewed sense of energy, and sneaks off into the darkness.

"WHAT THE HELL ARE you doing?" Tate asks through the crack in the door, voice gruff from sleep.

Masyn holds the Pepsi out to him. "Brought ya somethin'," she says, unable to contain her laughter as she leans on the door and stumbles past Tate into the guesthouse.

"Are you drunk?"

She wiggles her eyebrows and mumbles something along the lines of "I don't know, Hough. Are you?"

"You can't be here."

"Hold on, my phone has been blowing up." Masyn rolls her eyes and flings herself onto Tate's couch, squinting at the bright phone screen in her hand before jabbing it and lifting it to her ear.

"Hey, babe!"

From where he's standing, Tate can hear Clayton's voice on the other end of the line, asking Masyn where she's at.

"Oh, I'm at—"

Tate lunges to grab the phone, ending the call before Masyn can get them into more trouble.

"Excuse me! I was on a phone call."

"Just shut up and don't move." Tate walks into the small kitchen and emerges minutes later with a peanut butter and jelly sandwich, water, and some Advil. "Eat this. I'll take care of your boyfriend." He slumps into the armchair across from the couch, rubbing sleep out of his eye, and swiping open the phone. He looks up abruptly. "There's, uh, nothing I shouldn't see in this text thread, is there?" He winces.

Masyn smiles mischievously and then quickly deadpans, "You're disgusting."

"Probably doesn't matter anymore, seeing as VanDamme has sent you like a hundred texts since you got here."

Clayton: Where'd you go?

Clayton: Mase?

Clayton: Sorry, forgot. I meant Masyn?

Clayton: Are you okay?

Clayton: Babe???

Clayton: Why'd you hang up?

Clayton: Are you at home? I'm coming over.

Tate rolls his eyes and types out a response.

Masyn: Not home . . . at the Kensingtons'. Felt tired. Sorry.

Clayton: Why? Just go home. I'll meet you there.

Clayton: Is Nat home tonight? I can stay over.

Tate looks up at Masyn in disgust before turning back to the phone.

Masyn: I don't know. Don't come over. Phones dying. Bye.

Tate grunts before adding one last text.

Masyn: Also, don't ever send me nudes.

Then he smirks as he turns the phone off, dropping it into his pocket.

"That's mine," Masyn scolds between bites of her sandwich.

"You can't be trusted."

"Thief."

"I believe this makes us even," he says as he stands and grabs a coat.

"Where are you going?"

"To take you home. Like I said, you can't be here."

"You mean you don't want me here."

Tate drops his chin to his chest. "You're drunk, and you're underaged, and literally so much more."

"Not drunk." She holds up a corrective finger. "Tipsy. And I'm sobering up now, thanks to your buzzkill. Just admit it, you wish I wasn't here. You've barely said a word to me for weeks."

"Yeah. I'm your teacher, and you're my *student,* so you're right. I wish this situation weren't happening. Now, let's go."

"What happened to 'You're ours . . . stay . . . we need you.'"

"Both are true, but one of them gets me fired. Possibly arrested."

Masyn stands and walks to the door. "I'll let myself out. Thanks for the sandwich."

"I'm not letting you walk home alone."

Masyn can't believe his audacity. "I live next door. I'll be fine," she says, her features hardening.

"I told you, you're not going alone," Tate demands with more force than Masyn has ever heard from him.

She turns, finding him right behind her as he reaches up to brace a hand against the door, keeping her from opening it. "Why are you being like this?" she asks.

"It's pitch-black outside."

"No, Tate. You said you cared about me, so why are you doing this? Why are you pushing me away? Why are you turning cold?"

"Enough, Ace!" he yells, then drops his face in his other hand.

Masyn turns her back on Tate, wishing she could hate the way the nickname sounds on his lips. She takes a deep breath and wraps her arms around her torso. "I knew this would happen."

"What?"

"That you'd think differently of me. You found out who I was, and now you've given up on me, just like the rest of the world."

"Masyn—"

"Don't!" Masyn insists, swallowing the lump in her throat and pulling at the door handle.

Tate leans in further. "Let me explain."

"No! You don't even know the worst of it, so I'll save you the trouble. I'd hate to burden you with more of my failures. Why do you think I ended up here in the first place?"

Tate drops his hand and steps back, rubbing at his day-old scruff. "I'm an idiot. I'm such a self-centered idiot."

Masyn turns back to face him and slumps down until she's seated against the door. The weight in her chest is almost too much to bear and the ringing in her ears makes her claw at her temples. She shakes her head and closes her eyes.

It's weird, being able to physically feel the emotional turmoil raging on inside yourself before you're able to register it mentally.

When Tate speaks again, he's crouched in front of Masyn, his voice gruff, crackly even. "We hurt in the same ways. You know it's true. You saw it in me that first day on the beach, and I see it in you every single day—in your eyes, your voice, your demeanor."

"Yeah, I'm hurting. I'm glad you can see that. But so what? None of that seems to mean anything," Masyn says, moving to leave.

"Please, don't go. Let me explain, Ace." Tate falls to his butt, resting his forearms on his knees, and Masyn stills.

"Why do you keep calling me that?"

"Because that's who you are. I've watched your surf videos every night since I found out, and I have no doubt that out there on the water you are whole. I've seen it with my own eyes—the joy that burns through you when you're out there. I've been trying my hardest to keep my distance, and I still can't help myself from watching you surf in the morning. You could set the ocean on fire. What I want to know is, where do you go, Ace? What chases you away as soon as you hit the sand?"

Masyn shifts, blinking away tears. "You were on my back porch the other night. Why? What happened?"

"Don't change the subject. This isn't about me," he says, his grey-blue eyes piercing hers.

When Masyn doesn't respond, Tate extends his pinkie out to her.

She stares at it, and when she doesn't make any move to reciprocate the gesture, he leans down and captures her pinkie in his. She squeezes back ever so slightly, and he drops his hold.

"I've already told you. I thought I knew what I wanted but it turned out to be too much," Masyn whispers. "I'm still trying to balance the effects."

"What does that mean?" Tate demands, his voice growing in intensity.

The pause that follows causes Tate to grow frustrated again. He breathes a heavy sigh through his fist.

"Maybe it means that I'm not ready to talk about it. Okay?" Masyn yells, leaning in toward Tate. "It all got out of hand. I can handle the pressure, I can handle the competition, I can handle the ocean," she says, looking at her trembling hands, wondering how much more she'll admit to.

"There are certain people in the surf world that I can't handle," she whispers, fighting against a quivering lip and losing the battle to the tears now racing down her cheeks. "Certain people I can't go back to."

Tate narrows his eyes and nods. "Then don't. Forget them, start over. Start having *fun* again, whether that's surfing or something else."

"It's not that easy."

"I know, but it's possible."

"It just feels like every time I'm ready to rip off the Band-Aid and face my future, I force my wounds to cut deeper."

"Maybe you need to be patient. Let the stitches do their job."

Masyn shakes her head. "I never had a chance with the stitches. I was infected the second blood was drawn."

"No. I know you can overcome whatever this is. Tell me, and I'll help you," Tate pleads. Masyn shifts her attention to the floor. He continues, "You know what else I know? You'll never *not* be Ace Madden, but you'll *always* be more than a surfer. The Rip Tide team, or whoever made you believe otherwise, can go screw themselves."

Masyn shrugs, only half believing him, and thumbs at her tears. They sit in silence for a minute before Masyn speaks up. "What's going on with you? I know you're not drinking Pepsi anymore."

Tate's jaw tenses, but he doesn't say anything.

Masyn breathes out a laugh and picks at her nails. "I don't get it."

"Don't get what?"

"Where do you go, Tate?" she says, using his words against him. "It's like you show a little of your true self and then you go into hiding. You want to get to know me, and then you try to transfer me out of your class. You come to dinner, and then you storm off. You surf, and then you break down and go MIA. It's always been a two-way street between you and me, so now it's your turn. Why won't you tell me what is going on with you? What are you afraid of?"

Tate buries his face in his elbow and gently butts his head against his arm. "I won't put this one on you."

Masyn sighs and stands. "I'm going to go." She looks at Tate balled up on the floor and offers him a hand. He takes it, coming to a stand and squeezing her delicate fingers in his. When he moves to pull away, Masyn pulls him back in, feeling his warmth on every inch of her palm. "Don't do this."

Tate just stares at her.

"I didn't just watch when you caved in on yourself after surfing, Hough. I may not know everything going on inside your head, but somehow I feel it. When we were crouched down on the sand, I felt things right alongside of you. I feel things when it comes to you—I can feel again. I've never understood someone so deeply or felt so intensely understood by someone until I met you. Moving here, I didn't expect to meet someone who could throw me a lifeline with one look or anchor me with the crook of their pinkie. Someone who sees so much more than what I say but offers safety in their silence. It hurts! Do you get that? The way you force the emotions out of me is excruciating, but once they're out it's like . . ." Masyn quiets, searching for the right words.

"It's like your soul is finally free," Tate finishes for her.

Masyn closes her eyes against the warmth rushing through her and nods. "Why were you on my back porch, Tate?"

He bows his head, looking at their clasped hands, but doing nothing to break free. "This . . ." He swallows hard and raises their hands.

Something inside Masyn clicks. She looks at her dainty hand, secure in his hold, then back up to his face. His features are rugged, mature, and dusted with heat—completely at her disposal, but untouchable all the same. Every one of her senses is homed in on every heartbreakingly handsome part of him, but the infatuation in her heart turns to terror as she realizes she's felt this way before.

Her attraction to Graham was an allure, a challenge, a forbidden excitement. With Tate, it feels like an inevitable connection, impossible to ignore. Like a fated bond clicked into place the moment they locked eyes in the midnight ocean and dialed in with every encounter since.

But Tate's not Graham, so he must recognize her foolish affection toward him. He must be about to cut ties with her completely.

She sees it in the downcast hollows of his face. She can't lose him. It'll be hard to not allow herself to want him, but it would be excruciating to watch him go.

She adjusts her hand in his until their pinkies are hooked, and levels her gaze. "This, Tate, is nothing to worry about. A surfer's bond—nothing more. You have to believe me. I need you to know that we're on the same page. I can't lose you now."

Tate works his jaw before he closes his eyes and releases a ragged breath. "It's not that simple."

"It is. I won't come here again. I won't cry on your shoulder. You don't have to surf, just promise me . . ." Masyn's voice cracks and she lets her sentence trail off because she doesn't know what to say. Tate didn't say their friendship was over, but everything about this moment feels like a goodbye.

Tate's face remains solemn. When Masyn deflates, he places his other hand on her back and pulls her to his chest, resting his chin on her head. "I'm no good for you, Ace. So I guess I'm afraid of myself. Afraid of what I would do to you if I let my soul free." He sighs. "I'm better off alone."

How did this happen? Masyn thinks. How did she fall into the arms of a man the same age as the one who ruined her?

Masyn shakes her head against Tate's chest, giving him one final squeeze before breaking away. She silently makes her way to the door, turning back just before pulling it closed behind her. "Hough," she whispers. Tate looks up, forlornness shadowing his features. "Be careful. Our kinds of demons see best when they've got us in the dark."

Tate pulls his lips tight and nods once.

"And thank you." Masyn finally shuts the door and leaves.

Chapter Sixteen

In Chemistry on Monday morning, Tate does a double take when Masyn walks through the door, looking her up and down. When she scrunches her nose in confusion, he averts his attention.

"Nice jersey," Adison says as she shoulder-checks Masyn on her way to her desk. Masyn doesn't react in the slightest. Adison has left her alone for the past few days, likely realizing how close she came to spilling Masyn's secret and giving her all the attention. But Masyn knows their feud isn't over. She'd been waiting for the other shoe to drop since Clayton tossed Masyn his jersey right in front of Adison after soccer practice yesterday.

Masyn gets to work on her lab assignment, talking with McCall and redirecting Clayton every time he stops by her desk on his way to "gather supplies" while Adison rattles nonsense at the back of the room.

"... isn't chemistry so weird? You never know how a solution is going to react once foreign substances are introduced ..."

Whatever, Masyn thinks. *It's like she talks just to see who will take the bait and listen to her.*

A few minutes later, Jake lets out a low whistle. "Shoot, Clayton, you've got shoes to fill, bro. Masyn, how could you hide this from us?"

Masyn turns to figure out what Jake is talking about. The entire group at the back of the room is looking at his phone. Everyone except Adison and Clayton. Their eyes are fixed on Masyn.

Clayton gets up, but before he can stalk out of the room Masyn catches him by the elbow. "What's going on?"

He yanks his own phone from his pocket and tosses it down on her lab table, the screen illuminated with a photo that Masyn has never seen, but even upon first glance, it looks eerily familiar. She snatches the device and zooms in on different spots, all too aware of the phantom saltwater lacing through her tastebuds.

The picture shows Graham and Masyn in what can only be described as a loving embrace. Their foreheads are pressed together, and a bright smile takes over her features. She's not sure anyone here would recognize him, seeing as her arms are wrapped around his neck and his head is turned to the side, concealing most of his face. But his banded forearm tattoo is clearly visible, and she knows the leathery creases that frame his eyes and the alluring uptick of his lips all too well.

To make matters worse, it looks like artificial intelligence was used to change the background and clothing from the original photo, making their embrace look completely different than its reality. This version of Masyn wears a crop top and mini skirt, a red disposable cup in her hand. The skin is a little too glossy, lacking the freckles that dust her arms, and Graham's arms are buffer than they should be.

But to anyone who doesn't know the subtleties to look for, the photo looks like pure lust and party dust.

The actual picture was taken at a surf competition, Newport Pipe Pro. Masyn will never forget their first big win. She can still see the way Graham sprinted down the sand toward her as she came out of the ocean. He held her by the shoulders, his grip firm, proudly taking in every inch of her before pulling her into a congratulatory hug. Then he whispered against her ear, *"You and me, Ace,"* before lifting her up like the picture shows. They were both in a state of euphoria after the win, but as she looks at it from this vantage point, the memory is tainted.

None of it means what it used to.

Masyn bites her cheeks, unable to look at the phone any longer. Even though someone altered the photo, the truth is that it depicts what might have been the exact moment she and Graham crossed the line of professionalism. Their coach-athlete bond was too tight. By the time this photo was taken, Masyn was already enraptured with their partnership. She enjoyed every minute they spent together. She thought she wanted all of him.

Even now, after everything that happened and all the progress she's made to overcome it, she still feels a hint of that enamored pull deep in her gut. That fact alone fills her with utter shame.

"Madden!" Tate snaps at the exact moment Clayton swipes the phone from her hands and storms out of the room.

Masyn looks up, stunned.

"Mrs. Kensington called." He holds up the classroom phone. "Wants to see you in her office."

Masyn finds Karina's office empty, so she sits in a chair and rests her head on the desk, allowing the ringing in her ears to grow.

"Masyn? You okay, hun?"

Masyn lifts her head as Karina closes the office door.

"Tate said you called me out of class."

Karina purses her lips and looks around the room. "Mm, no?"

"Oh. Sorry. I guess I should have known he was just giving me an out." Masyn stands, swinging her backpack over her shoulder.

"An out for what?"

"Just Adison trying to make trouble. It's fine. Really."

"Okay, well, stay as long as you want, if Tate said it was okay," Karina offers, taking a seat in her leather desk chair.

"Thanks, but I have to go. The soccer team will be loading up for our away game pretty soon."

Karina nods, but Masyn can see her mind working to assemble the puzzle pieces behind her eyes.

At lunch, Tate beelines to Karina's office, slipping in just as a student leaves. "Is your phone not working?"

"It's working," Karina responds without looking up from the paperwork in front of her.

"Why haven't you answered my calls?"

"I've been with students." Karina moves her focus to her computer screen. "Yes, Masyn came in here during second period, if that's what you're after."

"And?"

"And what?"

"What did she say?" Tate demands.

Karina narrows her eyes at him. "I can't really answer that."

Tate hardens his glare, stepping all the way into the office and closing the door behind him.

"She's fine. Didn't talk much. On her way to a soccer game now," Karina finally says.

"Did she tell you what happened?"

This makes Karina abandon her task. "What happened?"

"You've got to be kidding me. Did you even look at her? Actually look at her? If you did, you would have known she was shaken up."

"Tate Houghton, you need to tell me what is going on, or get a grip on yourself."

"Karina, this is not just some random student you're counseling. Masyn is practically our family now."

"I know! Which is why I didn't try to cage her in. What happened? All she said was Adison was causing trouble, and we left it at that."

Tate sighs, rubbing his face. "I don't know, someone sent a picture around the class, and I could tell Masyn was really affected by it. She was withering before my eyes as she sat there and stared at it. I had to do something, so I sent her here."

"That's cyberbullying. We have a zero-tolerance policy. What was the picture of?"

"Don't know." Tate shrugs. "She went to a bonfire over the weekend. Could have been something to do with that."

"Well, go find it!"

"Me?"

"You were there. You saw who had it."

"Everyone in the school probably has it by now. I can't go around asking for a potentially scandalous photo of one of my students. Do you know what teenagers send to each other these days?"

"Oh, so you *do* know the boundaries. I was getting worried." Karina smirks.

"What's that supposed to mean?"

"I've seen you coming through the hedges a time or two."

"Her family dumped her here in pieces, Karina. She's all alone. I'm not treating Masyn any different than I would Kat."

Karina sighs and looks up to the ceiling. "Just be careful. She's not—"

"Don't tell me she's not Kat. I know she's not. But she cooks dinner with you every night, and she's got Red taming a devil horse and throwing airs on the waves every morning. I got back into the ocean for the first time in five years." Tate swallows hard. "She fits."

Karina stands, reading Tate's expression as she slowly makes her way to the door. She stops in front of her brother and gives him a sad smile. "You're right," she says, squeezing his arm. "Wait here. I'll be right back."

When Karina returns, she goes straight to her computer. "Okay, Clayton VanDamme graciously emailed me the evidence."

"What's the picture of?" Tate demands from the corner of the room.

"Why are you standing in the corner? I thought you'd be hovering."

"I'm protecting my innocence. Masyn went through a wild streak, you know; anything could pop up on that screen."

Karina looks up. "I thought you didn't read the file."

"I read the internet."

"Let's see what we've got." She tilts her head at the screen, then pats around to find her glasses atop her head. Tate folds his arms against his chest, clenching his biceps to keep himself from running to her side. "Looks like a picture taken at a party." Karina frowns. "I don't know what it is about this picture, but there's something..."

Tate pushes off the wall and strides over. He takes one glance at the photo and immediately curses, pounding a fist into the desk.

Karina startles. "What? What do you see?"

"That," he says, pointing to the inked lines wrapping around the thick forearm in the photo, "is Graham Gentry, Masyn's surf coach."

Karina stills, straightens, and steadies her breathing as she closes the image. "I think it's best if you let me handle this."

Through his rage, Tate's focus catches on the way Karina pins her lips together and averts her gaze. "You knew about this?" He whirls on Karina. She scowls, but Tate doesn't let her respond. "I'd speculated, but I could find no proof. You knew! For how long? Tell me you haven't known for months and have been doing nothing but watching her suffer all this time."

She looks straight through his anger. "Stop talking right now. You know that's not true."

"Do I? Because I've seen you do it before."

"Out! Now!"

Tate barges out of the office, slamming the door behind him, but his guilt doesn't let him get far, and he slumps down against the wall opposite the door. He had no right to accuse Karina like that. The sting of it pricks at the back of his eyes, and he swallows against the sudden lump in his throat.

"Thank you, Coach Nance. I'll talk to you later."

Tate looks up from where his head is buried in his hands to find Karina coming out of her office.

"She's not on the bus," she whispers.

Chapter Seventeen

"I'm sorry."

Karina doesn't stray her focus from peeling potatoes at the sink. Tate's in her peripheral vision, poking his head in from the back door. "Leave, Tate. You're not invited to dinner tonight."

"I had no right to say that. I know you did everything you could for Kat, and you were the best mom to her. You *are* the best mom for her."

Karina tries to remain stone-cold, but tears fall. Tate rushes to her side, pulling her into a hug. "Rina, I mean it. I'm such a jerk. I'm so sorry."

"I'm not watching her suffer. She knows I'm here for her. She knows it," Karina says, her voice strained. "And I'm seeing her make new friends and try new things. She's even surfing again. I thought I was helping her heal by letting her take the lead. I didn't think she would take off again."

"Hey." Tate brushes his sister's hair out of her eyes. "You're right. She's doing all those things, and she's lucky to have you. Wherever she is, she's going to come back."

Karina studies him for a beat before she speaks again. "She's at the equestrian center. Red's got her."

Tate's face falls flat. "You couldn't have led with that? When did you find out?"

"Just before you came in, and no. I was prepared to never speak to you again."

"You didn't, uhh, tell Red what I said, did you?" Tate winces.

Karina chuckles. "As much as I hated you for a moment there, I didn't want you dead."

"Thank you," Tate mouths before heading back out.

TATE WAITS IN THE guest house with his windows open until he hears Red's truck pull up the drive.

"Masyn come home with you?"

"Yep, she ran over to Nat's a few minutes before I pulled in. Said she wasn't willing to risk running into the guard dog." Red winks.

Tate ignores the jab, instead focusing on the urge to abandon this conversation and go check on Masyn. "How was she when you left?"

"I'd say she's as good as a teenage girl gets after a rough day at school. She's just got to sleep it off. She'll be fine."

"You think she's going to try to surf?"

Red coughs. "There's a storm coming in. She'd have to have a death wish to get in that water with the rip currents slashing through the waves the way they are."

The moment Red goes inside, Tate rushes through the hedges. He eyes the garage light shining through the door crack with suspicion, but when he pokes his head in, it's empty. Just as he's turning to leave, something catches his eye. There's a gap in the lineup of Masyn's surfboards. The absence of her favorite yellow shortboard like a ransom note pinned to his gut.

Tate grabs a board and bolts toward the beach. Red was right. The waves are choppy in their usual surf spot, broken up by at least three rip currents from what he can see. And the tide is going out, which means it's a full-out riptide. Panic rises as his quick scan for Masyn comes up empty.

By the time he gets halfway down the bluff, rain is falling in hard drops. He catches sight of Masyn's neon board slashing skyward through the heavy grey clouds to his left, wrenched from a wave like a beacon—or an omen. He curses against the sinking feeling in his stomach and quickens his pace.

The cold sand beneath his feet reminds him how much he hates the beach at night. The mute glow of the setting sun on the horizon is a weight pressing down on the water, darkening it with every passing second, letting its beauty subside to transform into the cold-blooded force it is.

Tate doesn't waste any time. Once he's close enough, he shucks off his hoodie and t-shirt and runs into the whitewash, duck diving under each wave as it comes. When he finally gets far enough to crest and catch a glimpse of Masyn, he yells out to her. She snaps her head up. The next thing Tate knows, she's paddling toward him. As her wave swells, she pops up on the board, never taking her eyes off him.

Tate watches as she maneuvers across the wave. She's approaching at speed, but he holds his ground. Masyn comes as close as she can then carves, drenching him with a spray of ocean water before squatting into a seat on her board.

"I don't want you here," she says, her face dead of expression. "I'm fine."

Tate studies her in silence—the rise and fall of her heavy breaths, the flat line of her lips, and the spark of electricity behind her eyes that eventually fades into nothing. It's all there. The hurt, the sorrow, the anger, all the broken pieces floating around her crystal blue irises.

"You're not fine," he finally says.

"I will be."

"Masyn, you have to fix this—actively work through it. It's not going to go away on its own."

"I don't want to fix it, Tate! I want to forget it. I want to be forgotten."

Tate frowns at her words and a strong wave sucks them toward its base as the swell builds. "You can't be out here," he calls.

Masyn looks at his bare chest, lacking the protection of a wet suit. "I'll be fine. *You'll* freeze to death."

"No, Masyn. You won't be *fine*. Not today! You do realize you're surfing against a riptide? There are cuts all along that side of the cove. It's only a matter of time."

"I KNOW WHAT A rip looks like, Hough. I'm perfectly capable of avoiding them. This is the only—" Masyn stops herself, looking out onto the now-dark horizon, then back at Tate. "I'm fine."

"Stop saying that. Stop lying to yourself."

Masyn rolls her tongue over in her mouth, weighing the odds of winning this fight.

"I'm not leaving you, Ace. You get caught in a rip, and I'll go in after you. I don't care how strong it is, it'll take us both. I'll make sure of it."

Masyn averts her gaze from Tate and focuses on her hand swishing back and forth under the water. He's right. It's too dangerous out here. But if she goes back in, she'll be forced to face her newest reality. She'll have to apologize to Nance for skipping the game and reply to McCall's one thousand text messages. Clayton will probably show up at her house demanding answers at some point. Plus, everyone at school will look at her differently—like she's a slut.

But what she's really afraid of is what happens next. People asking who the guy in the picture is. Wanting to know how they met, how long they hooked up, why they aren't together anymore.

That's the problem.

The taste of salt brings Masyn back to her surroundings. She looks up to find Tate latched onto her board and staring at her with concern flooding his face, and she realizes that the salty taste isn't the phantom sensation brought up from her memories, nor is it ocean water.

She's crying. No, she's *shaking* with sobs.

"Did he hurt you?" Tate asks, his voice barely audible above the roar of the waves.

Masyn tries to steel herself against her emotions, but her brow only furrows more, and her lips wobble.

"Did he hurt you?" Tate insists.

Her head tilts ever so slightly, her eyelids weighed down by shame.

"Lay down. I'm taking you in." Tate's demand is gentle, but Masyn complies.

When they make it to the sand, Tate tosses his board onto the beach and immediately moves to help Masyn. When he holds her by the shoulder, he searches her features as if assessing which emotional wound most needs healing. Instead, he stays quiet and guides Masyn up the beach with an arm around her. He stops where his clothes lay dry and forgotten on the ground, bunches Masyn's wet hair in his hands, and squeezes out the water. Then he takes the elastic from her wrist and ties her hair into a sloppy bun. He unzips her wet suit and helps free her arms from the sleeves.

"Dry off," he commands, handing Masyn his t-shirt. She does as she's told, then gives the shirt back.

"Here, wear this," Tate says, retrieving his hoodie.

"No, you—"

"Put it on, Masyn."

She obeys, and silence falls between them again as they head up the beach, Tate holding her up the entire way like he knows she's unable to walk on a broken soul.

At Nat's, Tate walks Masyn all the way into her house, flips on the electric water kettle, then leads her into the bathroom and turns the shower on. "I'm going to go change. I'll be in the living room when you're done."

Masyn nods and takes a hot shower that's not nearly long enough to wash away the pain pounding against her mind.

Once she's dressed, she comes out to the living room to find Tate right where he said he'd be, hunched over on the far side of the couch with his elbows resting on his knees and his hands holding his head. Masyn can't see his expression with his hood on, so she quietly takes a seat at the far end of the sofa.

Without emerging from his huddle, Tate slides a cup of hot chocolate over to her side of the coffee table.

Masyn takes it, relishing the warmth on her palms as she stares into the milky liquid. *Tate knows. He figured it out, probably after seeing the picture that went around school, which means everyone else will, too.*

She doesn't know how long she sits, staring into nothingness. When she looks up, Tate is focused on her, his expression as grim as she's ever seen.

He grabs the blanket draped on the couch behind him and throws it at Masyn. "Talk."

"About what?"

"Doesn't matter. Just talk."

"What if I don't want to?" But the real question is: *What if I don't know if I can? What if I don't know how to tell the person who seems to protect me the most the secret that I'm most ashamed of?*

Tate scowls at the ground. "I surfed. After five years of not touching even a grain of sand, I surfed for you. So, I'll sit here until you do."

Masyn stares at her drink for minutes on end, trying to figure out where to start. "He broke me." She chews on her lip, all her energy drained from that one statement. "But it was my fault," she finally confesses. "And it wasn't as bad as you probably think, so you can stop feeling sorry for me."

"Masyn, no," he blurts, fury taking over his features. "You're a teenager!"

Masyn grinds her jaw. "I know, okay? I know. Age of consent and all that. I've looked it all up, Tate. I know!"

"I'm sorry. I'll listen, but I saw the picture, and you don't get there on your own. He reeled you in."

Masyn's quiet for a while.

"We weren't at a party together. I have been to parties with him," she admits, "but we weren't partying when that picture was taken. The background was changed. That was a celebration on the beach after I won a competition. I was wet and salty and wearing a wet suit before Adison got her hands on it." She sighs and pulls her phone out to find the real picture. She knows Tate believes her, but it feels better to prove it. Or maybe it makes it easier to talk when she can omit any ounce of added scandal.

"He was my coach. I felt so lucky that he wanted to coach me—touring surfers never coach other athletes—and then, thanks to him, Rip Tide offered me a sponsorship. I've always dreamed of surfing for the Rip Tide brand . . . my dad was a Rip Tide athlete before he died. Anyways, we'd intertwined our passions, and we were riding the high of success every day—together. He was a part of my every thought, you know? Not because I was in love with him, but because he was a big part of what I loved—surfing, Rip Tide, and winning.

"I guess I just got that confused with attraction. I tempted him; I wanted him to want me, and I liked the way it made me feel when I knew I had his attention." Masyn peeks up.

Tate keeps his expression stone-cold, his jaw pulsing, but he listens. He nods for her to continue. "We went out for a surf one night. It was just for fun—we were on longboards—but Graham had been drinking. He unleashed and jumped onto my board. That's when I realized my mistake. His hands . . ." Masyn looks away and wipes a tear.

Tate scoots closer, reaching out a hand to comfort her, but stops short and rests his arm on the back of the sofa. It doesn't feel right to touch her when she's talking about her scars left by a man who's probably around the same age he is.

"His touch was different that night. He said we needed to strengthen our bond, really get us ready for the Triple Crown, but his hands were so big, so commandeering, so different on me than they had been before." Masyn scrunches her knees to her chest, shaking her head against them.

"Masyn . . ." Tate starts, unsure what to say. He wants to hear the rest, but he doesn't want to force her if she's not ready to tell it. She's already been through enough manipulation.

"I'm okay," she says, nodding as if trying to convince herself. "We tandem paddled back out to the section, and that's when it happened again. It was nothing serious, he was just trying to kiss me and, I don't know, touch me in a way I didn't want to be touched." Masyn buries her face in her hands. "Ugh, this is so stupid. I've been kissed before. I've kissed people I didn't necessarily want to. I should have just dropped it and moved on. I'm making a bigger deal of it than I should."

"No. What happened next?"

"I couldn't get him off of me, and I panicked. I think that's what's haunting me the most. It wasn't the kiss that scared me, it was his forcefulness in that moment; it was like he was going to get what he wanted no matter what happened to me," Masyn admits, rubbing her hands down her thighs. "The last thing I remember is salt burning down my throat. And then I woke up in a hospital bed."

"You were face down on a surfboard in the ocean when you blacked out? Are you fu—"

"Don't go there, Hough. I don't remember exactly what happened."

"You were trapped in the water under a man twice your size. I can tell you exactly what happened."

"He didn't! The testing at the hospital came up clear. He didn't—"

"He would have! He could have killed you!"

"Tate! I get to choose what I see in the blackness. Okay? I get to choose how much of the hidden truth I can handle." Masyn's chest heaves and shakes with every agonizing breath. "We were such a good team," she adds, her lip quivering. "We were supposed to be a team."

"He's a scumbag of a person, Masyn. Don't let yourself forget that."

"I know him better than I've ever known anybody. He's cockier than sin, but he's not . . . aggressive. We wanted what was best for each other, and I don't think either of us ever imagined that happening. It almost seems like my mind is playing tricks on me. Maybe I am blowing everything out of proportion."

Tate stands, his hands flying up in outrage. "Do you hear yourself? What are you even saying? You just told me how he used his authority over you to take advantage of you, and he drowned you in the process. You woke up in the hospital!"

Masyn follows, lurching off the couch. "I don't know, Tate. I've never allowed myself to relive it this fully. It's the first time I'm giving words to my thoughts, okay? I can't help what I feel. Isn't it possible that it was just a one-time mistake he made on a drunken night? Isn't it possible that maybe I can get over myself, so I can go back and be a Rip Tide surfer again?" Their shared exasperated breaths fill the silence. "When I surfed for Rip Tide, I belonged to something. . . I have to reclaim my name."

"You tell me. Your conscience knows what a mistake is. I don't think a little mistake leaves a person's soul at the bottom of the ocean." Tate groans and drags his palms down his face, clenching his fingertips against his sharp jawline. "I'm guessing your family doesn't know the truth?"

"They think we got caught in a rip current, just like the rest of the world. I think my mom might have caught on when I tried to tell her at the Triple Crown, but she wouldn't listen." Masyn huffs out a sigh and collapses on the couch. "If it were up to her, I'd still be surfing with Graham."

Tate shakes his head. "Ace, let me just clarify something. I don't care how much you flirted with Graham Gentry. I don't care if you pushed him up against a wall and came on to him. He should have *never* followed through. He should have never put you in this position. If he can't handle himself with alcohol in his system, he shouldn't have been drinking around you." Tate walks closer, reaching his pinkie out toward her. Once Masyn links hers with his, he continues, "You're just a kid . . . your people should be protecting you."

When Masyn doesn't respond, Tate drops her hand and flops onto the couch beside her. "Do you maybe want to show your classmates the real picture?"

"No!" Masyn says without hesitation. "They can't know anything about my surfing career."

"Why not?"

"The only thing they'll see when they Google search Ace Madden is my partying streak and how I disqualified myself from winning the biggest junior surfing competition in the nation, and then they'll see the pictures of *surfing's most dynamic duo*, and they'll recognize Graham from the fake party picture Adison made. It won't be long until they ask all the questions. Everyone will find out, and I'll have to wear a scarlet letter to school every day."

"So then what makes you think you deserve to carry around this burden in secret for the rest of your life?"

Masyn shrugs. "When I go back to California, everyone will already know my story. I just thought maybe I could live here for as long as possible without people thinking the worst of me."

"If you let people in, they'll get over the bad parts. You keep it inside, and *you* will *never* get over it. You've told three people since you moved here and look how far you've come."

"Three people who want what's best for me. This world isn't full of nice people, Tate. It only takes one person to take something from my past and drag me down. And with the way Adison is twisting it, this information could ruin me."

"You're a minor."

"It doesn't matter. Graham's not going to take the heat for this. If he goes down, he'll make sure everyone knows that I led him on. I'd never get another sponsorship again, and even if I did, I don't want the attention. I don't want it!"

"It's not fair! You shouldn't have to live your life haunted by a past you didn't choose."

"Aren't we all haunted by our pasts?"

Tate leans forward, cradling his head in his hands. "I just wish I could have known you before. I'd have made sure this didn't happen. I'd have protected you."

"Don't worry. I'll be fine."

"If I hear you say that one more time—" Tate cocks his head to the side, biting back his words. "Come on, let's go."

"Go where?"

"You're not sleeping here tonight. And I just fished you out of a riptide, so don't argue with me. Now, let's go."

"I'm not sleeping at your place." Masyn balks at the suggestion.

Tate deadpans. "Karina has a comfy couch."

Chapter Eighteen

In the morning, Red wakes Masyn up by throwing a pair of western boots on the couch where she sleeps. "Wake up, kid. We're hauling horses up north."

Masyn squints one eye open. "Do I have to?"

"Will you agree to come if I just say I want you to?"

"I guess . . ."

"Cool. Let's go with that."

"Where's Tate?"

Red looks into the kitchen, exchanging a glance with Karina. "Gone."

Masyn sits up. "What do you mean, gone? He was just here last night."

"Said he had to catch an early flight for a weekend getaway. He's a big boy; I didn't ask questions."

"A weekend getaway to where?"

Red pounds his fists one on top of the other. "I don't think I'm at liberty to say, kid."

"What did he say to you, Red?" Masyn frantically looks toward the kitchen. "Karina, what did he say?"

"Honey," Karina starts, rounding the island and tossing a kitchen towel over her shoulder. "Tate didn't give us much information, but like I said . . . he's a protector."

"Nah, I don't think that covers it," Red adds. "The fool thinks he's Batman. And whatever you said to him last night, well, he's dusting off his suit."

Karina eyes Red.

"What? She deserves to know."

WHEN THEY ARRIVE AT the hosting equestrian center, Red goes to the office to handle registration forms, and Masyn walks with Karina toward a massive dark-brown barn with iron accents.

"So, how are you doing after yesterday?" Karina asks.

"I'll be fine . . . I always am."

Karina wraps an arm around Masyn's shoulder. "Fine's a terrible thing to be, Mase."

Masyn leans in and grins, letting out a long sigh.

"So, I saw Tate flying down the bluff with a surfboard last night. Was that to go find you?"

Masyn grimaces. "Yeah, he wasn't happy about that, with the storm coming in and all. I just couldn't help it. Something about surfing seems to fix the problems caused by surfing."

"Even in a storm?"

"Something about a storm seems to calm all the other kinds of storms." Masyn shakes her head as she breathes out an embarrassed laugh.

"It's a thing. We revisit our trauma in an effort to accept it, make it right, change the ending. There are a number of reasons for it, but I won't bore you with that information. Just be careful. Sometimes revisiting the past prohibits you from overcoming it."

Masyn nods, and silence falls for a few minutes before Karina speaks again. "Hey hun, look, I'm just going to be honest. I'm worried about you being alone so much."

Masyn offers a small smile, nodding in agreement. She hasn't slept with the lights off since she's been there. "I can call Nat."

"I can get you a dorm if you want it. Or, if you'd rather stay put, I have a guest room. It's open to you anytime for however long—and I'm not just offering because I'm worried. We enjoy your company. I live for the days that we prep dinner together." Karina's wide smile scrunches her nose.

"Thank you. Really," Masyn replies. "Can I ask you something?" At Karina's nod, Masyn asks, "Did Tate really avoid the ocean for five years?"

"Wouldn't even look at it. I never thought he'd touch a board again."

"Is it because of Kat? When she passed away, was it—"

Karina nods, closing her eyes. "The ocean."

"Is this my dearest cousin?"

Masyn and Karina turn to see Adison strutting toward them in riding pants and tall boots.

Masyn groans. "Not now, Adison."

Adison sticks her lips out in an exaggerated pout. "What? It's perfect that you're here. I've been needing to talk to you about surf stuff."

Masyn scowls, trying to find Adison's angle.

Karina turns to Masyn. "Red's probably ready for our help now. Should we get going?"

"Oh, I'll be quick. Now that surfing is becoming a whole extended family affair, I thought I'd better brush up on my facts," Adison says through a cloying smile.

"It's okay." Masyn smiles at Karina. "I'll find you." Karina winks before walking off, and Masyn faces Adison. It'll be better to take her bait now than to let it fester.

"What on earth are you doing here?" Adison says through a clenched smile.

Masyn ignores her question. "What do you mean surfing is becoming a family affair?"

Heat flashes across Adison's features and she pops her lips to hide her creeping smile. "That was just a load of BS to get Mrs. Kensington out of here."

"You're lying."

"Ask your mother."

Masyn sucks her cheeks in. Discussing surfing with her mom is the last thing she wants to do. "I'm not talking to you. I know you made that picture and sent it to the whole class." Masyn starts walking out of the barn, forcing Adison to jog to keep up.

"I didn't *make* anything. I merely brought the truth to the surface."

"I don't know what you think you know, but I'm asking you to please stop. If you keep this up, I'll . . ." Masyn trails off, not wanting to admit what will happen if Adison keeps on down this war path. For all she knows, it will motivate Adison more.

"You'll what? Retaliate just like you're doing now?"

"What is it about my presence that you deem a form of retaliation? I wouldn't even be talking to you if you didn't approach me."

"Oh please, don't flatter yourself. It's not your presence. It's the fact that you're going out of your way to steal everything that's mine, and don't even act like you didn't turn right around the other night and tell Clayton about my parents' separation."

At the barn exit, Masyn looks back at the horses, wishing she could take one out and ride all the way home. "I don't spread rumors I have no business in. I know what it's like to have to hold my secrets in with all my strength."

She looks down as the realization hits her. That's what she's been doing this whole time. She's been trying to tourniquet her trauma—stave off the memories, in hopes of saving her passion. All the while, Adison's been threatening to rip it off and watch her failures spew out.

Masyn steps out of the open barn doors and turns the corner to find Clayton leaning against the wall five feet away. She freezes, but he shakes his head and rolls off the wall to walk in the other direction.

Masyn curses under her breath. "Clayton, wait."

"I can assure you he wants nothing to do with you," Adison says, stepping in front of Masyn.

Masyn rolls her eyes and pushes past her, grabbing Clayton by the elbow. "That picture was fake. You have to believe me. I don't have a boyfriend."

"Masyn, I don't have time for this. I have a polo match I need to warm up for. Plus, how am I supposed to believe that Adison would waste her time creating a fake picture of you? I've seen her Photoshop skills. They're not that good."

"Seriously? She hates me. She's been going out of her way to make my life harder since my first day of school."

"She's been a little petty, sure, but I've known her for years. She's not like that."

"Forget Adison. Can you just trust that I'm telling you as much as I can right now?"

He stops, searching her eyes. "No, Masyn, 'cause I know you'll never tell me the rest of it."

As much as Masyn wants to reach out to him, offer more information, he's right. But she never expected to feel her heart breaking for him. "Okay," she says. "Good luck then, on your polo match."

Clayton huffs. "That's it? You're giving up that easily?"

"What am I supposed to say?"

"Anything! Just tell me what's with the secrets? I'm standing here right in front of you, asking for you to let me in, and I can literally see you holding the truth on your tongue. If the picture is fake, then why was Adison hinting at your older boyfriend weeks before it came out? Why does she always claim that you're not who you say you are? Why do you flinch every time I touch you? Your body is like a minefield; at any second I can hit the wrong spot, and it will set you off. Call you the wrong name, and I get bitten. So, tell me *something*, Masyn, because I can't keep blindly trying with you."

"That was my coach," she blurts. "We weren't at a party; we were celebrating a win right after I . . . won. Adison reworked the picture to look like something it wasn't."

"Coach for what? Where was the rest of the team?"

Masyn looks down, grinding her jaw.

"I have to warm up. I'll talk to you at home," Clayton says after a beat of silence, swiping a heavy hand through his hair.

"Clayt, that information is . . . complicated."

He heaves out a laugh. "Of course it is," he says, walking away without so much as a backward glance.

Masyn stands there, arms slack at her sides, not registering what just happened. *Just tell me something*, Clayton had said. *Anything*. But that's just it. There's nothing—not a single something she could offer him that would make this situation better. Graham has polluted even the simplest details of her past.

"Oof, that's a burned bridge if I've ever seen one," Adison squawks, pompously strutting up with her hands behind her back.

"It's better this way. I always knew Clayton wouldn't be able to handle the truth—wouldn't be able to handle me," Masyn says, without looking at Adison. "You can have him."

Adison moves in front of Masyn so they're standing face-to-face and narrows her gaze. "What I don't get is why? Why aren't you flaunting your real identity to everyone in the school? You certainly seemed to be proud of it back in Cali."

"You of all people should understand that things aren't always as they seem behind closed doors," Masyn whispers, shoulder checking Adison as she walks away.

"Hey," Adison calls.

Masyn turns her head just enough to see Adison in her periphery.

Adison doesn't say anything more, just shrugs and sends Masyn a sad smirk, but the action is riddled with subtext. The kind of subtext that leads Masyn to give a small smile in return.

ON THE RIDE HOME, Masyn hardly says a word. She watches the thick woods blur past her window, trying to wrap her head around the fact that she nearly told Clayton she surfed competitively. If she'd let that slip . . . One Google search would tell him nearly every secret she's been keeping.

Red catches Masyn's eye in the rearview mirror. "Can I ask you a question? I'm not going to make you talk about anything you don't want to. But where's your family? Where's Nat?"

"My mom and stepdad have been busy with work. They own a surf company, and they've been traveling to a few different surf towns. Trying to expand their business or whatever. Nat's in and out . . . mostly out. I think she's in London right now."

"Well, if you need anything, you let us know. Our doors are always open for you. Understood?"

Masyn nods.

"I'm serious, kid. If your dad—" Red clears his throat and squeezes Karina's hand across the center console. "If your dad hadn't passed, we wouldn't be such strangers."

"Thanks, Red, but you've never been a stranger." Masyn smiles at him through the rearview mirror. "Have you heard from Tate?"

Karina shrugs, exchanging a quick glance with Red. "No, but we've gone much longer without hearing from Tate. I'm sure he'll be back for school on Monday."

Masyn nods.

"What is it, Masyn?" Karina asks.

"Nothing," she responds, settling in to sleep out this drive, but sleep doesn't come, her anger fueling a slew of questions through her mind.

What if he gets hurt? What if whatever Tate is doing just makes things worse? What about me? What if I didn't want a Batman?

Chapter Nineteen

THAT NIGHT, MASYN SITS on her front porch wrapped in Tate's hoodie and a blanket. When she sees headlights, she runs over to Tate's guest house and knocks on the door. It flings open immediately. It's dark inside and out, but Masyn can barely make out the silhouette of Tate's curls flaring out from under a cap.

"Shit!" He scowls and flicks his hood up, turning away from Masyn.

Was that a bandage covering his eye? "Hough—"

"You need to leave," he barks as he closes the door.

Masyn blocks it with her slippered foot, locking eyes with Tate. She takes in the bandage covering his temple and part of his eye. A gash peeks out over his brow. "What did you do to him?" she squeaks.

Tate's face twists in disgust. "Are you f—"

"Did you hurt him?" she demands, much louder now.

"He really has done a number on you, hasn't he? Not only did he take advantage of you, but he's brainwashed you, too?"

"You had no right to go out there and track him down."

"Are you hearing yourself? Let me make one thing clear. You're mine, Masyn. And I don't mean that in whatever sick and twisted way Graham Gentry meant it when he made you believe the same thing. You deserve to be taken care of. You deserve to feel safe. And nobody else seems to be stepping in, so yes, I did. And I had every right to knock some sense into that coward. He sure as heck knows now that you don't belong to him."

Masyn steps back, stunned. Tate looks at her for a beat before slamming the door closed.

"Tate, open the door."

"Go, Madden!"

Masyn pounds a fist against the door and turns to find Red standing a few feet away. She looks at the first aid kit in his hand before flicking her eyes up to his.

One side of Red's mouth pulls up in a half-smile as he holds up his supplies. "Batman."

"Tell him not to show up to dawn patrol tomorrow. If this is how he's going to act, I don't care if I ever see him again."

Red doesn't answer, just dips his chin in a nod and offers a fist bump, which Masyn accepts, wishing it didn't warm a piece of her heart as she continues to storm back to her house.

Chapter Twenty

When Monday comes and there's a sub teaching chemistry, Masyn can't help the annoyance that floods through her.

It carries through to lunch, when Adison is sitting in *her* usual spot next to Clayton. Adison looks at her with challenge in her eyes, but Masyn ignores her. Clayton hasn't said anything since Masyn last saw him at the equestrian grounds, so she goes to the furthest empty table she can find, wishing McCall was at least at school today to keep her company.

"Well, this is ironic. You're the hot topic of the school, and you're sitting alone."

Masyn looks up from her phone at Seager Brooks, who is leaning against her table. She's seen him on the football field, in a few of her classes, and even at the bonfire the other night, but they've never acknowledged each other. As is typical for him, he wears a letterman jacket over a black hoodie with an all-too-characteristic bad-boy gleam in his eye.

"Why am I the hot topic?"

"Like you don't know."

"I *don't* know, but whatever it is, I don't want to talk about it."

"I heard you bit VanDamme."

Masyn rolls her eyes.

"So you did?"

"Why would I tell you? We don't talk," Masyn snaps.

"We're in nearly every class together. I sit right behind you in sixth period."

Out of the corner of her eye, she catches Clayton striding over. "Seager, back off," he hisses. Masyn drops her head into her hand, peeking under the visor of her fingers to see Seager dip his chin toward her and smile. It's the kind of smile that's almost a laugh, the kind that two friends would exchange over an inside joke. It's not the kind of smile Masyn and Seager have any business with, yet she finds herself struggling not to return it.

"Don't you have weed to sell?" Clayton chides. This makes Masyn quirk her head to the side, and Seager's expression transforms into a sinister smirk.

"Madden, for the record, I don't blame you. This guy could use some roughing up." He claps his teeth at Clayton as he walks away.

"Are you guys friends?" Masyn asks.

"Seager doesn't have friends, or at least he doesn't keep them," Clayton answers.

"I didn't need you to come over here and save me."

Clayton pulls out the chair next to Masyn and takes a seat facing her. "I wanted to apologize. For pushing you further than I should have."

Masyn blinks. "Thanks, I guess."

"Can we go back to how things were?"

"Clayton," she starts, picking at the hem of her plaid skirt. "I've already told you I can't give you what you want. I'm not girlfriend material."

"I don't need a title," he says, wrapping an arm around her and pulling her into his side. "I just need you. I realized that this weekend. I really like you, Masyn . . . I mean it."

"I like you, too, it's just . . . I don't know. Things seem to keep getting between us."

The bell rings, and they agree to finish their conversation after school. However, Masyn doesn't see Clayton when classes end, and soccer practice runs late, so she doesn't get the closure she was hoping for.

Once she's home, she puts on a bikini under an oversized sweatshirt, deciding to squeeze in a quick surf session. The undercurrents following the last riptide have been creating some massive sets. Just as Masyn reaches the garage to grab a wet suit and a board, the growl of a motorcycle fills the air. She turns with a hand on the door to find Seager propping his bike up with one foot, ripping off his helmet. She takes in his tousled black hair, thick eyebrows, and the masculine lines of his neck as he stares back at her.

"What are you doing here?" she calls out.

"I came to see you."

"How do you know where I live?" she asks, walking over to him.

Seager walks around his bike to face her. "I have ears. You have a boyfriend who doesn't stop talking about all the times the two of you make out at your aunt's empty house on the bluff."

"Well, *why* did you come to see me? We're not friends, remember?"

He shrugs a shoulder. "Curious, I guess."

"About?"

Seager steps closer, his piercing stare and musky scent with a hint of motor oil invading Masyn's senses. Holding her gaze, he slowly reaches toward her collar bone and sweeps the collar of her sweatshirt to the side, hooking his finger under the string of her bikini. When he snaps it, a wave of chills runs through Masyn.

"Apparently, I'm the only one in the school who uses Google instead of social media as my primary search engine."

Masyn is sure stress hives are already breaking out across her neck where Seager's fingertips brushed against her skin. She takes a deep breath and swallows hard. "What do you want?"

Seager scrunches his face. "Nothing."

"Then what's the point?"

He pins his golden eyes on her like a wolf taunting its prey. "Like I said, I'm curious."

Masyn stares at him for a moment, biting her lip. Then she turns and walks back to the garage. She flings open the side door and looks over her shoulder, motioning with her head for him to follow her.

Once they're in the garage, Seager links his hands behind his head and spins around, taking in the wall-to-wall Ace gear. "Dang, Madden. This is no joke."

"You said you Googled me," Masyn says, resting her back against the door.

"Yeah, I Googled you. I didn't stalk you."

"Well, then, it's time for you to leave. I don't want to talk about it," Masyn says.

Seager's brows knit together as he walks over to her, coming so close their knees practically touch.

"Stop looking at me like you know me. We're not even—"

"We're not friends," he says, resting a hand against the door behind Masyn. "Trust me, Masyn, you don't want to be my friend."

Masyn's lips part as she catches a whiff of mint on his breath. She barely notices her chest heaving up and down as she stares into Seager's daring eyes. Clayton's signature double honk rings out in the driveway, startling Masyn.

Seager's eyes flick to her hand as it flies to the doorknob beside her. He rolls his gaze up and down her body before that sinister smile makes a reappearance. "Go ahead," he says, dropping his hand from the door.

Masyn turns to walk outside, her shoulder skimming Seager's chest, causing her to brush off the rising goosebumps as she walks toward Clayton's truck.

Clayton's focus catches on the garage. "What is he doing here? Were you guys in the garage alone?"

Masyn balks, covering the spot on her neck where Seager's fingers swept only minutes before. "It's not like that." She looks over her shoulder to find Seager strutting toward them with an Ace Madden sweatshirt flung over his shoulder.

"VanDamme," he says with a bro-nod.

"Are you selling her drugs?"

"Clayton!" Masyn shrieks.

"Well?"

Seager looks at Clayton and chuckles before leaning down to Masyn's ear. "I know nothing," he whispers.

Masyn shakes off the shadow of heat his breath left on her skin and looks straight ahead at Clayton as Seager mounts his motorbike and peels out of the driveway.

"He better not have laid a hand on you. I'll kill him."

Masyn shakes her head. "It's not like that."

"Can I come in?" Clayton asks, motioning toward the house.

"I don't think that's a good idea."

"Look, I'm sorry again for overreacting about the picture. I just want to go back to the way things were."

Masyn looks to the side, hesitating.

"If I have to fight Seager Brooks for you, I will."

This makes her stomach flip. If only he knew about the guys he'd have to fight to get to her. "Maybe we just don't give ourselves a title," Masyn offers, "for the first little bit at least."

"Fine. That's fine," he agrees, pulling her into a hug.

LATER THAT WEEK, MASYN wakes to a sky hooded with heavy grey clouds. A sight that brings a smile to her face—in Ellsworth, Massachusetts, big clouds equal big waves. Red practically has to drag her out of the water after dawn patrol. She'd convinced him to ignore the storm warnings and commit to their morning surf sesh, a decision they may both be regretting after emerging from the ocean raw with fresh surf rash.

Like any other day this week, Masyn expects to see a substitute teaching chem class, but her heart stutters when she walks in to find Tate sitting at his desk. She hasn't even seen a shadow of him around the Kensingtons' since that first night he got back, and Red has proven to be a poor source of information on the topic.

"I don't ask, and I don't answer," he says anytime Masyn prods. *"Double A."*

So annoying.

Masyn doesn't look at Tate as she walks past. He'll be able to see the salt-crusted waves in her hair and the red rash on her elbow, and know she was out in a storm again. *Good,* she thinks, a grin creeping up her face. She hopes he is mad. It would be all too satisfying to see him feel just a shred of the anger she's held toward him over the past few days. As if on cue, her smile turns into a scowl. She told Tate everything, and then he up and disappeared, taking *her* matters into his own hands. Then he refused to talk to her for the foreseeable future, only to come back, call her his, and disappear again.

She continues frowning down at her desk even after Tate rises to start class. A hush comes over the room, unlike any other school day, that causes her to look up. Her scowl quickly fades when she sees him at the front of the room, hands behind his back, wearing a cap and brandishing *the* black eye of all black eyes. He's covered it with makeup, but it isn't fooling anyone. The deep purple skin sagging under his left eye still peeks through. Masyn leans forward and squints. *Are those stitches under his brow?*

Tate's gaze darts toward her, and he quickly refocuses on the rest of the students. He points at the words *"DON'T ASK"* written in all caps on the board behind him.

"Okay, let's get started," he says, folding his arms against his chest and revealing a black cast covering his hand and extending halfway up his forearm.

Masyn's mouth drops open. Tate doesn't look her way, but she knows he must see her reaction in his peripheral vision by the way his neck reddens and his jaw ticks.

"Dang! You get hit by a bus, Houghton?" Jake shouts from the back of the class.

Masyn doesn't hear Tate's response. She doesn't hear anything for the rest of class. All she can think about is what Tate did in California. She never imagined it would result in stitches and broken bones. Tate and Graham are pretty evenly built, but Tate went in with the upper hand. If Tate looks like this, she can only imagine what cuts and bruises Graham has. Worry kicks at her gut.

When the bell rings, Masyn doesn't have any packing up to do. She swings her backpack over her shoulder and storms to the door while her classmates chatter.

"Madden," Tate says, his voice stern. He nods toward his desk, signaling for her to wait behind. Masyn freezes and steps aside as the same silence as before falls over the class while they pack up and head to third period.

"I'll wait for you in the hall," Clayton tells her as he passes with Jake and Adison. All Masyn can do is stare back at Tate. This is the first time she's seen him in the daylight since his trip. Even though he looks like he took a beating to defend her honor, she can't stifle the resentment brimming inside her.

"I'm not going to ask you what you did," she snaps once the class has cleared.

"Good, because I'm not going to tell you," he replies in a hushed tone.

Masyn glares back before moving to walk out of the room, but Tate catches her elbow. He leans down to whisper, "We need to talk; obviously, we can't do it here."

"Right, I forgot that's how this works. I tell you one thing, you disappear, when I want to talk you say no, and then when you're ready, you demand that I spill all my deepest secrets so you can disappear again to, what? Fix them? Retaliate? Get yourself half-killed?"

"That's not what this is—"

Masyn grabs Tate by the chin and jerks his face to the side. "Oh, really?" she mocks, getting a better look at the stitches slashed across his brow. "Don't lie to me, Hough. We don't lie to each other."

He swipes her hand from his jaw. "Just give me a chance to explain."

Masyn flares her fingers against the heat zinging up her hand. "I can't tonight."

"Why not?"

"I'm busy."

"Get unbusy," Tate demands, leaning in.

"On one condition," Masyn negotiates.

"No, Masyn, we're not . . . it's too dangerous. The rip currents still haven't settled from the storm."

"Red and I were out there this morning."

"And look at you. Your skin is raw," Tate says, motioning to her arms and legs.

"The waves reward bravery, Mr. Houghton. See you tonight," she mocks before turning her back on him.

Outside the threshold of the classroom, Clayton, Jake, and Adison are jammed together, not even pretending like they weren't eavesdropping. As she takes in the suspicious expressions on their faces, panic rises in Masyn's chest. She mentally hustles to recount the conversation and decipher if she let any confidential information slip.

"What was that all about?" Jake asks.

"Nothing."

"I know he's friends with your aunt, but that looked—" Clayton starts.

Jake takes over his sentence. "That looked . . . I'm not even sure how to say it. Cozy? Hot? Heated?"

Masyn shakes her head. "No, just . . . no. I'm not going to explain right now. I have to get to class."

"We'll see you at lunch," Jake says, pulling Clayton in his wake.

Adison, who's been smirking through the entire conversation, adjusts the oversized purse on her shoulder and chuckles. "My, wasn't that enlightening? I tried to warn Clayton that he was too young for you. I can't wait to say I told you so."

At lunch, Masyn fights the urge to sit by herself and takes a seat next to Clayton. Jake, sitting across from them, eyes her over his sub sandwich.

"Bonfire tonight," he says through a mouthful. Adison looks disgusted as she watches Jake from further down the table, but the way she looks at Masyn, anticipating her answer, feels suspicious. Masyn's not about to sign herself up for some sort of intervention with their posse.

"It's a school night, and another storm is coming in," Masyn replies, looking to Clayton, who shrugs.

"Are you a toddler?" Jake taunts.

"No, but I'm an athlete, and so are you. What's your plan? To pop an Adderall to get you through your hangover? Not to mention, rain doesn't really bode well for a bonfire."

"You're feisty today, and I'll have you know that I have a prescription. Thank you very much. But really, you have to come."

"I have better things to do."

"Clayton will be at the bonfire, so if kissing his face off is one of those things, take it off your list. Or do it *after* the bonfire. It doesn't take precedence."

Masyn looks sidelong at Clayton.

"Dude. Just let it go," he murmurs to Jake.

"Uh oh? Trouble in paradise? Did Masyn scare you off from kissing ever again?" Jake chides, chomping into the last of his sandwich.

Masyn looks down and thumbs the sleeve of her sweatshirt.

"Bro, just shut up," Clayton hisses.

Jake throws his hands up. "Sorry! It was a joke." He points to his lip and bites. "Come on. You guys need more fun in your lives. The bonfire is officially a definite yes for all of us."

Clayton stands and slings his backpack over his shoulder before reaching down to pick up his lunch tray. "I've got a meeting with Coach," he says, and walks away without another word.

Adison makes her way over to them, dancing her fingertips across Jake's shoulders. "Did I hear the bonfire is a go?"

Jake jumps in. "Yes! Other than Masyn is being a buzzkill and doesn't want to come."

"Mmm," Adison hums. "Yeah, Masyn is very busy these days juggling all her extracurriculars. Soccer, mucking stalls, Clayton—"

"I said I can't make it, okay? What's the big deal?" Masyn glares at Adison as she takes a sip from her water bottle.

"Okay, I'm just going to say it. Are you hooking up with Houghton?" Jake interjects.

Adison's hand clenches Jake's shoulder, and Masyn coughs, choking on her water. "Excuse me? Where would you get that idea?"

"Hey, I'm just looking out for my boy C. We all saw you after class today, and you two looked very familiar with each other, if you know what I mean. Plus, Adison said she *knows things,*" he adds with air quotes.

Adison slaps him on the arm before squaring her posture with Masyn. "Oh, I know things," she says through a tight smile, "but I'm just going to sit back and watch, because this is playing out so much better than I could have ever imagined."

Masyn stands, grabbing her things. "Jake, we're buds, remember?" Jake holds up a fist for Masyn to bump, and she continues. "If you ever say something like that again, I will kick you in the balls so hard—"

"Okay, okay. I'm sorry."

Chapter Twenty-One

"Stop! Turn into this driveway right here," Adison demands from the back seat, leaning her elbows on the center console of Clayton's truck and pointing to the house three doors down from Nat's.

"Who's house is this?" Clayton asks as he turns off the gravel road. "You sure we can do a bonfire here?"

"There never was going to be a bonfire, dude. It's our alibi. I thought you realized that," Jake says, leaning against the passenger window.

Once the truck is parked, Adison hops out and walks up to the porch, peeking in the windows. "This is a summer house. We're using it as our lookout point."

"Lookout point for what?"

Jake slaps Clayton upside the head. "Catch up, man. Your girl just fraternized with a teacher. We literally heard them saying something about meeting up on the beach tonight . . . we're spying."

"We'll explain more later, just come on, and don't talk so loud." Adison leads them around the house, through the backyard, and halfway down the staircase that descends the bluff to the large deck where each home's separate path meets before joining into one last staircase that zigzags down the rest of the bluff. She gestures to the small shed in the corner. "Hide in here."

About ten minutes pass before Jake turns from his post at the door crack and whisper-shouts, "She's coming."

Clayton remains seated on the floor of the shed, uninterested, but Adison crouches under Jake to spy through the gap. "No? Is that really—" Jake starts.

"Yep," Adison answers proudly. "Turns out she didn't meet Houghton at the beach. She met him at her house, which means they could have been doing *anything* together before now."

"Shhh, they're getting closer."

Mr. Houghton's voice fills the air, and Clayton finds himself straining to hear what he's saying.

"It's impossible to watch and listen at the same time," Jake wines.

"Just shut up and listen," Adison demands, and they press their ears to the crack in the door.

"Forget it, Ace. What are we doing? This is stupid. We shouldn't be out here."

"Don't overthink it. I know you want to as much as I do. Just, let me show you. Come on."

From his spot in the corner, even Clayton finds himself trying to decipher their words, looking at his friends to see if they have any idea what Masyn is really saying.

"I don't want anything to happen—"

"Oh, so now you're concerned about safety. But not when you went to California to beat the living daylight out of—"

"Why are you so worried about him? After everything we've talked about, it's still *him*?"

A pregnant pause rings through the shed, and Jake gapes at the others. Masyn continues, "I wish I wasn't, okay? I wish I wasn't worried about either of you. But I am. Now, can we please stop talking and cut to the fun part?"

"There are things we need to talk about before—"

"If anyone has something to talk about, it's me. Okay? I don't want to talk. For just once, I want to forget the noise around us. You and me out there. Don't even try to tell me you don't want this. I can see it in your eyes, Tate."

Jake turns his head to peep through the crack. There's another long pause before the footsteps fade down the stairs. Adison remains in place swallowing a smile, while Clayton sits paralyzed with disbelief.

Jake's mouth hangs wide open as he claps Clayton on the shoulder, shaking him. "Duuuuude, did you know your girl was foolin' around with a teacher? *Our* teacher?"

Clayton glares at him. "What did you see?"

"They were eyeing each other big time. Had some sort of pinkie promise going on. I don't know, but didn't you hear? He beat someone to a pulp over her!"

"Well, I think our job here is done," Adison says, standing and brushing dust off her clothes.

"Also, why didn't I know that she surfs? That's freaking cool," Jake croons, forming a hang-loose sign with his hand.

Clayton's attention snaps back up to Jake. "Were they going down to surf?"

"Let's go, you guys," Adison interrupts. "The details don't matter."

"No," Clayton demands, coming to a stand. "Were they walking down to the beach with surfboards?" He doesn't wait for the answer before bursting through the door of the shed to look down on the beach where Masyn and Houghton are already paddling out into the large swells. Clayton turns to Jake and Adison. "Are you two kidding me right now? That entire conversation was about surfing."

"With a teacher," Adison adds. "Who she calls by his first name, and who broke bones for her."

"Who freaking cares? I've only ever seen one person surf this beach. Houghton is probably the only surfing partner she has access to."

"You're in denial, Clayton. We all heard the same thing, and it was . . . scandalous." Adison scoffs. "I should have recorded it," she adds under her breath.

"Wait, you guys, look!" Jake exclaims, rushing to the edge of the deck.

Down below, Masyn pops up on a massive wave, carving and completing one maneuver after the other. She ducks into a barrel and reemerges with speed before gliding up the wave and into the air. Grasping the edge of her board, she does a 180-degree spin and lands smoothly in the foam of the wave. Her hands fly up in celebration before she jumps off the board and paddles back out toward Houghton.

The guys look at each other wide-eyed. "Holy frick, man! Did you know about this?" Jake asks.

Clayton shakes his head, stunned. "She's unreal."

"And, for the record, she just fist-bumped Mr. H," Jake says, leaning in toward Clayton. "I think we can all agree that's a pretty friend-zoney thing to do. I'll give you that."

Adison huffs behind them, and they turn to find her partway back up the stairs. She weighs something over in her mind before she straightens her posture and lifts her chin. "You've been calling her by the wrong name, you know? Gentlemen, allow me to introduce you to Ace Madden, Rip Tide's Queen of the California Coast." With an eye roll, she adds, "I'm sure you can figure out the rest on your own. I'm leaving."

Clayton pulls Jake's sleeve. "Come on, dude. I'll take you guys home."

"You're kidding right? How is this not the coolest thing you've ever seen? Your girlfriend is a surfing legend," he says, shoving his Google search in Clayton's face. "Don't you want to go out there and talk to her?"

Clayton studies the phone for a minute. "She doesn't want us to know, okay?" he snaps, shoving it back into Jake's chest. "If she wanted us to know about this, she would have told us, which is why neither of you are going to say anything to anyone, including Masyn. Got it?"

Jake turns on his heels and salutes. "Your relationship is so weird."

Chapter Twenty-Two

"THAT WAS AMAZING!" MASYN says, tossing her surfboard on the sand and pulling her wet suit down to her waist.

Tate follows behind her and chucks her a towel from his bag. "Did you have to throw air on every wave?"

"Oh, please. You'll catch up one day, you rusty kook."

Even with his cast, Tate loads both boards in his arms and heads up the beach, smirking over his shoulder at Masyn's joke. "It did feel good to ride a decent-sized swell again."

"You actually weren't as rusty as I'd expected. I'm impressed, Tate Houghton."

Tate smiles back. "If I had a free hand, I'd flip you the bird."

"Hey, I have to tell you something," Masyn says, changing the tone. "You probably know my dad died in a surfing accident." Tate nods, setting down the boards. "It happened in Hawaii, and I've never been able to bring myself to surf there. Even though winning a competition there would be huge for me, stepping on that beach just seems impossible. But seeing you come out here after everything you've been through with Kat's loss . . . I don't know, it's just been encouraging. So, thank you."

Tate wraps his uninjured arm around Masyn's shoulders. "Couldn't have done it without you," he says before squatting back down to grab the boards. Masyn hangs his bag over her shoulder and follows him across the sand. When they reach the top of the stairs, Masyn's focus is down at her feet. She doesn't see Tate stop short at the grass line of her backyard and collides right into his back.

"Dude, what the—" The slight shake of Tate's head stops Masyn midsentence. Now somewhat scared, she clings to him, latching one hand onto the wet suit material at Tate's hip and setting the other on his back. His muscles go taut. "Is something wrong?" Masyn whispers.

Tate doesn't answer.

Masyn plasters herself to his back and braces for something bad. "Tate, tell me."

He quickly repositions the surfboards in front of him and turns to face her. "Something will be wrong if you keep groping me like that! Did you know Clayton was waiting on your porch?"

Masyn steps back, a mixture of relief and newfound stress coursing through her body. "I thought there was a mountain lion! I was protecting myself!"

"You've got to be kidding me. A mountain lion? In Massachusetts?" Tate asks. Masyn bulges her eyes at him. "Just—Do you want me to cover for you?"

Masyn doesn't have time to decide before Clayton calls out, "Houghton, it's fine. I just want to talk to Masyn."

Tate looks over his shoulder, then back at Masyn. "I'll take care of these," he says, motioning to the surfboards.

Masyn nods before heading toward the porch to face Clayton. She stops on the steps a few feet from where Clayton sits on the patio sofa and leans against the pillar, readjusting the bag on her shoulder. Keeping her distance won't hide the fact that she was just surfing—she's wearing a bikini and a wet suit, for heaven's sake—but she can't help but be defensive in this moment. "What's up?" she asks.

Clayton sighs and swipes both hands down his face. "I think we should break up."

Masyn stands upright and takes one step toward him. "Clayton, we just decided to start fresh."

"I just—I think it's best if we give each other some space, and I wanted to make sure that was clear before I started distancing myself."

"Why?" Masyn asks, now realizing she wants to be with Clayton more than she's let herself believe.

"I don't want to force you to be more than you want to be for me."

"But I want to be together. I want to be . . . someone for you."

Clayton stands and walks over to her, linking his fingers in hers. "I know. But I'm starting believe you when you say you don't have the capacity to be who you want to be for me." He gives her hand a squeeze and adds, "I'm sorry," before walking away.

Masyn stills.

It's not until she hears Clayton's truck start and reverse out of the long driveway that she realizes she's still standing there. She wipes at the tears trickling down her face and moves to go inside.

"Ace." Tate's voice is quiet, but it's close.

She looks to the side and finds him at the edge of the porch.

"My keys are in my bag," he says, pointing to his duffel, still draped over her shoulder.

Masyn bites her lip and looks down at the bag, sniffling against the tears that won't stop. Tate's at her side now, her shoulder practically touching his chest. He's thrown on one of the Rip Tide t-shirts he must have found in the garage, and Masyn has to close her eyes against the formidable Ace logo threatening to slice through her new life. When she opens her eyes, Tate's examining her face. She can feel him ready to be whatever support she needs right now, but she shakes her head against his silent offer and hands over the bag before walking into the house.

She doesn't have the strength to talk this one out right now.

IF THERE WAS ONE word to explain this night, it would be *unexpected*. Masyn lies in her bed, looking up at the ceiling, a million emotions coming and going like the swash of the sea. She hadn't expected to catch waves that big—even more, she had forgotten how good it felt to be free enough to enjoy it. She hadn't expected Tate to let loose out there, either. She hadn't expected to break things off with Clayton, hadn't expected to be sad about it.

And, for some reason, every unexpected aspect of this night keeps bringing her back to thoughts of Graham.

Why? It makes sense to worry if Tate hurt Graham. That's human nature, right? But there's a more obtrusive feeling pulling at the back of her heart, her mind, her gut.

She couldn't possibly be missing him . . . could she?

Masyn turns onto her side, silently scolding herself, and opens her phone, scrolling through her contacts and stopping on Graham's name.

She clicks on his contact and a photo of him holding her in a piggyback shows up, causing her to clutch at the pang in her chest. This wasn't the first time she'd looked at his contact since moving here. However, it was the first time this picture had popped up, which means Graham must have recently assigned it to his account.

Does this mean Graham might be regretting things as much as she does? Is he sorry?

Recently, she'd unblocked his number and spent many sleepless nights looking at pictures of them, wishing things were different. But what irks her most is that she doesn't wish things hadn't happened; she wishes they were better for each other. They'd already become best friends and a killer coach-athlete combo. Maybe if she were a little older, or more mature, they could fit in that one last category and things could have worked out for them. Maybe they could be on tour, crushing surf competitions and continuing to grow into one indomitable force.

Masyn grunts. *It's demented to think like this.*

Graham rocked her world in the worst way. Masyn knows that. Looking back at how far she's come from those dark days after their kiss, Masyn knows she did what she had to. They never could have continued on Graham's terms, but that doesn't keep her from dreaming of a different future.

Masyn flops onto her stomach and folds the pillow over her head, resolved to put this out of her mind and go to sleep. However, minutes later, she finds herself doing the unexpected once again and hits *call*.

Graham picks up just as Masyn moves to end the call. "Ace?" His voice is like a long swig of your favorite childhood drink—nostalgic, but not quite right for your matured taste buds. Nonetheless, it's a reminder of simpler, happier times.

"Ace?" he tries again. "You there?"

A solid stream of tears streaks Masyn's face, and she lets out a shaky breath, unable to bring words to her lips.

Graham sighs on the other end of the line, and Masyn can picture him running a heavy hand up and down his jaw. "I miss you," he says.

Masyn squeezes her eyes shut, clenching her jaw to keep from sobbing. Graham would take her back with open arms, only looking toward the future. She knows it.

Is it possible that the one person who can fix me is the very person who broke me?

"Look, I'm sorry. We could have worked through it if you'd just stayed. We're *us*—Rip Tide's dynamic duo." Masyn stills for a beat, wondering what to say, where to start, and Graham continues. "If you don't want to talk, that's fine, but I'm telling you, I've tried to wait for you to take your time, have your space. Now, it's getting time to set things in motion. I've always told you we can't stay stagnant. And now I'm asking you, A-babe—come home. I don't want to be me without you. I want to be us. Let's be us again."

Masyn's breath hitches. She feels like she's stood up on a wave she's now realizing is a bomb. If she doesn't bail, she'll soar to the base until it caves in and foam rolls her—like it had before. Masyn slams her finger against the screen to end the call.

"*Let's be us?*" Ugh. She feels so stupid. She'd said the same thing to Clayton, not even realizing Graham had put the phrase in her head. "*We're us.*" Now that she thinks about it, he'd always said that. She should have seen the way he passively poisoned any chance she ever had of a relationship after him.

Before she can block Graham's number again, he calls back. Masyn, now enraged, accepts the call. "We're done, Graham. Don't try to contact me again."

"Don't say that. You called me. You picked up."

"There is no more us."

"Why not? What happened? Why do I have bloody knuckles for defending myself against a man I don't even know?"

Masyn can't even bring herself to scoff. He knows what happened. And now she can never go back. She can never go home. She musters up all the energy she has and says, "You want to know what happened? I trusted you. But you pulled me under, and I got caught in a riptide I can't escape from."

Chapter Twenty-Three

A FEW DAYS LATER, Masyn gets to skip class to meet up with the soccer team and drive to their out-of-town game. A win here will make them regional champions and earn them a spot in the state tournament.

After their team meeting, Masyn boards the charter bus with one goal: to sit as far away from Adison as possible. Masyn takes a seat next to McCall and overhears Coach Nance telling the bus driver that they're good to go. But Adison is nowhere to be found.

"Where's Adison?" Masyn asks McCall.

"Nance said she's driving with her parents." She shrugs and pops a headphone in.

Masyn frowns at the thought while she gets comfortable in her seat. Thirty minutes later, she still can't shake the feeling that something is off. Adison would do anything to avoid riding with her parents. She pulls her phone out of her pocket and, against her better judgment, sends Adison a text.

Masyn: Everything ok? You're not on the bus.

Adison: Great observation Captain Obvious. I'm coming later.

An hour later, the team arrives at their destination. As they unload and head for the field house, Nance holds Masyn back on the bus. She dangles a captain's armband from her finger in front of Masyn, who looks at the red elastic like it's the dark mark.

"What about Adison?"

"She's not coming. Sprained ankle." Masyn furrows her brow in confusion. Adison had just said she would be there. "Even if she were, I'd want you to be a co-captain for this game."

"Okay," Masyn responds hesitantly, taking the armband. As soon as she's off the bus, she texts Adison again.

Masyn: What's going on? I know you don't have a sprained ankle.

Adison: Try not to miss me too much.

Masyn and Coach Nance walk into the field house together. When they open the door to the locker room, McCall is lecturing the entire team from a raised platform.

"If y'all know what's good for you—if you want to win tonight—you will keep your mouths shut. Do you hear me? Not a word!" McCall stops and retracts her pointer finger when she realizes Masyn and Nance have come in.

The two stare at the scene in confusion while the team stares back with mixed expressions of humor and horror.

Nance chuckles. "First of all, I didn't know you had that kind of sass in you. Good for you, McCall! Now please don't do it again. Second, I don't want to know. From this moment forward, all we are thinking and talking about is the game. Speaking of, Masyn will be our captain tonight. Adison won't be here, so McCall, you'll be starting in her position. We have an hour until we warm up, so do what you need to do, but leave the drama out of it."

"What was that all about?" Masyn asks, joining McCall by her locker.

McCall rolls her eyes. "Nothing, it was just . . . I don't know . . . you know?"

"Uhh, no. I'm not following."

"People always have something to say about my brother. And Seager's just . . . I just wish they'd cut him some slack."

"Seager Brooks is your brother?"

"Yeah, why? Did you guys hook up?" McCall deadpans.

"Oh my gosh! No! I just didn't know, is all. He's so..."

"I know!" McCall slams her locker shut.

Masyn looks around at the team getting ready. "Why is everybody staring at me behind my back?"

McCall's eyes go wide for the briefest moment. Then she flicks Masyn's new armband. "I'm guessing this has something to do with it. They'll get used to it."

THE SOCCER GAME IS a constant switch between offense and defense for the entire eighty minutes of play. By the last time-out before overtime, every member of the team is covered in an array of mud, blood, and grass stains.

Nance looks to Masyn. "Tell me what's happening out there from your perspective. What's keeping us from scoring?"

"We need more room in the offensive zone. There's nowhere to run."

Nance taps her whiteboard before wiping it clean and scribbling again. "Okay, ladies. I know you're all tired, but we're switching up the formation, so I'm going to need every one of you to kick it into turbo. Instead of our 4-3-3, we're going to run a 4-4-2, but I want the midfield staggered—two defensive mids, two offensive. This will give us more room to run the ball in the offensive zone. Defense, you'll have extra help from the midfielders to keep the ball out of our half. Let's go!"

The change proves to be helpful. The girls get more strikes on goal, but none sink into the net. With one minute left before sudden death, McCall gets a corner kick. Masyn pulls away from the goal, knowing that just like every other corner they've had this game, the opposing team's giant defensive players will head the ball away from the net.

McCall looks at Masyn as she's setting up, and Masyn knows exactly what she's doing—or at least, she hopes she does. So when McCall kicks the ball, Masyn starts sprinting toward the penalty mark. The ball soars in a perfect arch over the clump of players, making them jump at the opportunity to get a head on it, but then it spins infield, just outside their reach. Right as they're all coming down from their jumps, Masyn launches herself into the air. She keeps her eyes pinned on her target as she reaches her peak and makes contact with the ball before propelling quickly into the throng of players and falling to the ground. She can no longer see the goal between all the bodies, but she doesn't have to. Cheers erupt, and her team grabs at her to help her up. They've done it.

By the time the charter bus arrives back in Ellsworth, the team is still on a high from winning the regional championship.

"There's a party in the West Woods," one of the girls calls out. "We're all going! Time to celebrate!"

Masyn grimaces, but she knows she has to go. Clayton will probably be there, and the way he looked at her as she stood in front of him in a bikini and a wet suit has been weighing on her heart. He'd run out of hope that she'd tell him about her past, and she has nobody to blame but herself. He deserves to know the truth.

Masyn pulls out her phone to text McCall, who rode home with her boyfriend.

Masyn: You going to the party in the woods?

McCall: Yes...phones @ 1%. Wait for me at the tree line. Have to tell you something.

Chapter Twenty-Four

MASYN'S EFFORTS TO WAIT for McCall are thwarted when the rest of the team insists on entering together. String lights line a path into the woods just behind the dorms, and the thump of music grows with every step. When the soccer team walks into the clearing, the partygoers erupt in congratulatory cheers. Even Adison, who Masyn assumed would be bitter about the win, seems proud. When she catches Masyn's eye, she winks over the fire in the middle of the clearing.

Not wanting to figure out what that means, Masyn makes her way to where Clayton and Jake are chatting with Seager and some other football guys.

"Hey," Masyn says to the group before turning her attention to Clayton. "Can we talk?"

Clayton exhales a breath. "Sure," he says, his tone flat.

They walk outside the clearing behind a line of trees where the warmth of the fire no longer reaches them. Clayton swings around to face Masyn, his previous annoyance visibly transforming into something like anger.

"What's wrong?" Masyn frowns.

"Nothing. Say what you were going to say."

"Clayton, are you okay?"

He widens his stance, folding his arms across his chest and responds with a stiff nod.

"Um, okay. You asked about my coach . . . from the picture—about what sport I played." Masyn peeks up from under her lashes to find Clayton scowling down at her, but she surges on. She's already committed to telling him. "I surf. Or I used to . . . I don't know. I know surfing's not really a huge deal out here, but in California it is, and I've kind of become meta-famous for being the best junior surfer in a long time."

Clayton adjusts his watch and lets his arms fall slack to his side, his expression now cold and unimpressed. "Cool."

Masyn rears back. "Cool? You've been dying to know my secrets, and when I finally build up the trust and courage to tell you, you say *cool?*"

"The timing of it is just weird. Are you telling me just because I saw you surfing, or because I broke up with you? Or are you telling me because now everybody knows, so you figure you might as well get the credit for *trusting* me with your hidden past? Which, by the way, I don't think being Ace Madden, the best surfer in the nation, warrants so much secrecy."

Masyn's face falls flat. "Everybody knows? What are you talking about?" she asks through shaky breaths.

Clayton tosses his hands up, cursing under his breath. "It's all anyone has been talking about today—you, or Ace, or whoever.

Even the soccer girls are over there talking about it." Then he retreats, and Masyn knows he's walking away for good.

She clutches at her ribs. That must have been what McCall was lecturing them about. Add one—or twenty—to the list of people that lied to her face. She scans the crowd, looking for Clayton again, but halts her search when she finds Seager watching her through the smoke. Keeping her glare locked on his, she storms back over to the group, not stopping until she's grabbed Seager by the lapel of his leather jacket and dragged him aside, behind a tree. "You 'know nothing,' my—"

"Hey, hey," Seager says, stepping closer and leaning down to come eye to eye with her. His dark golden eyes are hooded by thick brows as he searches Masyn's face.

"How could you? I never should have told you."

Seager puts a gentle hand on her upper arm. "I think you should know—" He stops and looks to the side, swallowing hard as Clayton comes into view.

Clayton looks from Masyn to Seager and back again. "I can't believe this," he spits.

"What?" Masyn yells. "What can't you believe?"

Clayton stares at Seager, his hand still on Masyn's arm.

Masyn moves toward Clayton, grabbing his forearm, and trying but failing to peel his focus off of Seager. "Tell me, Clayton, because I promise you I'll clear it up."

Seager clears his throat. "I was just trying to mess with Clayton's head, I didn't mean for other people to overhear and blow it out of proportion," Seager tells Masyn, but he's looking at Clayton. Their eyes bore into one another's as if throwing telepathic punches.

"What are you not telling me?" Masyn asks, looking between the guys. Neither one acknowledges her. Instead, they continue their silent assault.

"This is unbelievable. Who has secrets now?" Masyn cries. "I'm going home." People holler after her as she runs away, but she doesn't stop for anything, not even the name "Ace Madden."

THE EMPTINESS OF AUNT Nat's house caves in on Masyn as she flips through channels, trying to find a TV show to distract herself. It doesn't take long for Clayton's truck tires to scrape against the driveway. Seconds later he knocks on the door.

"Seager?" he asks as soon as Masyn opens the door.

When she doesn't answer, he pushes past her and leans against the back of the sofa. "You told *Seager*?" he tries again, this time laced with defeat.

Masyn closes the door, then walks past Clayton and sits on the sofa, hugging her knees to her chest. She bites her lip to keep the knot in her throat from growing. "Seager was just—He and I aren't even friends."

"It sure sounds like you're friends," Clayton snaps. "Sure looked like you were friends when you were locked in the garage together the other day and when you were convening behind a tree in the woods."

Masyn catapults off her seat, and Clayton meets her in a stand, the couch acting as a barrier between them. "How dare you imply something like that when we've been alone together. You're the only one who knows—" She squeezes her eyes against the threat of tears. "It's just not true. You're so concerned with how things look to other people, that you can't see for yourself what's really happening."

Clayton hangs his head. "Why did he know before I did?"

Masyn shrugs. "He figured it out, showed up at my house, and asked me straight up. So, I showed him my boards in the garage."

"Why?" Clayton demands with a raised voice. "Why *him*?"

"I don't know, Clayton. I just felt like it. Do you know how hard it is to be buried alive by your past? Not being able to tell people who you *actually* are because you know that *you* are the one thing that will eventually ruin yourself?" Masyn pauses, her heart pounding beneath quick breaths. "Seager wasn't demanding anything from me. He just wanted to know, and I just wanted to stop my secret from shoveling another load of dirt on top of me."

"You could have told *me*, Masyn. That's what I'm so upset about. I *wanted* you to tell me. I *asked* you to, over and over."

Masyn sits and wipes at the tears that have escaped her eyes. "I'm sorry. I didn't think . . . I didn't want you to stop liking me."

"Why would I do that?"

"Because of the way it ended."

Clayton pauses before reassuming his position against the back of the sofa. When it's clear that she isn't going to say more, he looks out the back windows and sighs. "We saw you out there the other day."

Masyn eyes him, and he continues, tipping his head down. "Seager didn't leak your identity. Jake and Adison wrapped me into some sort of spy plan they came up with. There was no bonfire the other night. They were baiting you because they wanted to catch you meeting up with Houghton."

"Was Seager part of it?"

"No."

"Then why would he try to cover for you?"

Clayton shrugs. "Seager and I...We have history."

Masyn narrows her eyes, waiting for more clarification.

"I watched from the deck on the bluff. You were amazing." Clayton huffs out half a laugh. "Of course you were."

Once again, Masyn remains silent, so Clayton goes on. "That's when Adison told us exactly how good you are . . . you know, good enough to be Ace Madden, sponsored by Rip Tide."

"So that's why the whole school knows? Because you guys decided to spy on me? You're the one who told everyone?"

"Don't put this on me. I didn't hang around, because I knew you didn't want me to know. I made us all leave."

"You could have stopped them in the first place."

"I didn't know, Masyn! Geez! You should be grateful we found out the truth. This narrative is a whole heck of a lot better than the original one Adison had planned for you. If I hadn't looked at the context clues of what you were saying to Houghton out there on that deck, you'd be rumored to be hooking up with a teacher right now, which honestly, isn't unbelievable if you ask me."

This strikes a chord inside Masyn, and her tears quicken. "Go! Leave! We're done talking."

Clayton pushes away from the couch and walks toward the door, pausing with his hand on the handle. "I'm sorry, Masyn, for how this came about. For what I just said. But have you ever considered that maybe, if you gave people the chance, they would like you for who you are *now*?"

Masyn keeps quiet even as Clayton shuts the door and leaves. When she hears his truck pull out of the driveway, she relocates to the back porch, unable to put up with the suffocating silence inside the house. She stretches out on the patio sofa, allowing herself to feel the gravity of the situation. Covering her face with her hands, she lets the tears suction her skin together.

When her crying finally subsides, she lies there, focusing on the nocturnal baritone of the ocean waves. The sound shouldn't be comforting. She should be afraid of the ocean's night mask that nearly drowned her under Graham's force. But the opposite is true. The moments she feels the most panic out in the ocean are the moments in broad daylight; when she's running out into the water, when she's about to pop up on her board, or when she's gaining momentum to complete a hard maneuver. Ironically, these are the very moments Masyn used to feel the most excitement. It's almost as if she's not afraid of the ocean—she's afraid to be happy again. Afraid to be free.

Not even the sound of footsteps on the deck or the sight of Tate hovering over her from between her fingers can jolt her out of her daze.

Tate takes a long swig of his soda and lifts a hand off Masyn's face. They stare at each other wordlessly before he drops her hand back into place and takes a seat at the other end of the sofa, lifting her feet and repositioning them on his lap.

Masyn lets herself be comforted by his presence for a few minutes before breaking the tranquility. "You shouldn't be here, Tate."

Silence rings out between them, prompting Masyn to prop up on her elbows and study him. He's relaxed against the sofa, his head turned to the side and looking down at her. He maintains eye contact while reaching forward to grab the small remote from the ledge of the propane firepit in front of them and clicks it on. Then he flops back against the backrest as he was.

Masyn traces the line of his five o'clock shadow with her eyes, watches his jaw tick, his Adam's apple bob. She sees the burn of pain in his eyes, like a heart scraped raw. He's not trying to hide it like he used to.

He squeezes one of her feet and lazily rolls his head back to center, looking up at the stars through the gaps of the pergola. "You gonna kick me out like you did the last?"

"No."

"Why not?"

"Because you're not okay," Masyn whispers.

He blows out a sigh. "Neither are you."

Masyn swings her feet around and readjusts so her head rests on Tate's thigh. She inhales, finding comfort in the scent of his detergent mixed with ocean water.

He rests his casted hand on her shoulder, rubbing his fingertips along the faded fabric of the old Rip Tide hoodie she's wearing—his hoodie. "You wear this a lot," he says.

"Yeah, I guess I do." Masyn rests her hands under her chin. "Why?"

After a beat, she answers, "Have you ever tried to heal from something you're trying to keep hidden? I don't think it's possible. When you bury a secret, it doesn't rest. It shakes like an awakened mummy in its tomb. When my secret started shaking, I built more walls—I decided the safest thing to do was to not let anyone close enough to see it. But that night on the beach, when we first met, you walked right through my walls like they weren't even there. I tell you things . . . I *want* to tell you things. And you don't get scared off. You listen. When I'm feeling stupid and alone, sometimes I need to know that someone like you exists for someone like me."

Tate reaches down with his free hand and hooks his pinkie in Masyn's. He doesn't say anything, but his gentle squeeze feels like a silent promise. He'll always see Masyn for who she really is. She has no doubt about that.

"What's wrong, Masyn?"

"They know about Ace."

"Who's they?"

"Everyone. The whole school."

"But what is *wrong*?"

"There's not enough good in me for them to focus on. The bad things won't fade to black. They'll rip me apart until my mummy breaks free."

Tate pulls Masyn into a sitting position, holding her by the shoulders and moving in front of her. "That's not true, Ace." Masyn looks down, and Tate jolts her. "Look at me," he snaps. "You burn. Okay? You burn inside everyone you meet."

Now Tate is the one to look down. Shaking his head, he slowly brings his gaze back to Masyn. With a shine in his eyes, he continues, "You have so much goodness inside of you. People are drawn to you. Impacted by you."

Masyn leans forward and rests her head on Tate's shoulder, shaking it back and forth and squeezing her eyes shut to keep the tears in.

"I'm sorry, Masyn. I'm sorry," he says against her temple.

Masyn realizes that she's not the only one trembling. She pulls away to find Tate shaking. "Hey," she says, tipping his chin up so he meets her eyes.

Tate stills. His eyes search hers before dragging down to her lips, and he stands abruptly. "I can't," he says, pacing. "I'm failing you. I'm failing." His words grow in intensity until he buckles, crouching to the ground. "I've failed you."

"What are you talking about?"

"I've been stuck. For five years, I've been stuck grieving Kat. And that night, when I looked at you, it was like I was seeing her. And I just thought to myself, *don't mess this up*. It was almost like it was a message from her. Then in just one glance, you understood my soul and I knew I wanted to do my best to keep you, know you, protect you. But I haven't done any of that. I haven't been able to protect your secret or stop your pain. I've become selfish. And after everything you've been through . . . I shouldn't be here."

"Tate, stay! Don't go!"

"I'm sorry," he says, turning to leave. "I won't let myself do this to you."

"Tate!" Masyn cries, clutching at her hoodie, and storming after him. "You're not failing me. Please!"

He pauses at the edge of the porch, speaking over his shoulder. "Masyn, you don't understand."

"Then tell me. I want to understand."

"I can't . . . I won't. You said it yourself; I shouldn't be here."

"I need you," she whispers to his back, voice cracking.

Tate whirls on her. "No, Masyn. You don't! Okay? I need you to know that. I need you to know that you don't need *me*. You have Karina and Red, you have friends your own age, you have your family, even though it may not seem like it right now. You don't *need me.*" Tate pauses. "I would fail you all over again if I let you need me."

Masyn remains still, looking up at Tate only inches away from her. She takes in his response, wishing she could reject every part of it. The moment she thinks he's going to finally leave, she stops him again. "Tate, what else?" she asks softly.

He parts his lips but bites his response back, taking a step to distance himself.

"Okay then," Masyn says and walks into her house without a second look.

Staying here tonight was never her plan. Masyn quickly changes into sweats, grabs her comfiest blanket, and jogs over to Karina's, making herself comfortable on the couch.

She'd hoped being at Karina's would help her avoid her nightly check-up on Graham, but not ten minutes later she's scrolling through pictures of them. Masyn flicks her eyes up at the sound of the back door opening. Tate slips in and slumps onto the couch opposite her.

"This room's taken," she chides, hoping it sounds more rude than humorous.

"Shut up," he quips, pulling a blanket over himself.

"You can't be serious, Tate. What are you doing here? You just told me to leave you alone, which—just so we're clear—I told you to leave me alone first."

He clicks on the TV and levels a gaze at her. "Remember what you said about our kind of demons?"

Masyn's features soften.

"I just need tonight."

At that, she flops back onto her pillow, resigning to his company.

"Plus, I wanted to make sure you didn't run away or something stupid," he adds, earning a throw pillow to the face.

Chapter Twenty-Five

MASYN WAKES TO WATER dripping on her head. When she cracks an eye open, Red is next to her, holding a straw over her head and releasing another drop with his finger.

"Why, Red? Why?"

"Dawn patrol," he says, a smirk lighting up his face, then he gulps down the water in his cup before walking over to the other couch where Tate lays face down on a pillow, feet hanging over the armrest. He grabs an ice cube from his glass and puts it in Tate's collar. "Dawn patrol!"

"Uhhh!" Tate yells out. "What the heck, Red?"

"That's what you kids get for not inviting me to movie night."

"I didn't expect company," Masyn says, wrapping a blanket around her shoulders and walking into the kitchen where Karina's already frying up bacon and eggs.

Last night, her sympathy for Tate turned into anger as he settled onto his couch and turned a movie on. Why should he get to decide who she does and doesn't need in her life? Him coming to stay with her at Karina's proves they need each other; but instead of admitting that, he blamed it on her needing to be looked after every time something doesn't go her way.

"No? What movie did you watch?" Red looks from Masyn to Tate, who's now standing by the back door.

"She wouldn't know. She refused to watch it because she was too busy pouting."

Masyn plucks a piece of crispy bacon off the plate on the island and glares at Tate.

Karina chuckles. "Pouting about what?" she asks Masyn.

"We weren't having a movie night. I was being babysat." Masyn chomps into her bacon, watching Tate shake his head and Red fail to hide his laughter. "I'm going to go get ready."

"Hey, just meet us down on the beach. Let the babysitter bring your board down." Red's laughter bubbles up again before he even finishes his sentence.

"No, no. I've got it," Masyn says, walking toward the back door. When she comes shoulder to shoulder with Tate, she pauses, locking eyes with him in a piercing glare. "I don't *need* you," she adds under her breath.

ON THE FIRST WAVE, Red throws and lands a 360, whooping and hollering like a kid on Christmas morning. When the next wave comes in, Tate paddles and pops up, quickly positioning himself to duck into the barrel. Masyn, paddling for the same wave, sees him deep in the barrel and decides to drop in. As soon as she pops up on the board, she huddles into the sweet spot to finish the barrel.

Having not expected him to make it through, she startles when Tate yells from right behind her. She's even more taken aback when he reaches out and grabs her board, causing them both to get eaten by the wave.

Masyn comes up coughing and jumps on her board, chasing after Tate, who's already paddling back out. "Are you kidding me?" she calls out to him.

"You dropped in on me!" Tate yells back before duck diving under the incoming wave.

Masyn follows suit. "You were in too deep. You were never coming out of that."

"I was riding the foam ball. I would have made it if I didn't have to slow down for you."

Masyn separates herself from Tate by paddling around to the other side of Red and turns her back to the incoming waves, shaking her head. A massive wave starts building up behind them. "You want this one?" she asks, looking at Red.

"All yours, kid."

Masyn doesn't wait a beat before lying flat on her board and paddling as hard as she can. She catches it at the perfect time and gets to her feet, riding the wave for a second to feel it out before deciding how she wants to rip it. With her back to the break, Masyn glides down to the base to throw a bottom turn, but when she goes to carve in, her board nearly collides with Tate's. He's dropped in on her, carved around her, and has now poached her wave. Masyn bails, jumping off her board and over the wave.

The fight for waves continues until Red lands another 360 and signals for them to come to shore, where Karina sits with a propane heater and a bag full of breakfast burritos.

"That was *some* surfing out there," she says.

"Why is it that you two seem to be secretly conspiring together one day and on opposite sides of a battle royale the next?" Red asks over a mouthful of burrito, then turns to Karina. "Did you see my 360?"

"If she's going to poach my wave, I'm going to do it back. You saw her drop in on me." Tate looks over his shoulder at Red from where he stands with his back to the fire, trying to free his cast from the watertight protection sleeve.

"Oh, I saw it," Red laughs.

Karina chuckles with him. "Let me guess. This all started with Tate running his mouth, and now Masyn doesn't want to put up with it."

Masyn points at Karina. *Bingo!* "Tate doesn't think I can hold my own. Had to prove him wrong," she says, throwing on a parka and unwrapping a burrito. "And I only dropped in the first time after I saw that he was getting eaten by the barrel."

"You guys gonna go at it again at sunset?" Red asks.

"I'll probably be hanging out with friends my own age." Masyn flashes a smirk at Tate.

Tate yanks his bag off the ground. "Quit taking my words and rubbing them in the dirt. It's childish." He takes off toward the house, calling over his shoulder, "And don't come looking for me when you want someone to surf with tonight."

Masyn looks to the Kensingtons, embarrassed that they're there to witness one of her and Tate's fights. "Sorry, that really got him riled up."

Red waves her off. "Ehh, he's probably still recovering from yesterday."

"Yesterday?"

"It was the sixth anniversary of Kat's passing," Karina says.

Masyn's hand flies to her mouth. "I'm sorry. I didn't know."

Red claps a hand on her shoulder. "Don't apologize. This . . . Surfing, riling Tate up, and having a beach breakfast is exactly what Kat would have done if she were here. We needed this, so thank you."

Karina smiles and nods. "Hey, Masyn, before you go," she says, "if you ever need a place to sleep—comfortably—we cleared out the guest room for you."

"And by cleared out, she means she painted it and completely redecorated it with you in mind." Karina slaps Red, and they both look at Masyn.

"Thank you," Masyn says, taken aback. "I . . . I can't wait to see it."

Karina smiles and winks. "And we can lock Tate out if you want us to. Just let me know what you need."

MASYN GETS TO SECOND period early and storms up to Tate's desk. "You didn't tell me what yesterday was."

"Didn't want to."

Masyn glares back at him.

"I don't need to tell you everything. I need you—" He stops himself, blowing out a breath. "No. We're not doing this. Have a seat," he orders, standing and walking over to the whiteboard.

Masyn follows him. "I'm done being the only one who shares things."

"Good, now you know how VanDamme feels."

Masyn's mouth drops open. "You're a real jerk, you know that?"

Tate ignores her and writes *"Pop Quiz"* on the board as the class swarms in. "Take your seat, Masyn Madden."

"That's Ace Madden to you," Jake jokes as he comes in. Tate zeroes in on him. "I mean, to everyone, since we're all just finding out, and it's cool and everything. Wasn't telling you how to live your life, Mr. H. By the way, where'd your cast go?"

"Cut it out."

"Yourself? Sick! Why?"

"I meant that directed to you. Cut the crap. But, yeah, I took it off this morning . . . got too salty," he adds with a sideways glance toward Masyn.

McCall leans in toward Masyn. "Since you haven't made an official statement on the A-C-E issue, everyone is still talking about it. By the way, when were you planning on telling me about that? I thought I might be the first to know the details, you know, since I fought the whole team to save you from despair at our last game."

"It's not just you, McCall. I haven't talked about it to anyone. I was hoping I wouldn't have to."

McCall winces. "The rumor mill is working overtime. You have to say something to someone before it blows up. Just maybe not my brother this time . . . he doesn't tell anyone anything, even if it's true."

"Okay, sit with me at lunch."

"Ehh . . . " McCall hesitates.

"What? Why not?"

"Because Seager sits at your table." Masyn gives her a look, silently trying to piece together what she means. "I don't mind, he just likes to have his own sphere. He'll be all silent and broody at his end of the table, talking to nobody, but secretly having an opinion about everybody, and it'll throw off his groove if I'm there."

McCall was right. Seager was sitting at his end of the table, and he was visibly disturbed when McCall sat down next to Masyn. Masyn leans over the table, looking down at Seager, and furrows her brow once his eyes meet hers. He fixes his eyes on his lunch and continues eating.

Masyn: I invited her to sit with us. Get used to it, and be nice.

Seager: I know.

Masyn: How? How do you know?

Seager: You just stared me down and basically said that with your angry little eyebrows.

Masyn slides her phone back into her bag, trying to suppress a smile. It shouldn't make her happy that Seager knows her thoughts without needing to voice them, but it does.

Jake's voice breaks through the chatter of their table. "Ladies and gents, we finally have the opportunity to sit in the presence of living legend, Ace Madden, herself," he says, starting a round of applause.

Though Masyn's stomach drops at the subject, she knows Jake is only playing around, so she smiles and reaches over to nudge him on the shoulder.

"Seriously though, Masyn. We have questions. Namely, why didn't you tell us? And why are you here when you should be shredding it up in SoCal?"

Masyn shrugs, looking around the table. All eyes are on her, but she stops on Seager's when she recites her practiced answer. "I didn't think anyone out here really cared about surfing. And umm, I don't know. My sponsorship ended, so I decided it was time to focus on academics. It's hard to make a career in surfing."

"Not if you're the best in the country, it's not." Masyn shifts her gaze to Adison. She's smiling sweetly, but Masyn knows better. "Nobody beats Rip Tide's dynamic duo. Isn't that what they say? I can't believe they would let your sponsorship go. Seriously," Adison says, looking to the rest of the table with the fakest surprised expression Masyn's ever seen. "You guys have to see the videos of Masyn surfing. Should we watch some?"

Masyn balls her hands into fists to keep from calling Adison out in front of the entire lunchroom. She knows right where Adison is headed. There isn't a single surf riptide of her that doesn't pan to Graham every few minutes. It's as if Ace Madden doesn't exist if Graham isn't in the picture. Politics aside, Masyn can't survive talking about Graham right now. She looks around, trying to calm her racing heart and begging for a distraction.

"Hey." Masyn flinches, more from the startle of Clayton's voice than the hand he places on her shoulder. They exchange a glance that makes Masyn feel like she's disappointed him all over again. "Can I sit here?" he asks, pointing to the seat between her and Jake.

"Yeah, sorry. I was just spacing out."

"Where've you been, dude?" Jake asks.

"Freaking Houghton. I was begging him to drop my grade from that stupid pop quiz. He has it out for me." Clayton shoots Masyn a sidelong glance. "He didn't give any other class a pop quiz today. Just us."

Wrong distraction.

"No joke! Masyn, what'd you do to Houghton to make him so mad? You holding out on him?" Jake razzes.

"Dude!" Clayton hisses, giving him a look that says, *What are you doing?*

"Oh, there's no way that *she's* holding out on *him*," Adison says.

"What? I was talking about surfing!" Jake shrieks.

"Oh, yeah, so was I." Adison stands to leave, and looks Masyn square in the eyes. "Actually, wait, I don't think I was."

Heat floods through Masyn, and she swallows hard, searching for a way to defend herself against the hostile accusation. Her eyes flick to Seager, whose head is bent low, brow furrowed, and once again she wonders why she cares what he thinks about her. All eyes at the table bounce around, trying to sift out the truth in Adison's wake.

Masyn stands to leave, but her frustration boils to the surface before she can gather her things. Why should she have to keep running away from Adison's rumors?

"I surf with Houghton and his brother-in-law, Redford Kensington, every morning because they're my next-door neighbors. If you guys want to make drama out of that, go talk to Adison. She's probably brewing up her next rumor as we speak," she adds as she plops back down in her chair.

Masyn's hope of some alone time before soccer practice is crushed when she sees Adison's mom walking out of the field house with Coach Nance. Thankfully, Nance herds Shaylynn in the opposite direction, even as they both eye her, but she runs into a bigger hurdle when she gets into the locker room. Adison is sitting in front of Masyn's locker, wiping tears from her cheeks.

Masyn walks over and drops her things on the bench. "What? Are you like cursing my locker or something? I doubt those are the tears of a virgin."

Adison rolls her eyes. "I just sat down, okay?"

"What's wrong?" Masyn asks, stifling a groan.

"Nothing!" Adison snaps. Masyn raises her brows and turns her back to Adison to start getting changed. "You're all anybody cares about now."

Masyn freezes, not knowing what to say. She didn't ask people to talk about her. She'd prefer they didn't.

"Even my family. I saw my parents talking to each other the other day at my dad's. I thought maybe they were getting back on good terms, but when I got closer, do you know what they were saying? They said I'd have no chance sharing the limelight with you, but even worse, that now that you're here, they can't get the divorce they wanted because our family would be the screwed-up one. It's like, maybe if I were better at something, they'd want to stay together, but at the same time, I'm the reason they can't get what they want . . . because I can't compete with *you*."

"Adison, I'm sorry. Honestly, I hate hearing the name Ace Madden out here. I wish nobody knew." Masyn pauses, cocking her brow at the fact that Adison is the sole reason everyone knows.

"Whatever!" Adison retorts.

"I know how it feels when your parents care about your success more than your feelings. So . . ." Masyn considers inviting her to Aunt Nat's but thinks better of it in light of recent events. "If you ever need some extra time away from home, we can go for a joy ride at the equestrian center or something."

"I have my own friends, thank you. And you're lying. Why would you hate that people know you're a surfing goddess sponsored by the biggest beach brand in the nation, and in love with your smoking hot coach?"

Masyn quickly looks over her shoulder to see if anyone overheard. "Would you shut up? We were not in love, and you have no right to talk about any of this. It's my life, my business. Stay out of it." Adison scoffs, and Masyn sighs in frustration. "Look, if you don't want it to get attention, don't give it attention. It's that simple." Masyn grabs her bag to go change somewhere else, turning once more before she leaves. "Adison, as much as you don't want people knowing about your family's split, I don't want people digging into my partnership with Graham Gentry. I'm asking you, please, just leave him out of it?"

If Masyn thought any kind of olive branch was extended between her and Adison in the locker room, she was wrong. Once Nance kicked off practice with the announcement that Masyn and Adison would be co-captains for the rest of the season, the claws came out. Now back in the locker room after practice, Masyn's covered in sweat and bruises.

"I'm showering at home," she tells McCall as she gathers her stuff. "Have you seen my phone?" McCall shakes her head while Masyn presses the ping button on her watch. They search for it, then stare at each other wide-eyed when they realize Masyn's phone is ringing in Adison's locker.

"Oh, are you looking for this?" Adison asks all too knowingly. She throws her hands up in surrender against the immediate distrust that's written all over Masyn's face. "You left it behind earlier, so I kept it safe for you."

Still skeptical, Masyn collects her phone without a word.

"Seriously. Check it if you don't believe me."

Masyn ignores Adison. She walks out of the field house as a new dread rises in her gut, and she wonders what her cousin is up to now.

There's not much left that Adison hasn't already discovered. Is there?

Chapter Twenty-Six

Afraid of running into Tate at home, Masyn goes straight to the equestrian center after practice.

Red stops short when he sees her in the barn and reroutes to talk to her. "Fancy runnin' into you here. Haven't seen you around since you became a soccer star."

"Hey, Red. I thought it was about time I paid Phee a visit."

"He misses you. Don't ya, boy?" Red says, reaching out to pat the horse's head. Phoenix bobs his head and bares his teeth. "Screw you," Red says to the horse, and Masyn laughs. "So, what's wrong?"

Masyn snaps her focus to Red. "Nothing's wrong."

"Pssh, don't even. This horse has practically turned into your emotional support animal. If you're here after practice looking like that, something's up," he accuses, pointing up and down her legs.

Masyn rolls her eyes and looks down at the green stains streaking her knees. "Some people need emotional support animals twenty-four-seven. A need like that should not be shamed."

"Spit it out, kid."

"Just stupid high school rumors."

Red raises an inquisitive brow.

"The whole school knows I'm Ace now."

"Ahh. Is that what brought on your little spat with Tate this morning? Did he let it slip?"

Masyn shrugs and sighs. "No. Tate can't make up his mind whether he thinks I need to grow up or be babysat, and he's punishing me for it. He gave my class a pop quiz today and nobody else."

Red laughs. "That is a very Tate thing to do."

Masyn just shakes her head. "I better not stay after all. I have homework to do. Chem homework!"

"Hey." Red stops her before she leaves. "I know Tate can be a pain in the neck, but I have to thank you—dropping in on his waves, banning him from dawn patrol, and whatever you two talk about during your late-night porch conversations . . . you've brought him back. We're all really glad you're here, and not just for the surfing. It's been . . . everything, getting to know you."

Masyn smiles. "He brought me back, too. You all did."

MASYN SITS IN HER car, facing the far pasture and thinking about what Red said. She's glad she's here, too. She never thought she'd say that, but the Kensingtons have given her more support than she ever got at home. The dinners on the patio, all the mornings out on the waves, the multiple times they've stopped what they were doing to help her, the guest room; it's all been—healing, Masyn realizes.

I'm healing.

A knock on the passenger window snaps Masyn out of her reverie. She lifts her head from the steering wheel to find Clayton opening the passenger door, still sporting his polo attire complete with helmet hair.

"Can I sit with you for a minute?"

"Sure." Masyn's heart starts to pound, a reaction to Clayton's proximity or the thought that this might be yet another tough conversation.

Clayton turns in his seat to face her and then looks at the radio, smiling. He turns up the volume, and the lyrics to "Golden" by Harry Styles fill the car. They both smile until laughter escapes them.

"I miss you, Clayt."

Clayton nods and pulls Masyn's hand into his. "I miss you, too, Buttercup. I really miss you."

"I'm sorry," Masyn says, dipping her head and peeking up at him from beneath her lashes.

He cups her face with his other hand and gently strokes her cheekbone where he once rubbed ointment on her road rash, chuckling to himself. "I know," he whispers and then he closes the distance between them, their lips locking instantly.

This kiss is different from any they've had before. It's not soft or cautious, there's need behind it—desire. Clayton pulls Masyn to him. She deepens the kiss and tugs at his shirt as his hands explore her back.

She pulls back just enough to say, "This doesn't change things. I can't be your girlfriend."

"I know," he responds, nibbling at the spot where her neck meets her shoulder. "It's okay, Mase."

Masyn kisses him again, leaning into him, before she pulls away once more. "We can't do this here. *I* can't do this here."

"You're right," Clayton huffs, his breathing fast and heavy as Masyn sits back in her seat. "This wasn't my intention, just so you know."

"I know." Masyn smiles and grabs his hand.

"We probably shouldn't do it again."

Masyn pauses. "I know," she adds with a whisper. "So we're good?"

Clayton winks. "Golden."

The smell of barbeque lures Masyn to the Kensingtons' before she even steps foot in her own house. The kitchen is empty, but trays of pulled pork, cheese buns, and coleslaw are covered in foil on the island. Masyn makes herself a plate and starts eating as she leans against the island.

"Well, aren't you a sight for sore eyes?"

Masyn thumbs at the corners of her mouth and cranes her neck to glare at Tate entering from the back patio. "You don't live here. Go away."

"Neither do you."

"Actually, I do," she goads, turning to him with a hand on her hip. "I have a room now. In the actual house."

Tate keeps walking toward her until his chest is inches from her shoulder. He leans past her to grab a plate, then straightens and pokes Masyn's neck where Clayton had been kissing earlier. "You plan to do *that* in your new room?"

Masyn slaps his hand away. "You can't say things like that to me."

"Since when did *we* have restrictions on what we say to each other?"

"Since you decided to be just my teacher and not my friend."

Tate grinds his jaw and folds his arms against his chest. Then he looks down at the bruising on his wrist and back up to Masyn, clearly making a point. "You call that not friends? You call last night not friends?"

"Fine," Masyn snaps, enraged by the butterflies coursing through her. She tosses her now-empty plate in the trash and throws her hands up. "You want to talk? You told me to get friends my own age, so I did. This is what friends my age do. You got a problem with that?"

Masyn's phone vibrates on the counter. A picture of her and her mom on the Huntington Beach pier lights up the screen. "Ugh. I have to answer this," she says, picking up the phone and settling into a chair on the back patio. "Hi, Mom." If her tone comes out clipped, her mom doesn't notice.

"Honey, how's it going?"

"It's been fine . . . good. It's been good. I think I've officially settled in."

"Yeah? I've been hearing you're quite the soccer star."

"Oh, I don't know. Today was kind of a rough—"

"Look, hun, I don't have much time. There's something I need to run by you."

"Oh," Masyn says, jostled by the abrupt change of subject. *So she doesn't actually care about how it's been going?*

"You've talked to Graham," her mom says—whether it's a statement or a question is unclear.

Masyn's heart drops, and she subconsciously flicks her fingers to fight off numbness, though it hasn't presented in a while. "Is that a question? Have *you* talked to Graham?" She shakes her head in confusion and does a double take when she catches Tate leaning against the doorframe in her peripheral vision. She shoos him away, but he comes closer, his frown deepening with every step.

"I talk to Graham every day. You know I have business in the surf industry, and our dealings overlap."

Masyn doesn't say anything. She knew her parents' surf brand was growing quickly, but she didn't realize they were making deals with the devil.

"Masyn?" her mom snaps.

"I'm here."

"We've been meeting with Rip Tide and have come to a deal. I think we can get your sponsorship back. You can come home."

"I don't want my sponsorship back. Not yet. I'm not ready. I want to stay here. You can't make me come back," Masyn argues. Tate closes the distance, sitting on the armrest of her chair and leaning in to hear the other end of the call. Masyn pushes against his thigh, even though she knows it's no use. From the look on his face, she could run and hide in the bathroom, and he'd still follow her in to catch this conversation.

"Honey, don't be silly. That sponsorship was one of the best things to ever happen to your surfing career."

"It's not about that, Mom. I'm not doing it."

"Okay, well, I'm out of time. I'm coming to your state championship game. We can discuss this in person," she tells Masyn. "Your father would want you to do this," she adds and hangs up.

"There's no way in *hell* that I'm—" Tate's voice is deep and protective, but Masyn cuts him off.

"I'm not ready to talk about this." She folds herself into her lap, tipping over until her shoulder blade rests on Tate's thigh. She gives herself three deep breaths to calm down and then silently stands and walks to Aunt Nat's, feeling Tate's eyes on her and the lingering warmth of his support the entire way.

Chapter Twenty-Seven

THE NEXT FEW DAYS pass without Masyn having to face Tate, but only because she's timed them out perfectly. In the mornings, he's respectful of the nature of dawn patrol and doesn't ask. Masyn leaves chem right when the bell rings, and after soccer practice, she goes straight to Red's office at the equestrian center. Red's always out and about, checking on horses and watching polo practices, which makes it the perfect place to do homework and hang out until it's time for bed. She might see Adison or Clayton here, but if she goes home, she risks running into Tate, and he's harder to ignore.

Masyn chuckles at the makeshift *Masyn's Hideout* sign Red put on the door and pushes past it. She drops her backpack and soccer duffel on the ground and sits at the desk, pulling out her phone. Since their conversation the other night, Masyn has called her mom more than she has the entire time she's lived out on the East Coast; however, she hasn't actually talked to her. If her mom answers, it's only to say that she's running into a meeting and will call back later. When yet another call is declined, Masyn looks around the office and accepts the fact that today is the day she is desperate enough to call her stepdad. Not surprisingly, the call forwards to voicemail on the second ring, and she immediately gets a text from her mom.

Mom: Sorry, can't chat. Boarding a flight to Sydney for a business trip. See you at the game next week. Hope to have big news!

Masyn: I need more details about what we last talked about. What do you mean you've been talking to Rip Tide? I'm not going back!

Mom: Graham said he would call you. I'm sure he wants to be the one to tell you. Gotta go.

Masyn: Graham?? I'm not talking to Graham!!!!

When no return text comes in, Masyn throws her phone on the desk and pulls out her laptop. She's deep in a Google search of Graham Gentry when the door swings open. She's finally getting close to figuring out the current dynamic between Graham and Rip Tide, so she doesn't even look up from the article she's reading when she jokes, "Nice sign, Redford."

"So, you admit it. You *are* hiding from me."

Masyn's eyes fly up and she slams the laptop shut. Her shock quickly turns into annoyance when she sees Tate standing with his arms folded and a smirk on his face.

What ever happened to double A, Red?

"Whatcha lookin' at?" Tate asks, his smirk evolving into a full-on smile. "More stuff kids your age do?"

"I'm not hiding from you. I'm coming here because I know that you don't. Now leave, and don't be annoying."

"That's called hiding," he says, coming around the desk.

She places a hand protectively on her laptop and eyes the open door. "It's more like blatantly avoiding."

"Come on, let me see." Tate pulls Masyn's rolling chair, but she extends her arms and anchors her fingertips into the desk.

"Mind your own business, Tate."

"Why?"

She levels him with a glare over her shoulder. "If you see what's on my screen, you'll get mad and overreact. I didn't ask for your involvement on the subject, because I don't *need* it." Masyn scoots her chair back to its original position and leans back, folding her arms with as much attitude as she can muster.

"Stalking a boy?" Tate jokes.

No, Masyn thinks, but what she says is, "Maybe," in hopes it will scare him away. She sort of is stalking a boy.

Tate leans down, resting one palm on the desk and the other on the back of her chair. His eyes light up with mirth only inches from hers before he flicks the laptop open. The article's featured image of Graham, chest bare with his wet suit bunched at his waist and holding an Ace Madden surfboard, fills the screen. Tate looks at Masyn again.

All she can do is stare at the dusting of freckles that has appeared over his cheeks since he started surfing more.

"Have you talked to him?" His voice is low and gruff.

The answer pricks at Masyn's lips, but she's paralyzed by the disappointment that's taken over Tate's eyes. There are depths to the silver in his irises that she hasn't seen since the first night they met; almost as if life is betraying him all over again in this moment.

"Answer me, Madden. Have you contacted him?"

Masyn's eyes dart around Tate's features, analyzing his body language. His fist is clenched, his jaw is taut, breaths quickening. Her gaze drops when she realizes there's nothing she can say to answer that question truthfully without letting him down.

Tate swallows hard against the silence, then cocks his head to the other side, stands, and walks out.

Masyn remains frozen in her chair, unsure what to do or say. She won't let herself feel ashamed for calling Graham. She had every right to seek closure. And now that her mom has implied he might contact her in the coming days, she has every right to research him—to prepare herself for what to expect.

"Tate!" she calls out, but her voice is far too weak for the charged way he stormed out. She pushes away from the desk and stands. "Tate, come back!" Masyn shouts through the door. She braces her hands against the desk, letting her head hang as she curses at her circumstances. When she looks up, Adison is with a group of girls all wearing varied expressions of shock and amusement, craning their necks to look in like Masyn's life is a reality TV show. She can practically see the rumors sparking behind their eyes, but reacting would only kindle them. Masyn glares back before Red's broad frame fills the doorway.

"What was that all about?"

Masyn flings her arms up in defeat and deflates into the chair behind her, shaking her head.

"Your tiffs don't usually last this long."

"I think I'm about to be shipped back to California."

"Why?"

"To be Ace Madden 2.0. My mom's been talking to Rip Tide . . . and Graham." Masyn peeks at Red, curious if the mention of her former coach strikes a chord with him.

He furrows his brow and folds his arms across his chest, thinking.

He doesn't know everything, but he knows enough, she determines.

"Are you okay with that?" he asks.

Masyn shakes her head, keeping her eyes down.

"Well, do you want to stay here?"

"I don't want to—" Masyn pauses, and picks at the hem of her practice jersey as she bites at the inside of her cheeks. "I can't go back. I won't be able to be who I used to be."

"Let me handle Tate. Just give him some space. It'll be okay. We'll figure out the rest . . . together."

Over the next week, Masyn sleeps at the Kensingtons' every night, afraid of even the slightest possibility that Graham will show up at Aunt Nat's without notice. She doesn't speak to Tate. As much as she wants to, she's trying to do what Red suggested and give him space. Even more, she's trying not to *need* him, whatever that means. McCall's called her out for shooting daggers at him in class more than once, but Masyn can't help it. The longer he ignores her, the more she wants him to notice her. But no matter what she does, she can't get him to look at her for longer than a split second. She even wore his old Rip Tide sweatshirt to school one day. It clearly caught him off guard, seeing as he stammered through the rest of his sentence once he noticed, but he shook it off and continued on as normal.

Today, she's forced herself to turn over a new leaf. With the championship game at their home field tomorrow, it's time to focus. Soccer is something Masyn built on her own—no family ties, no scholarships, no professional support. Winning the state championship would be huge, purely because it would be something she did for herself. It would prove that surfing didn't define her. She could be more than Ace Madden, maybe even better.

As the class comes to a close, Tate passes out graded exams. On the second page of Masyn's, there's a note in red ink. *"See me at lunch."*

Masyn's heart lurches. Of course, he's ready to talk now that she's surged past the whole ordeal. When she walks out after the bell rings, she stops at Tate's desk. "I think you graded mine wrong."

When he turns the page, he'll find her handwritten reply. *"No."*

AFTER SOCCER PRACTICE, THE team goes to one of Ellsworth's quaint Italian restaurants for their final pre-game dinner. The smell of basil and wood-fired pizza makes Masyn's mouth water as she scoots into a seat in the middle of the long table reserved for them.

"I came by your house last night. Your car was there, but you weren't," Masyn hears Adison's voice across the table, but doesn't register that she's speaking to her until the accusation has silenced the group.

Masyn leans forward to look down the table at Adison. "Are you talking to me?" she asks, to which Adison flares her hands and raises her eyebrows as if to say, *who else?* "I was probably at the Kensingtons' for dinner."

"So, you eat dinner with him now?"

Masyn juts her chin back. She doesn't want to entertain Adison with the details of her personal life, but she's not letting Adison do this again. She refuses to watch her spin rumors by asking a biased question that will put the wrong ideas in the minds of everyone else present. "Does it hurt your brain to constantly come up with false implications?" Masyn asks. "When I'm invited, I eat dinner with the Kensingtons—who are my neighbors—and sometimes Mr. Houghton joins us because he lives on the property and is also Mrs. Kensington's brother. But no, he was not there last night."

"I'm just confused how it happens."

"I just told you how it happens."

"So, do you chase them, or do they chase you?"

"I don't even know what you're talking about now. Where are you going with this, Adison?" The eyes of all their teammates are on them as they, too, try to make sense of Adison's question.

"Your older boyfriends. Graham Gentry I can see liking his girls young, but Houghton? You must be working overtime to keep him wrapped around your finger."

Masyn stands, her chair screeching against the tile floor. "Where do you get off, Adison? You have no right to even speak on the subject of my life, let alone spread volatile rumors around the whole school. I know you have no concept of the real world outside of high school, but I do. I have business deals to uphold, scholarships and sponsorships to secure. My reputation matters to me because my last name isn't going to do me any favors the way yours will. And, for the record"—Masyn looks to the rest of the table—"I'm not involved with either of them. You have nothing close to proof because it simply doesn't exist."

"Ladies!" Nance hisses from behind them. "Are you trying to get us kicked out of here? We're supposed to be bonding, not fighting."

Masyn eyes Nance. She was prepared to leave, but out of respect for her coach, she silently takes her seat again and refuses to so much as look in Adison's direction. However, that doesn't keep her from overhearing Adison's final comment.

"Oh trust me, it exists. Living, breathing, rock-hard proof."

Chapter Twenty-Eight

AFTER THE DINNER, MASYN goes straight home, grabs a few things from her room at Aunt Nat's, and walks around the hedges over to the Kensingtons'. She takes a shower and is setting her things out for the next day when she hears distant shouting. She looks out her window facing the guest house. Tate is nowhere in sight, but she definitely hears him. On her way out to see what's going on, she finds Red and Karina in the kitchen.

Both of them do a double take. "We thought you were out there harassing Tate again," Red says, pointing next door.

Karina's eyes go wide. "Don't tell me he's yelling like that at poor Clayton VanDamme."

"Oh, this is good." Red smiles as Masyn hurries toward the front door. "Hey, hey, not so fast! I'm in charge of Tate, remember?"

"Red, if he's yelling at my friends, I'm at least coming with you."

"Okay, fine, but let me do the talking."

Masyn rolls her eyes and follows him out the door, with Karina bringing up the rear. They jog toward the shouting up ahead on the gravel road. Coming closer still, Masyn can begin to make out Tate's pointed cuss words, but the other person's response stops her dead in her tracks, causing Karina to bump into her. She didn't hear the exact words, but she'd recognize the timbre of his voice anywhere.

"You show up here again, and I'll kill you," Tate's threat rings out in reply.

"Stay here," Red demands and cuts straight through the hedges.

A door slams. A few seconds later, a red sports car speeds past the Kensingtons' driveway, and Tate rounds the corner at a run. He jumps into his Jeep, stopping short when Karina and Masyn call his name. He looks angrier than Masyn has ever seen him. So angry that not even the warmth of Karina's arm wrapped around her shoulders can keep goosebumps from covering Masyn's skin.

Tate's eyes bore into Masyn's. "I get you want your old life back now, but you're playing with fire, Ace. Stop it!" he warns before he slams the door and speeds off after the Mustang.

Red emerges from the dust with a concerned look on his face.

"Who was that?" Karina asks. "Were they next door?"

"They were out on the road, but I didn't get a good look. I can't be sure."

"It was Graham." It's a statement, not a question. Maybe even a challenge. "Wasn't it?" Masyn finally asks. The whiff she got of his cologne trailing behind the car was faint, but unmistakable. And where Masyn's concerned, there's only one person Tate would threaten.

Red holds Karina's gaze for a beat before looking at Masyn and clutching the back of his neck. "Yeah, it was Graham."

"Masyn, should we be concerned about your safety?" Karina asks.

Masyn shakes her head, but Red leans in, holding Masyn by the shoulders, his expression earnest. "I need to know. Why is Tate threatening to kill him?"

Masyn eyes Karina before answering Red. "My relationship with Graham wasn't always appropriate."

Red cusses under his breath. "I'm going after him."

"Red, wait!" Red turns, and when Masyn looks into the fire in his eyes, she sees her father for a split second. She can't let him think the worst of her. "You know Graham and I were close. He was a really good coach, and we were winning every competition. It almost felt like the closer we were, the better we would do. I didn't mean to cross a boundary. Once I realized it had gone too far, Graham already had his eyes locked on our future as a team—we both did. It's not completely his fault." Masyn shrugs. "It doesn't have to be a big deal."

An ache washes over Red. Masyn can see it in the way his shoulders slump and his eyelids sag, but it doesn't slow his response. "It's *completely* his fault, Masyn. When it comes to something like that, it is completely on him." Red squeezes Masyn's shoulders even tighter. "But I'm not going for Gentry. Not now. I've got to stop Tate."

When Red releases his grip, Masyn turns and walks into Karina's warm embrace.

"It is a big deal," Karina whispers, swaying gently before resting her chin on Masyn's head. "When you walked up to me on your first day of school, you were a shell. Empty, but so, so heavy. I could see it. I could feel it. That experience changed you. He took the light right out of you."

Masyn looks down, remembering those first weeks after it happened, when she would sit on the beach completely numb. "Yeah, I guess I forgot how much it affected me."

"That's good—means you've been healing. But I want you to always remember, it was a big deal, and it shouldn't have happened." Karina gives her one more loving squeeze. "Are you staying with us tonight?"

"Yeah." Masyn looks out toward the road. "I'm just going to go grab a few things from Nat's. I might be in and out for a bit."

MASYN WAS IN AND out for as long as she felt it was necessary for Karina to stop worrying about her whereabouts. Now that it's past ten and Tate still isn't home, she slips out of the Kensingtons' house one last time and heads straight to the guest house.

She plops down on the sofa, preparing to wait for Tate to get home, when her eyes catch on something by the door. Two large suitcases, a few boxes, and Tate's surfboard in its travel case. Masyn walks over to the kitchen and opens the fridge—empty. She goes to the bedroom—spotless. Then, opens the medicine cabinet in the bathroom—bare.

Tate's leaving.

Masyn walks mindlessly back into the living room and paces as she tries to wrap her head around everything.

Tate's taking all his stuff . . . he's leaving for good. And he didn't even bother to mention it to her.

Masyn steps toward the door, but it swings open before she can even grab the knob.

Tate charges in, causing Masyn to backpedal. He stops when he's inches from her face. "Get out of my house," he growls.

She straightens, a silent refusal to back down. His face is so close to hers, she can see the silver flecks in his blue eyes and the individual lashes poking every which way, something she's never noticed before. Her eyes move to the scar under his chin—new since his spontaneous weekend trip—then to the tightness in his jaw.

As she takes in these new discoveries, she realizes there's still so much about him she doesn't know. "I'm trying to," she snaps, bumping into his shoulder as she moves around him, but she doesn't get far. She stops at the door and turns back to Tate. "Tell me what's going on," she demands, confusion and the desperate desire to grasp control of something overrunning her mind.

Tate laughs, but not at all like he thinks the situation is funny. "Don't play with me, Madden."

"Well?" Masyn's tone is laced with sinister sarcasm. "Did you find him? Did you beat him up again? What did you do, Tate? Tonight, and back there in California?"

"I'm not going to sit here and watch him back you right back into the black hole I found you at the bottom of."

"Then don't!" Masyn stalks toward him. "I didn't ask you to fight this for me." She pushes against Tate's chest, which only makes him come right back into her face.

"Someone has to!"

"No! That's where you're wrong. I don't need you, remember?"

Tate paces the floor. "Yeah, well, when I said that, I didn't realize you'd been calling him. What were you thinking, Masyn? You clearly need some supervision."

She was caught in a moment of weakness the night she unblocked Graham's number. That's all. Right? Suddenly, it feels like more. Like she has been longing for a simpler time, a better life.

Or, maybe, she was caught in a moment of electrified juxtaposition when she finally felt free again, but the unexpected devastation of her breakup with Clayton and the idea that he knew her gateway secret was trapping her all the same.

Maybe her subconscious is treacherous and has a habit of always bringing her back to the sources of her troubles.

The last was probably true.

But she can't say that to Tate. Not right now.

"Ugh!" Masyn groans. "You're impossible! Can you get out of your arrogant head for one minute and put yourself in my shoes?" She moves toward the door once more.

Tate doesn't miss a beat and swoops in front of her, his back blocking the exit. When he speaks, it sounds like all the angry energy has left him. "Then tell me, please. What were you thinking, contacting him?"

Masyn swallows, not wanting to admit her vulnerability.

Her silence seems to refuel his temper. "Whatever it is, you're too late. He's gone. I can't believe you'd be so . . ." He waves his hands in the air, looking for the right word until he finally spits out, "So desperate, so callow."

"Why do you care?" Masyn shouts. Tate works his jaw as he stares back at her, but Masyn doesn't give him the chance to answer. "Oh wait, you don't. I'm not—" Masyn looks to the side, trying to bar her tears.

"Not what?"

She catches sight of Tate's belongings by the door, and in a whisper, she finishes her sentence. "I'm not Kat."

Tate closes his eyes against the statement and bites his clenched fist. When he opens his eyes, they're filled with a mixture of hurt and concern, and Masyn can't stop the tears from racing down her cheeks.

Tate can treat her like the girl he misses so much, but one thing sticks out in Masyn's mind. "You would stay for Kat. You would never leave her."

Tate puts a hand on Masyn's biceps, squeezes, then lets his arm fall slack to his side. "You're not Kat. You're so much more."

"My entire life as I knew it ended when I ran from that beach," she says. "Everything I was passionate about and everything I loved about myself was Ace Madden. I thought it was all gone. I thought *I* was as good as gone. But then I realized I was wrong. My everything isn't gone, it's just held in the palm of Graham's hand. So sue me for briefly wondering if there was some way I could get back the pieces of me I thought I had lost."

Tate momentarily surrenders, pulling her to him, and Masyn lets his loose embrace comfort her for one silent sob before she pushes back and smacks his chest. She does it again, but Tate just watches her, taking in every bit of her emotion before he steps forward and pulls her in again. This time his embrace is tight and secure, unwavering.

Masyn tries one last time to push against him.

"Masyn, why does it feel like you're about to run out of here and try to leave Ellsworth for good?"

"I *have* to."

"No. You don't. You have the state championship game tomorrow."

"It doesn't matter anymore."

"It does, Ace. It matters. You brought the team to the championship. *You* did, and you worked from the ground up to do it. You need to see it through, for your team and yourself."

"It's different now. There are much more important matters at play than a stupid soccer game."

"Look at me, Masyn," he says, pulling back so she's forced to make eye contact. "You're not a runner."

"How can you say that? I ran away from everything."

"You weren't running away. You were chasing a better life. Do you understand?" Tate lifts her chin and looks deep into her eyes. "Don't let a broken man ruin what you've worked so hard to build. Again."

He lets her go and steps back, rubbing his hands down his face.

"You're leaving." Her statement isn't accusatory. It's just that: a statement.

"I have to."

"No, you don't."

"I won't let myself be the broken man to get in your way."

"You can't go, Tate. You can't! I need . . ." Masyn trails off, not wanting to give rise to Tate's fear. "I *want* you. Every day, I wake up wanting to see you, surf with you, talk to you. If you hadn't found me, I'd have been lost out there in that ocean. But now, when the hard feelings come, I don't want to run into dark water. I want to run to you."

Masyn takes in the crease between Tate's brow, the burning in his eyes, and reaches for him. "Please don't do this. Please don't leave me."

"Masyn." Tate shakes his head. "It can't be us. Not right now. Not like this."

She sighs in submission. "If I stay, you'll at least be at the game tomorrow night, right?"

Tate shrugs. "It doesn't matter. There are plenty of people here who are rooting for you and supporting you. You can't let me be your deciding factor. Do you understand that? Do you understand how unhealthy that would be, considering your past? I'm not going to ask you to stay again because you're more than capable of making your own decisions, but I hope you will. And if you do, I know you'll kill it."

Tate reaches back to usher Masyn toward the door, but rather than following his lead, she slumps into him, focusing for the first time on the way his solid body feels against hers and trying to memorize it all the same. "What if I do need you? What if I need you, and you're not here?" she whispers.

"You have to find someone else to be your person." Tate swallows hard and his next statement is only a strained whisper. "Promise me you'll find someone else to lean on."

"I don't think I can."

"Remember how I told you the waves reward bravery?"

Masyn nods against his chest.

"It was never about the ocean . . . Just be brave. You'll make it through." Tate locks his arms around her and presses his lips to her forehead. The quiver of his bottom lip against her skin, like he's fighting to get a grip on his emotions, is all it takes to release the rest of the tears that Masyn has been holding back.

Chapter Twenty-Nine

Masyn makes it through the next day doing all the things she's expected to do. She goes to class, sits at her normal lunch table, and even attends the state championship pep rally, and all the while her heart feels as if it's beating in waves. Like an internal call to the ocean—her safe haven. It's all she can do not to run to it, but she's trying her hardest to focus on the championship game tonight.

That's exactly the battle raging in her head as she sits in her car after school. She's supposed to be at the family luncheon the school is holding for the team before tonight's game. Her parents are probably in there, wondering where she is. Either that, or they're enjoying their freedom to brag about her without her there to stop them. Not because they're proud, but because her previous success has boosted business sales or something. Masyn rolls her eyes at the thought and begrudgingly drags her body out of her car and toward the banquet hall.

When she walks in, the room is full and buzzing with chatter. She doesn't see her mom or stepdad, but Red and Karina are chatting with a family a few feet away. They immediately end their conversation and walk up to greet Masyn.

Karina wraps her into a hug as Red says, "I thought I was going to have to send a search party out to the beach for you."

Masyn shoots him a look of understanding. "I was tempted, but I wouldn't be surprised if Tate was out there sitting watch."

Karina winces, causing the next wave of Masyn's heartbeat to crash prematurely. "He left already, didn't he?"

Karina nods and rubs Masyn's shoulder. "We tried to get him to stay for the game, but you know Tate. Once he makes a decision, he doesn't turn back."

Red hooks an arm around Masyn's shoulder and pulls her in for a hug. He dips his chin to whisper in her ear. "Hey, this is just Tate being Tate. We've always known he was a pouty-puss sitting out there behind the waves." Masyn laughs and Red pulls her closer, mussing up her hair. "We're the real team, kid. Let's raise hell out there on the field tonight." Red offers a fist bump and Masyn accepts, but before she can reply to his comforting words, she hears her mother behind them. She tenses on instinct.

"Redford Kensington." Kennelly's voice is light, almost a broken exhale, but the emotion behind it catches the group's attention.

Masyn and both Kensingtons turn toward her. Her face is blanched, her eyes watery. Red searches her up and down, trying to figure out the connection. Masyn is the first to speak. "Mom? Are you okay?"

"Kennelly Madden," Red says in surprise. "I'm sorry I didn't recognize you. It's a pleasure to meet you. You recognized me?"

"Wingate," she says and swallows hard as some of the color returns to her cheeks. "It's Kennelly Wingate now."

Red nods kindly and Masyn, not knowing what to say, tries to shrink behind him and Karina, but Karina stills her with a hand at her back.

"Dan had pictures of you two everywhere, but your mannerisms . . . My, you're just like him."

A smile lights up Red's face. "Dingo. We were brothers, maybe not by blood but by everything else." He reaches back to grab Masyn's hand, and she squeezes it hard, not knowing she needed the comfort.

"He talked about you nonstop. I just . . . I can't believe it. You're so much like him."

Red squeezes back and smiles at Kennelly. "No, no. Now this one," he says, yanking Masyn forward, "is his clone through and through."

"Hi, Mom," Masyn whispers, hesitantly using the momentum to give her mom a hug.

Kennelly takes a deep breath and smiles politely. "There's no arguing that," she replies, and Masyn wonders if she's the only one who detects the dismay laced beneath that statement.

Headmaster Wingate and Masyn's stepdad join the circle, followed by Adison's parents, and, finally, Adison.

"Aunt Kennelly, I can't believe you came all this way," Adison sings as she waltzes into the circle.

"Hello, Adi," Kennelly replies.

"There are actually a few people that have come from California. You know, college scouts, brand reps . . . " Adison turns her attention to Masyn before adding, "Coaches."

Masyn's heart skips barrels, and she bites her cheeks, suppressing the urge to put Adison in her place on the spot. "I better go. It looks like the team is eating together."

Masyn's stepdad turns to his wife. "Did you talk to her?"

"Oh, that can wait."

"It really can't. It has been waiting. And waiting, and waiting."

"We shouldn't be waiting, we should be celebrating," the headmaster adds.

"Well, yeah. Masyn, can we chat after you eat?" Kennelly asks.

"About?" Her stomach flips.

Her mom looks around the circle before her gaze lands on Masyn again. "Rip Tide. It's all good things. I don't want to stress you out, but we do need to have a discussion."

Masyn clenches her teeth. Her eyes flick to Karina's and Red's before finding her mother's. She dips her chin in a nod and walks as fast as she can to the team table. Once all eyes are off her, she runs out the door.

She only makes it down the first corridor before Coach Nance rounds a corner, nearly colliding with her.

They stop and stare at each other until Nance speaks up. "Tate Houghton called me today. Want to know what he said?"

Masyn shrugs.

"He suggested I lock you up in the field house until kickoff." Masyn remains still, eyes set on Nance. "I told him it's a free country." Nance comes shoulder to shoulder with Masyn. "I gave you my cleats that first day of practice—I'm counting on you, Masyn Madden. I believe in you, but I know that life is bigger than a sport, so if running away from this game and the crowd it brings is what you really feel like you need to do tonight, I'm in no position to stop you."

Chapter Thirty

THE STADIUM IS FULL by the time warm-ups start. Masyn catches one glimpse of her mother and instantly vows not to look into the stands again. She never returned to the luncheon and can only imagine that now she'll be getting a lecture on embarrassing her mother in front of their peers and family on top of whatever else she's been waiting to talk to her about. She's grateful now more than ever that in soccer, unlike surfing, there's a gate between the players and spectators with rules that forbid them from crossing paths until after the game.

McCall jogs up and takes her spot in line behind Masyn for their first drill. "Adison is crafting stories about you again."

"I don't want to know. Not right now."

"Um, you might want to hear this one."

Masyn drops her head back and groans.

"She's telling everyone that Graham Gentry is here. Like, in town, and that he and Mr. Houghton are fighting over you."

Masyn searches the stands without responding. When she doesn't find Graham by her parents, she sprints toward the goal to run the drill. McCall follows, and when they're back in line, she continues, "You weren't surprised. So, it's true?"

"It was true. But now it's over. I guess Houghton saw him pulling up to my house last night and ran him out. He left town, too. They're both gone."

"Why is our Chem teacher fighting another man for you?"

Masyn scowls. "Don't get wrapped up in the drama. The fight might have been because of me, but it was not *over* me. Just don't listen to her. We have a championship to win."

"I get that, but why? Does he know Graham Gentry? Do you hate Graham Gentry that much? Do you and Houghton, like, talk? About Graham Gentry?"

"McCall!" Masyn shrieks. "If I hear the name Graham Gentry one more time, I'm going to go rogue. I will tell you everything later, I promise. Just please, drop it for now."

McCall throws her hands up in surrender and respectfully backs down.

THROUGH THE FIRST QUARTER of the game, the opposing team's strategy is clear: take out Masyn Madden. Amid their aggressive stance on Masyn, double-team plays, and unnecessary slide tackles, Masyn keeps the ball primarily on the offensive side of the field. She even gets a few shots on goal. But every time the announcer says her name, he says Ace Madden. And every time it makes her picture Graham by her side.

When Masyn grabs the ball for a throw-in right by her team's bench, "Number Nineteen, Ace Madden, with the throw," rings out in the stadium.

"Can you tell them to stop calling me that?" Masyn yells to Nance.

"If you can hear the announcers, your head's not in the game. Don't worry about who's in the stands; don't listen to the announcer. You hear me? Get in the game, Madden."

Masyn throws the ball and jogs in to join the play. The ball gets kicked into the defensive zone, and Masyn waits in position to go help out on their half or make an offensive run. Number Three on the opposing team marks her, fisting Masyn's jersey.

"If I were hooking up with a professional surfer, I wouldn't be complaining about the nicknames he comes up with for me," she says.

Masyn ignores her and yanks free of her grasp. She can see the referee eyeing them from the centerline. *Keep your head in the game. She's just trying to get in your head,* she reminds herself.

"Come on, everyone knows you secretly like it. The two of you are all over each other in every picture I've seen online."

Masyn reels on the girl. "You have no idea what you're talking about, so I suggest you keep your mouth shut."

A whistle blows, and the referee runs up to the girls, hand in his chest pocket. Masyn flings her hands up and backs away in defense. She can't get a yellow card this early in the game. "Just a misunderstanding, ref," Number Three says to cover.

"I don't play around. Next time it'll be a card," the referee warns Masyn.

This gets her fired up. "Are you serious? Her hands were all over me. My jersey is literally untucked because of her."

"Watch yourself, Nineteen."

Masyn turns and balks behind the ref's back while Adison runs to her side before the next whistle blows to resume play. "It's a good thing you have thick skin tonight," she says as she backpedals. "Looks like you're gonna need it." She points to the stands, but Masyn refuses to follow her gesture.

In the next ten minutes, Masyn finds her groove, setting up several shots on goal and getting a few more in herself. As she receives a pass from the defensive zone, she finally sees a hole in the other team's double-teaming strategy: if she passes to McCall, who's playing left wing, they can run a give-and-go play, allowing Masyn to outrun the two defensive players coming at her from her right side. Masyn signals to McCall and takes off dribbling as fast as she can. Then she passes the ball to McCall, wrapping around her other side. McCall dishes the ball right back to Masyn on the line and takes off toward the open goal. Right as she looks up to gauge where she should aim her shot, pain shoots through her ankle and she's swept to the ground. The fall is hard and unexpected, but it's over as fast as it happened. Masyn rolls onto her stomach and blinks against the spots in her vision. In the background, Nance is shouting at the ref about an illegal slide tackle. Masyn was approached from behind and the player made contact with her body, not the ball. That's definitely illegal. But that's not what Masyn is caught up on.

When she looked at the goal, right before she went down, she saw someone standing behind it, just outside the perimeter fence. She didn't focus on them, but the figure was eerily familiar.

Tate said Graham was gone. He was sure of it, she assures herself. Still on her stomach, Masyn cranes her neck to look back at the goal. Nobody's there besides the goalkeeper.

"Waiting for your knight in shining wet suit to come help you up?" Number Three, who just took Masyn down, crouches in front of her. She's flanked by her teammate, who also chimes in.

"If he comes, tell him to take you back to where you came from. Sharks don't belong on land," she mocks.

Masyn flies to her feet, ignoring the pulse in her temples and the bright spots that speckle her vision. "What makes you think you can talk to me like that? You spoiled rotten—" The blow of the whistle quite literally cuts between the players as the referee moves in, turning to face Masyn and flinging a yellow card in the air like he's been rehearsing to do it all night.

Masyn's jaw drops, and Nance is immediately at her side, yelling at the ref. "Are you senile? She got tackled from behind on an open offensive breakaway, and you've carded *her*."

"Get off my field or you'll see the same yellow card for yourself."

"Like hell I will—"

Once again, the ref flicks the card to the sky, this time facing Nance.

Masyn groans and pushes Nance back. "It's fine, Nance, it's fine. I can do it again."

Play resumes and roughly five minutes later, Masyn is proven to be right. The same opportunity presents itself. She gets the ball, attracts the defenders, passes to McCall, and sprints around the outside. This time when she regains possession, there's one lingering defender applying pressure. Masyn slows and sweeps her feet around the ball twice, stumping the defender before charging toward the goal again. She watches the keeper's feet bobbing side to side, ready to dive. Masyn plants her left foot, and shoots with her right, sweeping the ball up with a spin as she looks to the goal.

He's there.

Graham Gentry is standing directly behind the goal, holding his hands in an upside-down heart over his head and smirking at Masyn like he knows every part of her.

She should be focusing on what's happening on the field. She should be following up on her shot. She should be moving out of the way of the giant defender barreling toward her. But she's rooted to the spot, eyes stuck on the man who broke her.

Until all at once, she's numb.

And everything goes black.

Chapter Thirty-One

MASYN KNOWS THE ROUTINE: First, she'll feel disoriented, then her ears will ring. She'll probably see Graham in her mind's eye until something breaks her out of her subconscious or she wakes up in the hospital. She remembers it all too well.

"Stay here, Masyn. Stay here. Come back and finish what you started." It's Tate's voice in her mind, so vivid she can practically feel his presence.

Masyn tries with all her energy to open her eyes.

I can't do it, she thinks.

"You can do it. You don't need me. Just be brave."

She tries again, this time feeling the cold, hard earth underneath her. Something's bracing her head. Finally, bright streaks pierce her vision, and though it's hazy, she can tell there's a group of people huddled over her as she lies on her back. She waits, but the scene fails to come into focus. All she knows is there's a man crouched directly over her, holding her face, pressing something to her forehead. Masyn latches on to the strong forearm, finding familiarity in its warmth. She rubs at the muscle striations with her thumb. She knows this forearm. She's taken refuge in these arms time and again.

She knew he'd be here.

"Masyn? Can you hear us?" she recognizes the voice coming from behind her as Joe, the athletic trainer.

She tries to crane her neck to look back at him, but he stops her. "No, no, it's okay. You stay still. We've got someone supporting your head and neck, and I'm working on getting some equipment out to check your vitals. Just hang tight."

Masyn nods, grasping tighter to the strong arm by her head like it's the only thing anchoring her to reality. She feels him shift and latch onto her, reciprocating her hold. Their bond springs new confidence into her.

He didn't leave me. He's here. I can do this. I'm okay, she thinks. When she opens her eyes again, her vision warps. Masyn focuses on her hand as she swirls her thumb back and forth over the prominent muscles at her aid, but when her vision finally flickers into focus, her heart stops. Beneath her grasp on the man's forearm is a banded tattoo.

The person huddled over her isn't Tate.

It's Graham.

Masyn swats his hand from her forehead and tries to sit up. A chorus of "not so fast" and "don't do that" echoes around the huddle, and Masyn obeys, mostly because everything hurts.

Graham's face appears right over hers. "Just relax. You got hit hard."

Her eyes lock on his, not because she trusts him to take care of her in this moment, but because she's trapped. Masyn locks her jaw against the heavy breathing that's suddenly taken over her, cursing her body for taking comfort in Graham's presence. She was so sure it was Tate. Until she figures out what she's feeling, she refuses to speak. She forces her eyes to latch onto something else. The scar slashed across his eyebrow. It's new.

Did Tate do this?

"Do you remember what happened?" Graham asks.

Masyn nods, even though she's not quite sure.

"Are you hurt?"

She doesn't answer.

"Masyn, where does it hurt?" Joe cuts in.

"Good luck getting that out of her. She won't admit to pain. Never has, never will," Graham says, patting her knee like he knows her. But what's more annoying is that he does. He's right, and he knows it. They've been through things like this with each other.

"Leave," Masyn demands from between clenched teeth.

"Masyn, that was a hard hit. I'm going to have the paramedics load you onto the stretcher to get you off the field and check you out," Joe cuts in.

Masyn sits bolt upright. "I'm not going to the hospital. I'm playing the rest of the game." Her vision blurs, but she doesn't let it show. She's not about to let Graham Gentry send her to the hospital and keep her from finishing what she started, again. "I'm fine," she says, coming to a stand to prove it.

The crowd cheers, and Graham nonchalantly steps to Masyn's side, supporting her when she wobbles. "You're not fine, Ace," he says into her ear. "I would know. I know your limits better than anyone here."

"Don't," she growls before turning her attention to Nance and hoping she can't see the way her eyes don't completely focus. The ground sways beneath her. With no other option, Masyn begrudgingly tucks her arm around Graham and grips him for balance. "I'm fine, Nance. Tell them I'm fine."

Nance looks to the trainer and the paramedics who've arrived on the scene.

"Okay." Trainer Joe sighs. "Masyn, we've got to make your safety our top priority."

"I have to finish this game," she pleads, motivated now more than ever to prove she doesn't need Graham Gentry to win.

Joe raises a hand to stop her. "It's almost halftime. We'll take you to the field house, check you out there, and if we see fit, you can play the second half. I'd never hold an athlete back with that look in their eye."

Masyn accepts the deal. Though she's still unsteady, she breaks free from Graham to walk across the field where the trainer's golf cart is parked. Joe and Red swoop in, catching her at the armpits and swinging her arms over their shoulders.

Graham steps in front of them. "I can help."

"No," Masyn and Red say in unison.

Graham leans in toward Masyn's ear closest to Red. "Unless you want Kennelly out here, I suggest you let me help."

Red stares at Masyn, gauging her reaction, then leans over to talk to Joe. "Why don't you go grab the cart? We'll meet you halfway."

Joe does as he's told, and Graham takes over his place on Masyn's right side.

"What is going on?" Red growls. "Tell me now or get the hell away from her."

Graham scoffs. "As of recently, there's a certain image that needs to be upheld. I'm under contract not to say anything until the press is notified."

"Contract?" Red asks.

At the same time, Masyn blurts, "The press?"

"Just trust me, okay? Our little soccer star is indebted to Rip Tide, so you want me to be here mending her image in any way that I can."

Masyn tries her best to shut out their conversation. She should be focused on one thing right now—the game that's only halfway finished. As they walk across the field, Masyn side-eyes the bench. Every one of her teammates is staring with wide eyes and open mouths except Adison, who stands smugly by the water table as her rumors gain credibility right before her eyes.

When they get to the golf cart and Masyn takes her seat by Joe, Red leans in. "You okay?" he asks.

"I don't know."

"You're okay," he wills. "Conquer it."

Masyn nods, then turns her attention over Red's shoulder. "Graham, get in."

Red doesn't move, just squints at Masyn. It's not until Masyn offers him an assuring fist bump that he pats the top of the golf cart, signaling to Joe they're good to go.

Masyn knows how bad this looks. Of all the adults who could be on this golf cart with her and Joe, she asked Graham to come. There's no doubt in her mind she just made things worse for herself, but if she wants to play her best in the second half, she has to sort through the chaos crowding her mind.

Chapter Thirty-Two

"You're not here for my support. You're here because I can't play the second half with my head in the game until I get this out."

Joe has finished his exam and left Masyn to hydrate and rest for a few minutes before he comes back to check her balance and blood pressure. He left strict instructions for her to stay on her back and relax, but instead, she's sitting upright, gripping the edge of the sports therapy table, as she grills Graham.

"Please. You know you're glad to see me."

Masyn scrunches her nose in response to his cocky wink. "You're not supposed to be here, Graham. Is it not clear that I want nothing to do with you? I left California to get away from you. Why can't you leave me alone?"

Graham leans his forearms on his knees and narrows his gaze at Masyn. "No, it's absolutely not clear, because you've never had the balls to talk to me like an adult."

"You had no right to do what you did to me."

"What *I* did to you? What *I* did? Oh please, Masyn. Take some responsibility."

Masyn's jaw drops.

"Why is it such a big deal? We kissed. We—" Graham stands and waves his hand around in the air. "That's really all we did. We could have easily forgotten it and moved on. Had I known you would handle it like a child, I would never have played into *your* games."

"I never kissed you, Graham!" Masyn's voice wavers. "Does that not say enough? You were behind me the whole time. Everything you did once you laid your hands on me was completely unreciprocated."

Graham's gaze drops to the ground and his brow furrows as if he's trying to remember exactly how that night played out.

"Even if I had, it's not about the kiss! It's about the fact that I almost drowned because of your selfish desires, and it's a big deal because I trusted you!" Masyn snaps. "I had no one, and I trusted *you*. You should have known it was too much for me. You should have realized you were taking advantage of our coaching relationship."

"Enough with the taking advantage crap. If anyone was being taken advantage of, it was me. You know me better than anyone on this planet. I let you find the parts of me no one else knows about. And don't say I'm wrong because I saw the way you found the one thing that was different about my appearance after months of not seeing me. You noticed it right away," Graham says, pinching the scar on his brow. "And then you decided that wasn't enough. Do you realize how long I had to resist your ploys to get my attention? I remember good and well the countless times you jumped into my arms, wrapping your legs around my waist. You flirted with me, asked me to stretch out your muscles, watched footage at my house. The bikini you wore that night . . . it was for me—I know it was. So don't tell me that I took advantage of you, because we both know it was all done in mutual effort."

"It didn't end in mutual effort," Masyn says, her voice raised. "You wouldn't stop. I tried to get you off of me, and you pinned me—"

"I saved your life!"

"No!" Masyn interrupts before he can keep talking his way out of this one. "Admit it. Your hands were all over me, even after you knew I didn't want to go any further."

Graham studies her with sadness in his eyes, then paces the floor. "We got caught in a riptide, and I saved your life. I took you into the hospital just to make sure everything was all right, knowing I would have to tell them I was intoxicated and alone with you. Knowing what kind of heat I would get for that, what rumors would spread. If they found any morsel of evidence that they thought proved foul play, I could have gone to jail. I knew all that, and I took you in because you matter to me."

"You didn't save me, Graham. Riptide or not, as far as I'm concerned, the ocean was the only one doing me favors that night, taking a part of me before you could take the rest." She looks down at the floor and shakes her head. "Everything that I was when I was with you drowned that night, so if you're here to find the Ace Madden we created, then you've come to the wrong place."

When Graham steps closer, Masyn wishes she could look away from his eyes. He looks more than sorry—he looks wrecked. "Maybe I screwed up," he says. "But then, why did you ask me to come? Why have you been texting me, saying you miss me, and you want back what we had before, and all that crap?"

Masyn's face falls, more confused than anything. *Is this gaslighting? Is this some story he made up?*

If so, Masyn has no chance. People will believe him. People will *want* to believe this.

"You told me there could still be an us," Graham says, resting his palms on either side of Masyn's thighs.

"What are you talking about?" she asks, leaning away, venom lacing her tone as she prepares to fight again.

"Don't play the victim, Ace," Graham retorts, though his tone lacks the energy of Masyn's. "I have the texts to prove it." He pulls out his phone and scrolls through a never-ending text thread. Then, he presses his thumb to the screen to stop the scroll and hands it over.

Ace: If we win, the state championship will be in a couple weeks. Come? For me?

Graham: Are you really asking me to fly across the country to watch a soccer game?

Ace: No, G. That's not what I'm asking at all.

Graham: Then?

Ace: I was hoping we could start back up where we left off.

Masyn doesn't even register the knock on the door when Nance peeks her head in as she scrolls to the very top of the conversation to figure out how this all started.

Ace: Hey, I've missed you. This is my new number.

Graham: Who is this?

Ace: Serious, G? It's me. Ace.

"Madden," Nance interrupts. "We're getting ready to head back out. You coming?"

Masyn looks up, still in a daze, as Graham snaps, "We'll be right there."

Nance sets her jaw. "Madden. If you want field time, you come now. I'm sending Joe in."

Masyn nods even as she clicks on the contact number. It's a Massachusetts area code. There's only one person who would have done this. The same person who "found" her phone at practice a few weeks ago.

"I'll be right out," Masyn says to Nance, and though she tries her best, she fails to hold eye contact because she can see Nance looking straight through her.

It's already happening.

By now, everyone knows Graham was her coach. But surf coaches don't fly across the country to watch high school soccer games. His presence here insinuates they were something more, and now all Masyn feels is naked and exposed. Ashamed.

When the door clicks shut, Masyn hops off the table. She passes the ensuing stumble off as an intentional shove at Graham and presses the phone into his chest. "This isn't me, you idiot. Have I ever called you G? You've been texting Adison Wingate—the person who hates me the most—and no doubt feeding all her rumors. What did you say on here?"

Graham swipes his face, cursing under his breath. "Nothing, I don't think I said anything. Something always felt … off. I've always wanted to talk to you in person."

Masyn moves around him and walks toward the door. "Well, let me save you the trouble. You're dead to me. I want nothing to do with you."

"Look I'm sorry, okay? How many times do I have to say it? It went too far, I know that. I'm sorry! These texts, and everything … I just want *us* back. We're the dynamic duo—Rip Tide royalty. Let's go back home and surf some titles together."

Masyn keeps her back to Graham, not wanting him to see the part of her that's fighting to give in. The part that wishes they could rewind time and go back to how things were. "Goodbye, Graham. I have a championship to win."

"Wait," he says, stopping Masyn at the door. "There's more. I know this is important to you, and I'm going to let you go, but what I said out there to Redford, I'm guessing you don't know anything about it. I know you don't believe me, but I care about you too much to tell you why I'm really here until after the game. So, rip into me. Do what you need to do to win, but just know we'll be speaking afterward. We can't not work through this. It's just not an option."

Masyn chooses to ignore Graham and opens the door, only to come face-to-face with Joe, who points her back to the table.

"Ugh!" she complains, turning and pushing past Graham.

"Do you want me to leave?" Graham asks, voice low. "Because I will, if that's what you want. Unblock my number, and we'll talk on the phone."

Masyn flops onto the table. "I don't care what you do, Graham. I literally don't care. Joe, if you don't clear me to play, I *will* kill him."

Chapter Thirty-Three

MASYN JOGS ONTO THE field with the crowd cheering behind her, stopping once she's in position next to Adison for the kickoff. The score at half is tied one to one, so there's no room to slack off.

"What are you looking at?" she asks as Adison stands with a hip popped, looking her up and down.

"No lip gloss smudges, no hickies. Maybe you weren't doing what we thought in there."

"Shut up, Adison."

"Oh, come on. You're seriously still not admitting that you and Graham Gentry are lovers? After all that? He knighted you. If you had to go to the hospital, he would have knocked out an EMT to ride in the ambulance with you."

"Is this game not important to you? You do realize it's the state championship, right?"

"Speak for yourself. Thanks to Granddad's bank account, after tonight, you're going back to California to be the Queen of Rip Tide. Here's a newsflash for you: there's no way you're going to be able to keep up your front when you and Graham are the joint face of the company. People are going to see right through you two, just like we did tonight."

The whistle blows, swooping them into play, but all Masyn can do is jog up center field. She can't form a play in her mind, she can't even see the ball, as realization shackles her from the inside out.

Her parents bought Rip Tide.

She doesn't know how she missed it. James Wingate's involvement, all the talk about meetings, traveling to Sydney where Rip Tide's headquarters are, their big news, and alleged reason for celebration. This must be why Graham is really here.

The ball gets kicked out of bounds, and Masyn looks up to find Graham. His expression is fraught with tension as he gives her a tight nod like he's confirming her suspicions. Masyn finds Nance, rolls one hand over the other, and silently walks off the field.

"Sub!" Nance calls, as Masyn takes a seat on the ground next to her. There's no way she's surrendering herself to the bench with her teammates currently amped up on rumors and adrenaline.

Masyn sits for minutes on end with her head between her knees, until Nance pulls her from the shell she created. Crouched in front of Masyn, her back to the game, Nance analyzes her from head to toe. "What is it?"

Still stunned, Masyn responds more to the white sideline than to Nance. "They're here to take me home. I have to go back."

Nance searches her face again. "Look, Masyn, I don't know what has happened or what is going on in your life, but I don't like what I see right in front of me. There are scouts here, you hear me? Scouts for the national team and the best schools in the nation, and they're asking about you, the rookie. If you can play like you played in the first half, you'll have more options than you know what to do with. Options that not a single person in this stadium would turn down. Do you understand what I'm saying?"

Masyn's mind is going a million miles a minute, but she catches on and nods at Nance, a new fire raging to life inside her.

I have to play. I have to win.

TEN MINUTES AFTER MASYN re-enters the field, the ball is thrown in and deflected toward the opposing team's goal. Masyn is nowhere near the closest player to the ball, but it's out in the open and she takes off at a sprint. She doesn't know if she's running toward the goal or away from her recent revelation, but when she makes it to the ball, she knows one thing is for sure: she will get this thing in the net.

One lone defender surges toward her and buckles down for a slide tackle. Masyn cuts to the side, moving around her as she sweeps past, and moves on to face the goalkeeper who retreats into the net, arms spread wide. Masyn slows, and when she's close enough, she quickly plants her left foot and swings her right as if to shoot. The goalie goes flying to Masyn's left in anticipation of the shot, but Masyn doesn't follow through. Instead of sweeping the ball up into the left corner of the goal, she fakes the shot and guides it to the right with a swift kick using the outside of her foot, giving her so much more satisfaction when the ball rolls into the bottom of the net.

The crowd erupts and Masyn's teammates race toward her, jumping up and down until they've fallen in a heap. Once the celebrating subsides, the girls run back and set up for the next kickoff. Masyn stops where the center circle meets the midline and bends down to fix her shin guards as the other team gets into place.

"I thought you would've run over to kiss your boyfriend." Number Three leers at her from a few feet away.

Masyn glares and ducks her head back down to continue adjusting her socks as a blush of anger heats her ears.

"You're totally showing off for him," Number Three taunts again.

This time Masyn's temper gets the best of her. She's on her feet and across the centerline before she can think better of it. "What is wrong with you? I don't even know who you are." Masyn juts her chin out. "Maybe that's because you haven't even made a half-decent play. The announcer has no reason to say your name."

As soon as Number Three shoves Masyn on the shoulder, the ref is between them, blaring his whistle. He glares down at Masyn. "Why is it that you are always in the middle of the trouble on this field?"

Already heated from her encounter with Number Three, she reacts by flinging her arms out wide. "How is this my fault?"

"I didn't see how it started. All I know is that you're one quick lip away from a red."

Masyn sets her jaw and backs up to her side of the field. Once the ref retreats, Adison comes up to Masyn's side, draping her arm across Masyn's shoulders. "You're one quick lip away from a lot of things, aren't you?" She turns Masyn toward the bleachers, points at Graham, and waves. Masyn remains stone-cold, shrugging Adison off.

Even though it's too far to hear from here, the roar of the ocean sounds in Masyn's ears, and a wave rolls in her stomach. The sensation sends her looking left to right, first finding the direction of the beach, then the exit. She wonders if she'll ever overcome the desire to flee when things don't go her way.

Don't run, she thinks. *You're not a runner.*

No matter how many times she repeats it, her mind refuses to believe it, so she gives it what it wants, and she runs. Not away, but everywhere she can in the game. For the rest of the half, she runs up and down the field, switching between defensive and offensive zones as needed. She sprints to intercept passes and makes one breakaway run after the next. When the final whistle blows, a huge sensation of accomplishment washes over her. They did it; they won two to one.

I did it.

The fans rush the field, and the next half-hour is filled with congratulatory hugs, photos, and handshakes with college scouts, but the stadium isn't clearing out and Masyn knows everyone is waiting to see how she'll interact with Graham.

After saying goodbye to a Dartmouth scout, Masyn turns to find all eyes on her. Graham is walking toward her, flanked by Masyn's parents like he's their favorite part of her. Adison's revelation flashes in Masyn's mind. They're here to take her back to California and force her to team up with Graham again.

Masyn turns, looking around for an exit, and finds Joe perched on his golf cart as he taps away on his phone. "I need you to take me to the field house," she says before she's even seated.

"You okay?" He frowns.

"Now, Joe! Please?"

Chapter Thirty-Four

McCall delivers Masyn's bags to Joe's office. "The coast is clear!" she announces. "Stadium's empty, and I saw Adison leave about ten minutes ago."

"Thank you!" Masyn says, lifting her head from its resting position on Joe's desk.

"No prob, but uh, there's a certain hot surfer waiting outside the door."

Masyn lets her head drop back down with a thud. "Why is this happening to me?"

"Okay, be honest. Does any part of us maybe still like him? He's like *the literal* hottest human I've ever seen."

Masyn sits up. "No," she says flatly, then rolls her eyes. "I don't know."

"Can you tell me why?"

"Yes?" Masyn tries, because she trusts McCall. She just doesn't know if she has the energy to relive it again.

"Later?"

Masyn nods, and McCall goes on her way.

Not long after, Masyn follows. When she gets to the threshold of the door, she pauses, takes a deep breath, and walks briskly out, as if she can sneak away in the blink of Graham's eye.

"Wait." His voice stops her in her tracks, but only for a second as Masyn remembers she doesn't have to listen to him anymore. She takes another couple of steps toward the parking lot without acknowledging him. "You round that corner and you'll run right into your mom. Rumor has it you've left her in the dust not once, but twice tonight."

This stops Masyn for good. She was hoping she could escape this night without having to talk to her mom. Kennelly has had plenty of opportunities to call Masyn and tell her about the Rip Tide deal since her trip to Sydney. It's not fair for her to do it now and spoil the win. She turns to face Graham, who's still leaning against the building in the dark corridor. "You knew? The whole time?"

"Don't put this on me. I would have told you if you gave me the chance, but you ran."

"I had to!"

"No, Ace! You didn't. You broke my trust just as much as I broke yours." He steps away from the wall, coming chest to chest with her. "We were a team, and you abandoned me."

"We stopped being a team the night you took advantage of me and sent me to the hospital!"

Graham huffs and shakes his head. "Not this again," he bellows. "Grow up. You were a tease. You wanted me to make the first move, and you know it."

Masyn swallows. He's partially right. She knows the part she played, but she knows now that as the adult—as her coach—he should have been playing referee. There are certain lines he should have known to never cross. And she refuses to let him push her into taking the blame again, because she knows good and well that it's too heavy for her.

"Sure, Graham. I teased you. I was sixteen, and I seduced you, my twenty-four-year-old coach, who should have known better. You're right; whatever, I'm done with you."

"We're not done!" Graham looks to the sky and drags his hands down his face. When he meets Masyn's eyes again, the last traces of the remorse he had the last time they had this conversation melt away as a sinister glare heats his face. "I'm done apologizing because we're just getting started again, A-babe."

He reaches out and hooks a finger under Masyn's chin, tilting her face up to his. "You're a big girl, it's time to act like it. You and me—Ace Madden and the King of Hearts—the new faces of Rip Tide. So, play the victim all you want, because trust me," he whispers, leaning down to her ear. "I'll prove to you just how much you wanted me. You won't be able to resist me again."

"I'm not going back to California. They can't make me," Masyn spits, yanking her chin away from him.

"They own you," Graham says.

Masyn storms off around the corner and, sure enough, her family is waiting for her with the Kensingtons. Her mom spreads her arms out wide and comes in for a hug.

"There's our girl!" she says. Her voice is soft, but her eyes are menacing. "We're so proud of you. Who knew you had the soccer gene in you?"

"Thanks, Mom." Masyn grins, not knowing what else to say.

"Masyn worked really hard all season," Karina says with a smile.

"Thank you for taking her under your wing. I know she'll miss you a lot."

The Kensingtons look at each other in confusion, and Masyn frowns at her mother. "I'm not leaving."

"Honey, you got it out of your system. It's time to go back home and finish what you started. Didn't Graham tell you the plan? I assumed that's what was holding you up over there."

Masyn squeezes the strap of her duffel. "I'm not doing it."

"Masyn! We worked hard to get you your sponsorship back. We've all made sacrifices. You *will* come home with us."

"By 'sacrifices,' do you mean you bought out Rip Tide just so you could force me back into a role I want no part of? So you could, what? Make money off of me? You didn't even ask me about any of it."

"We had no choice," Kennelly blurts. "Rip Tide is suing you. They filed a lawsuit against you, Masyn. A lawsuit." She smooths her coat, and then looks up, flashing a polite yet slightly embarrassed smile toward the Kensingtons. "We've been looking at taking over Rip Tide for years—the timing just worked out. Don't be so ungrateful. We're not the only ones that put our necks on the line for you. This whole family has pitched in to support you. Graham included."

Graham's practically family. Graham sacrificed for me. Graham is going to turn me into a rising star once more. Everyone should be so thankful for Graham. Blah, blah, blah.

Masyn's fury grows as Graham walks around the corner with his hands linked on top of his head. He raises his eyebrows and pulls his lips in a straight line as if to agree that Masyn's being a stubborn pain in the butt.

"I'm not doing it. You can't make me," she refutes.

"It's already a done deal, Masyn. You are legally required to serve restitution for the company, no matter who the current owner is. At least now, we have a say in what that restitution is. And might I remind you that after the stunt you pulled, you need this Rip Tide deal to fix your reputation, or your future will flush right down the toilet you threw it in." Kennelly sighs and turns her palms to the sky. "You're a minor. I signed on the dotted line weeks ago."

"You've got to be kidding me," Masyn implores. She snaps her attention from her mom to Graham, but he just shrugs. Even more enraged that he's suddenly pretending to be sorry for her when he was just playing twisted games around the corner, Masyn turns to her mom. "No, Mom, I don't need Rip Tide. I'm at the top of my class, and I just won a state championship. I talked to three different Ivy League scouts who are interested in me. My life isn't surfing anymore . . . I'm more than Ace Madden, and I have options. I want to talk to the old Rip Tide owners—figure something else out."

"That's simply not an option."

Red side steps behind Masyn and puts his hands on her shoulders like a father might. He dips his head and speaks low so only she can hear him. "Masyn, I'm on your side here, but I think they've got us backed into a corner. Maybe we can come to a compromise. I can help."

Masyn gives him a slight nod as she internalizes his words and tries to picture what a compromise might look like, though nothing that could brighten this situation comes to mind.

They own me.

Graham drops his hands from his head and rests them on his hips, catching everyone's attention. "I say we let Masyn make some of her own rules, as long as she follows some of ours."

Masyn glares at him from under her lashes. She doesn't know what he's up to, but after the last remark he made to her, it's definitely something.

Graham takes in everyone's confused expressions. "What? If we're talking legality, a lawsuit can't impinge on a minor's ability to get an education. If she wants to stay here at her fancy-pants boarding school and get straight A's and college credit, it'll only help her reputation. Besides, these days there are surfing competitions up and down the East Coast. So, we fly her out for promos and West Coast competitions, and she can stay here and surf the East Coast competitions, too. It would actually grow the brand more than if she were just on the West Coast . . . as long as she agrees to show up and keep a good reputation."

"But you're her coach," Kennelly argues. "You can't be on opposite sides of the country."

Masyn scoffs, but her expression lightens with Graham's next words. "I can find her a different coach." He shrugs, and there it is again: a flash of the sadness Masyn saw in his eyes in the training room. "I have friends."

"I'll pick the coach," Masyn butts in.

"Not a chance."

"Why not?"

"Who do you have in mind?" Graham folds his arms against his chest. "Let me take a wild guess."

"No," Masyn says, averting her gaze at the thought of Tate. "I don't know. I just want a say in it."

Graham laughs, but Kennelly speaks up. "We have a flight to catch. Masyn, I'll give it a try as long as Graham is okay with it. We'll sleep on it before setting any ground rules, and maybe we can all hop on a conference call in the morning."

AFTER SAYING GOODBYE TO her mom, Masyn hangs back, waiting for the stadium to clear completely so she can escape to her car without having to say another word to anyone. When she finally makes her way to the parking lot, the stadium lights click off, casting a dark shadow over the few vehicles that remain. She freezes when she recognizes a familiar figure leaning against her car. Loose hoodie, boardshorts, backward trucker hat.

Don't do this to me, Tate.

She already used up all her strength to say goodbye to him. She can't do it again.

The roar of an engine hums to life in the distance, and seconds later a single headlight shines in their direction, illuminating Tate's features. He remains motionless, his stare communicating a hundred different heartbreaks. Masyn bites her lip against the desperate misunderstanding in his expression.

He showed up for her. Tate came to support her, and instead he was forced to watch Masyn cling to Graham, lean on him for support, and ride off into the night with him. She let Graham be her savior. That's what it would have looked like from Tate's perspective.

Masyn itches to run to him and explain everything, but he's already made his decision. He chose to put her out of his life, and she chose to put her trust into herself.

She needed to find closure with Graham to win that game. She doesn't owe Tate an explanation.

The noise of the engine grows closer. When Masyn looks over her shoulder, Seager Brooks kicks a foot out to balance his motorcycle and holds a helmet out to her. Before she realizes it, she's moving toward him, accepting the helmet, and mounting the bike behind him. Masyn pauses, looking back at Tate. "I'm sorry," she mouths. Then she clutches herself to Seager's back and forces her eyes closed so she won't have to witness the hardest goodbye of her life for the second time in twenty-four hours.

Once they've hit the main road and the stadium is out of sight, Masyn finally speaks up. "What's all this about? Why were you at the stadium so late?"

Seager slows the bike to a stop at a red light and turns to look at her. "It looked a little bit like bombs were flying at you from all sides tonight. I thought you could use an escape." He shrugs, his eyes searching hers with a need for something she can't quite figure out. "I don't know why, Masyn, but I keep wanting to be that person for you."

Acknowledgements

I'll thank my Heavenly Father first every time. It is because of Him that I have the opportunity not just to write, but to share my stories with the world. And I think it's also because of him that this story will get into the hands that need it the most. I am eternally grateful to have His divine support.

Of course, I'm filled with thanks to my wonderful husband. However, this time I think he should be thanking me for ignoring him—I mean, working—so diligently that he had the excuse to buy an Xbox. You're welcome. And thank you, for fueling my passions, but also for teaching me when to slow down. You encourage me every single day, and I love you for it.

Can anyone write an acknowledgment for anything without thanking their mom? I don't think so. Thanks, Mom, for all your support, for helping me meet deadlines, and for raising me to have a brain that knows how to string a few sentences together (although my first drafts would say otherwise).

I have to acknowledge my entire family. My sisters, brothers-in-law, cousins, grandparents, aunts, and uncles on all sides have shown me so much love through this publishing journey. I'm so lucky to have you all on my team. Love you long time!

With every book, there come moments of doubt, and this one is no exception. There have been many times when I've let the negative overthinking drive me into a ditch, and it's been my new hype girls who have pulled me out. And they don't even know it! The girls who text me play-by-plays while they're reading, who share the heck out of my updates on social media, who won't allow me to let an opportunity to share about my books slip through the cracks. Alexia, Christina, Delaney, Kassi, Jocelyn, JanaLe, and so many more—your kind hearts and positivity have lifted me up through the publishing process of this book! Thank you!

And last but not least, my editor, Lindsey Hinkel. Reading your editing comments is always so entertaining in the best way. It is so fun to work with someone, whose personality shines through and brightens your day, even when the comment is saying something like *this is not as funny as you think it is*. Once again, I've learned so much from you, and I am grateful for the partnership we continue to build.

About the Author

Samantha Russell is the author of the Rip Tide series and *Social Craze*. She lives in Arizona with her husband, three wild-hooligan children, and everyone's favorite family member–Rook the Vizsla. She's a creature of habit, equal parts homebody and adventure seeker, and shamelessly addicted to soda. In her free time, she enjoys running, playing cards, and reading.

Writing a book was never in her plans–especially not when she chose her college major based on the least amount of writing possible. Thanks to love, and a certain global pandemic, she ended up an English major. Only after having a daughter, twin boys, and a medical resident for a husband did she decide to write. What better time, hey?

Samantha's books are filled with stories that brought her smiles and sanity through some of the harder, hair-pulling days of life. It is her hope they will do the same for you.

Instagram: @SamanthaRussellisanAuthor.
TikTok: @SamanthaRussellisanAuthor